Dog & Pony

Aloha

by

Richard Herr

PRANKISH PUBLICATIONS

ISBN-13: **978-0-9912981-2-9**

AUTHOR'S NOTES

First off, I want to give an F-Bomb alert. There are people who might object to some of the language contained in this book, and I wouldn't want them to be surprised by its contents.

In my defense, it's not as if *I* would actually use this kind of language. However, the greater part of this book takes place in New York City. I found it necessary to quote residents of the Big Apple. At times they use language that is rather salty, so I bit the bullet and recorded their words precisely. I could not in good conscience act as censor. Scholarliness is the only reason why I quote their language verbatim.

There are many people I need to thank for helping me create this book. The very first one is my wife, Deborah, my Alpha Reader, who plowed her way through crude first drafts and made them presentable to polite society. She has also interpreted pantomimed gestures and turned them into actual, solid words. She's always been encouraging. She's also bagged and contained many a bad joke before it was let loose on unsuspecting readers.

I'd like to give thanks to Eric Nelson, my editor, of Rabiner Lit (ericn@rabiner.net) for doing an absolutely super job of pulling my muddled thoughts together to make them comprehensible to people besides myself.

I also want to thank Gary Tenuta at GVTGrafix for the wonderful cover and all of the patience he displayed with an author who had that most dangerous of things: a little knowledge.

Let me acknowledge my co- father-in-law, Allan Halperin for serving as my Yiddish expert. (You can't write a book set in New York without using some Yiddish.)

I would also like to extend my thanks to the members of Montclair's Write Group and the members of the New Providence Writers Group who helped me in so many ways with the development of this book.

A scene in this book takes place in a mythical dollar store set on 14th Street in New York City. This dollar store is frequented by a number of ladies who could only be found in the Big Apple. They were inspired by someone who touched my life. Very briefly.

It happened back when I was living on the Lower East Side of Manhattan. I was walking down 7th Street when these two ladies, residents of the neighborhood, passed me. They were 60-ish, sturdily built, wearing housedresses (look up *housedresses* in a dictionary of antiquities), and were in conversation. I heard only one thing one of them said, but it imprinted itself on my memory to the point of becoming the inspiration for my dollar store ladies. As these darlings navigated their way to their mortal destiny past me, one said, about a nearest and dearest friend for sure, "She drinks, and she's got a nasty fucking mouth. Pardon my French."

You see? I'm just quoting.

TABLE OF CONTENTS

Part 1

...getting into Trouble

Chapter 1

The Voice of God boomed through the loudspeakers, "We've got five frigging minutes to the doors opening." Okay, so it wasn't some celestial messenger, just Sidney, my technical director.

At that moment a stage light crashed onto the stage floor next to me.

But I didn't let that bother me. Uh-uh. Not me. I *couldn't* let that bother me because I was right in the middle of a conversation with Cornelius van Patten, Chairman and CEO of Patten Products, my client *du jour*.

"There! Look at that!" I proclaimed. "Isn't that spectacular? I wanted to show you just one of the many effects we'll be using to wow your audience in this presentation." I pointed down to the mass of twisted metal and broken glass that lay awfully close to my tender and sensitive body.

"That looks like it could be a little dangerous," Mr. van Patten said, with doubt furrowing his brow. He might have got the clue that something was wrong because all of the stage hands were yelling and dashing about.

But they'd been doing that all night.

"Not in the least," I assured him. "Did you see me flinch when it landed there? I'm calm and relaxed because we're in a controlled environment."

Lies, lies, lies. There was flop sweat coursing its way down the small of my back, and my pant legs were hiding quivering knees.

But then lies and fear were the crux of my business. I do industrial presentations, Dog & Pony shows as they're known in the business. And they are always a last-second rush. To say that midgets were tap-dancing in my stomach would be an understatement. It was more like giants doing a Zulu war dance--and enjoying it.

"You're sure of that?" Mr. van Patten asked.

"Of course I am." I stepped in closer to him and changed the subject. "Any minute now, the audience is going to enter. It might be best for you to head out front to greet everyone, and we'll pull the curtain closed. After all, you don't want the audience to see the new product before the right moment." I held out a hand and led him toward the front of the house. With the other hand I gestured frantically behind my back for the crew to close the curtain.

After I guided Mr. van Patten past the lectern on the downstage corner and to the steps leading into the auditorium, I dashed back and inserted myself upstage between the two ends of the closing curtain. With the client no longer there, pandemonium seethed out of the wings as a whole crowd dashed out, trying to put things in order.

Leading the surge was Laura, my producer. She was usually contained, neat and impeccable. But this morning her hair might have been a little mussy; there may have been a small wrinkle in her skirt. Worst of all she might have been losing her temper, and I sure as hell didn't want that. "Harry, who ordered all of these crew members? The payroll is going to be way over budget."

We were staging this presentation in a Broadway house. When a show like ours books into a theater, the stagehands' union always assigns more people than is needed. But on this show it looked like the full cast from *Ten Commandments* was trying to squeeze themselves into the wings.

"Don't' be silly," I said, "I sent the union our requirements myself."

"Not according to what they say," Laura pouted.

People all over the place were shouting instructions about putting up drapes, focusing lights, placing props. Along the backstage wall, a totally inappropriate backdrop depicting Venetian canals was spread out between the wings.

Before I could continue with Laura, Joel, my designer, dashed up to me in a high snit. "Harry, they got the colors all wrong!" He pointed back to the product display the stage hands were wheeling out to center stage. There had to be a battalion of union guys pushing this ten-foot unit. "I sent them the info listing the specific PMS colors!" Joel wailed.

In accompaniment, I heard several people saying "Aw shit," off in the wings. I didn't know what their particular problems were, but my experiences during this night made me sure they were entirely aw-shit-able.

The inappropriate Venetian backdrop was flying out to be replaced by an even more inappropriate scene of a dungeon tower.

A few more aw-shits hit the airwaves.

Right in the middle of all of this clatter, my cell phone rang. I answered.

"Harry, where's my alimony?" It was Mirabel.

"I didn't check with my atomic clock," I said. "How many picoseconds late is it?"

"I expected that money ages ago. If I miss out on achieving my fifth-level Mage ranking, there'll be hell to pay, and you'll be paying it."

My blood began to boil as Mirabel prattled on about her damned phony magic. "Yeah, that ranking, and a MetroCard, will get you a subway ride."

"I'll have you know my Wizard Master said that I show great necromantic skills. I need the money to take more courses."

That was it. When Mirabel talks about her damn magic, I totally lose it. I silenced the phone by clobbering it across the nearest hard object I could find, the backside of the display piece. The phone shattered into a lot of small bits.

One of the union guys yelled out, "Props! We need the floor swept."

Somebody in the wings yelled, "Who's got the fucking broom?"

Joel had given up on me, and he was opening his carry-bag to fish out one of the many small cans of paint he carried around in there. He was climbing up on the display piece, trying to apply a few extra brush strokes to fix the colors that were wrong.

"Hey! Be careful," another stage hand warned him.

"Harry," Laura asserted herself through the many voices shouting, pleading, and arguing around us. "What are we going to do about this union bill?"

"I don't know," I said. "Isn't there a union rep around here?"

"Yup. Yup."

The guy who spoke up was off in the darkness of the wings. I couldn't really see him. From what I could make out, he wasn't all that tall, he had a bulbous nose, and his clothes looked--weird, like he was on his way to a Renaissance Festival.

"You've got too many people on this crew," I told him.

"There be enough," he said with an affirmative nod of his head. He stayed back in the shadows.

"No there aren't. They're tripping over each other as it is," I argued.

"They be needed for the end," he said.

"For the strike? You gotta be kidding me. We just have to

roll a few pieces out the door."

"Ye'll need more," he said, puffing on a curled pipe he held in his mouth.

"Hey, Buddy!" one of the stagehands commanded him. "You can't smoke that back here!"

"It be fine," the guy said.

"Oh. Yeah. Right," the stagehand said, almost trance-like, and wandered off in another direction.

"What do you mean I'll need more...," the walk-in music started out in the house. I swung my head around in a panic. That meant the doors had opened and the audience was coming in. I cursed; I had several floors to go up to get to the booth in the back of the auditorium. I turned back to the little guy--

But he was gone.

Whatever! I dashed off down the twisting corridors that led up to the booth, wondering what the hell the union was doing sending Rumpelstiltskin over to be the rep, anyway?

When I got up to the booth, panting, Sidney was in what would be described as a brisk conversation with the guy from the scene shop. "I told you guys we could get into the theater by midnight! How come your driver didn't show up till three? Do you know how much that cost us?"

"I never got anything about a midnight load-in," the guy replied.

Sidney threw up his hands, and settled down to business. He put on his headset, as we got ready to run the show. I did the same, sitting next to him, by the booth window. I saw Laura in the back, with her com on her head.

We all exchanged glances. Could we pull this train wreck into shape?

Chapter 2

Eugenia Coxmoor entered the booth. Eugenia was our client contact. If Mr. van Patten signed the checks, she authorized them. She had a generous decade on me, but that hadn't slowed her down from trying to insinuate her way into my affections. She started out being warm and friendly, however as time wore on and the end of the project loomed, she'd upped the pressure. Today was the last day; she was making an all-out effort.

Eugenia strolled up behind my chair, leaned down and nuzzled my neck. She slid her hands down from my shoulders, along my chest, and was proceeding at enough speed that I knew she couldn't brake in time for the belt buckle barrier. I reached down and snatched up her hands before they went crashing down heedlessly into the Valley of Hoo-Hahs. "Good morning, Eugenia," I said.

"Hi, Harry," she gushed. "Is everything OK?"

"Just fine." Biggest lie I'd told all morning.

Sidney looked over at me, then turned his head away and whispered into the headset mic, which meant he fed straight into my ear without anyone else hearing, except of course, everyone else wearing a headset. "Man, Harry, you sure are cougar kibble. I didn't know you had a taste for older women. Hasn't Eugenia used up most of her allotment of years where she starts her age with the number 4?"

Laura's voice filtered into my ear. "Don't be so hasty, Sidney. Eugenia's so desperate, she might even take him to bed. Think of what that might do for his disposition."

"Do you think that'd be good?" Sidney asked.

"It could only be an improvement," Laura replied.

"Yeah, that's right, Dude," Sidney shot a glance at me. "You are pretty snarky."

"Well, Sidney," I said aloud in my most pert and businesslike tone, "it looks like the audience is all in. Why don't we start the proceedings?" Meanwhile, the looks I gave my producer and my technical director told them I was figuring out chores for them in the morning, maybe braving wild and unsettled lands to clean out the back of the office refrigerator.

Sidney pushed the button on his Voice of God mic, and announced, "Ladies and gentlemen, please welcome our Chairman and CEO, Cornelius van Patten." He had a voice that sounded like a million bucks, even though he looked like something that had stumbled out of a bikers' bar, which wouldn't be too far from the truth.

We had stayed up all night mounting and lighting this presentation. We'd gone through missed signals on supplies, wrong equipment being shipped, lighting instruments falling out of the flys, and any number of calamities that inflict us in the business. But that was all over. We settled back with our frayed and sleep-deprived nerves to listen to that thing called a business presentation.

There's a special language that they use in the world of commerce called Corporate Speak. It's an argot that cryptographers are still trying to figure out. It requires casting aside simple, direct, Anglo-Saxon words that everyone is familiar with and substituting vague, barely understood terminology. The best practice in this verbal flim-flam is to take a noun and turn it into a verb.

For best results, mix in a monotone.

Cornelius van Patten droned on to his captive audience about the "synergies" that surrounded his "marketplace ventures" and other such vagaries meant to dull the senses of anyone within earshot.

That included me, and I'd been up all night trying to herd cats. I sat up very straight in my seat, opened my eyes wide, and stared down intently at Mr. van Patten as his voice droned on hypnotically.

And I really meant to continue, to stay Mr. Bright-eyed-and-bushy-tailed. However, my eyelids began to slowly creep down and my eyes began to lose focus. I revived myself several times, but the boredom began to overwhelm me...

Chapter 3

Unrelated objects drifted in a jumble through a gray cloud. A dog sailed through the air, his face wrinkled in a curious frown that asked why he couldn't just sit around and scratch fleas. A pony bobbed along, an incongruous derby squashed down on his head; his eyes flashed around as he tried to figure out what outlandish trick he was supposed to perform next.

Mirabel, my ex-wife, flashed through on what looked like a broom, except it also bore a resemblance to a piece of male anatomy. She was clutching onto a little hapless boy doll that bore a querulous expression. "Harry," she shrieked, "you've got to learn about magic."

Suddenly the little, male doll spoke up and said, "There's no such thing as magic!"

It was me.

A turtle floated through. He had Mr. van Patten's face. He said, "Synergized marketplace throughput."

The dog and the pony floated by in opposite directions. They both said, "Help!"

Mirabel swooped through again. She pounded the doll on the male broomstick. "You never, never, never understood. You just couldn't bring yourself to the magic."

The little doll repeated, "There's no such thing as magic."

Suddenly an eagle swept through--a bearded eagle with Sidney's face--and it said...

Chapter 4

"Stand by for product reveal."

"I hate magic!" I yelled out.

"Huh?" Eugenia said, from her seat right behind me.

"I said, 'Yeah, let's have it!' The product reveal," I supplied.

"Yes, of course," Eugenia said, taking the opportunity to reach a hand forward and caress my shoulder.

Sidney gave me a quick look then turned his attention back to the stage. I spoke into my headset, "Stand by to open the curtain."

I noticed they had chased Joel off the display piece onstage, and he'd come up to the booth and was seated to my other side.

Mr. van Patten was winding up. "And so it gives me great pleasure to introduce Patten Product's newest offering on the marketplace, Hot & Spicy Tequila!"

What happened next was the reason why we earn our money in this business. The curtain opened to reveal the backlit outline of the product display as it rolled downstage toward the audience.

Sitting next to me, Joel gave a tortured gasp at what he considered hideous colors, shut his eyes and averted his head. But that was Joel. To most people the colors were beautiful. However, none of the rest of us are in the habit of sleeping with a full Pantone color chart underneath our pillow.

Latin music, which had started out quietly under the end of Mr. van Patten's speech, began to swell in volume as the beat reverberated through the bass speakers, shaking the theater in tempo to the music. Vara-lights began to sweep across the stage, looking like a coordinated group of synchronized aerobatic planes, zooming tantalizingly toward the display only to dash away, changing color. True, the lights operated in a Missing Man Formation, since their comrade had fallen in action, right beside me on the stage floor.

Suddenly, an arc spotlights in the booth next to us, speared a beam of blue-white light down to highlight the bottles of tequila piled on the display. The Vara-lights then swooped in to wash the product display in a fiery red light. Several more spotlights hit it from different locations in the theater. Fireworks began to pop and explode all around the display. A video projector displayed a video on the back cyc of a bottle of Hot & Spicy Tequila with flames shooting up around it.

The audience loved it. They were on their feet applauding the whole thing. We had earned our money.

The fireworks finished with an overwhelmingly big explosion and gout of flames. My eyes were blinded by the flash, but I thought I saw the little union gnome stepping in from the wings to set off the last explosion.

The audience loved it; they cheered even more. Eugenia gave my shoulder a squeeze of appreciation (and invitation).

"What the fuck?" Sidney said, with a worried look on his face.

Eugenia's grip on my shoulder suddenly included some fingernails.

"What's the matter?" I asked.

"That last explosion was a surprise to me," Sidney said. "There wasn't supposed to be any big closer."

"What's happening?" Eugenia asked as she brought her second hand, complete with nails, up to my other shoulder.

"It's dropped some flames onto the display piece," Sidney said. "Good thing it's flame proofed."

"What do you mean?" the guy from the scene shop spoke up.

Sidney swung around to the guy. "I sent you the request."

"I never got no request," he replied.

"Oh shit!" Sidney said.

"What's happening?" Eugenia's tone had gone up several octaves.

Sidney stared down at the stage. "Some of the bottles broke, and the tequila is starting to burn."

That was startling news! We'd had those bottles onstage the whole night, surrounded by a very large union crew. What was wrong with them? How could it be that they hadn't stolen off the booze and substituted water for it?

It was the union's fault it was catching on fire!

I watched the flames growing onstage. The next item on the agenda was for Mr. van Patten to invite everyone to adjourn to the lobby to be served some new Hot & Spicy Tequila. He had been enveloped in a cloud of smoke, and he was standing behind the microphone having a coughing fit.

I lunged over in front of Sidney and punched the talk button on his VOG mic and said, "Ladies and gentlemen, please join us in the lobby where we'll be serving the new Hot & Spicy Tequila." The crowd surged toward the free booze, exiting the theater in a rush.

By this time, Eugenia was pounding on my shoulders with both fists screaming, "What are you doing? What are you doing? What are you doing?"

I then said into my headset mouthpiece that traditional and time-honored theatrical expression: "Close the curtain before we burn up the whole fucking audience."

Chapter 5

We all rushed down to the back of the auditorium to find the audience had cleared. Mr. van Patten was the only one there, wandering around aimlessly, a typical means of locomotion for corporate CEOs. Sidney had left the volume up on the music and it was doing a fair job of drowning out the crashing behind the curtain. It sounded like a whole battalion of stage hands was attacking the blaze with fire axes.

"Well, that seems to have gone fairly well," Mr. van Patten said.

"Yes!!" we all chorused together in much too loud a voice. This included Eugenia who had the corporate wisdom to know if there was no apparent disaster, there would be none that she could be associated with.

I herded my two clients together and pointed them toward the lobby. "Why don't you go out front and mingle with your associates? We have to clear up a few things onstage."

I heard the far-off wail of several fire trucks, but that was a common sound in New York. They weren't coming here!

We rushed onstage and inserted ourselves behind the curtain.

The place was even worse than when I'd left it earlier this morning. Everyone was running around shouting and screaming orders at each other. A number of the stage hands had torn off pieces of drapery and were using them to try to whack out the flames. Several artillery companies of stage carpenters were manning as many fire extinguishers as they could find. The display piece had been smashed into numerous bits that lay out around the stage, resolutely burning.

Joel stared at the rack and ruin of the display. "Harry, I realize it was a hideous color, but did you really have to kill it?"

Sidney dashed over to me. "I hear the fire engines getting closer. You'd better see what you can do about keeping things calm out front."

I raced back out the curtain and headed down off the stage, when Eugenia came rushing back from the lobby. "They're drinking the product up faster than we expected. Can you bring some from the display onstage?"

"You bet!" I enthused all over her.

I went back into Action Central, and got a stage hand to carry out one of the bottles. The label was singed at the edges, and wisps of smoke were circling around it. The stage hand used a piece of smoldering drape like a pot holder.

When we dashed out into the lobby, the fire engines were screaming up to the front of the theater. The first thing I had to do was set up a cover for us. "Watch out, folks, here comes some Hot & Spicy Tequila."

The bartender surmised that it was best to take the bottle along with the drape to keep from getting his hands burned. When he set the bottle down on the bar top, the varnish began to pucker and blister.

At that moment, several N.Y.F.D. guys came bursting in the lobby door, one of them carrying a nozzle with a trailing hose.

"Right this way," I directed them into the theater.

"You gotta get these people out of here," one of the firefighters said.

I swerved to face the crowd, and found myself nose-to-nose

with Mr. van Patten and Eugenia. I leaned in confidently toward them. "I could tell that these people were going to just hang around here for too long, so I thought I'd arrange this little show for them." I then turned toward the group and saidin a loud voice. "Okay, folks, this Hot & Spicy Tequila is *so* hot, it's made this place dangerous. Let's leave in a calm and orderly fashion right away. And when I say 'orderly,' I mean go out there and start getting those *orders* for this great product."

This did manage to launch most of the people out the door. The few who would have stayed longer, knew they wouldn't be served because the first person to leave the place was the bartender. He was a New Yorker; he'd seen the smoke; he'd watched the bottle blister the varnish; he was leaving.

I clapped my hands together and said to Mr. van Patten and Eugenia, "Well I think that pretty well took care of things. I'm heading back to wrap up the last few loose ends."

I smiled brightly and strolled over to the door into the theater. Once I cleared sight lines, I sprinted back to the stage.

When I arrived behind the curtain, the sprinkler system went off, soaking everyone onstage.

What followed was a marathon of hosing, extinguishing, dousing, and hollering. The high concentration of stage hands in the area had them bumping into each other every time they turned around.

Finally things seemed to be pretty well in control. The scene was declared safe. The fire fighters turned off the sprinkler system, and everyone started to assess the damages.

At that moment, Mr. van Patten and Eugenia must have decided to come back and give us thanks for a job well done. They stepped in between to two halves of the curtain, and their jaws dropped at the mess they beheld. Then one of the Thirty-Three Stooges released one last, errant blast out of his fire extinguisher and coated my two clients with a layer of foam.

That was the last that I saw of them.

Chapter 6

The next few hours were taken up dealing with the damages. I spent a lot of time signing different papers; most of them saying I had to pay money. I had to cover the water damage and replace all of the burned draperies, which included a backdrop for *The Gondoliers* and one for *Il Trovatore*. I was going to be in serious financial trouble and would have to look for quite a lot of new business.

Legal issues were bypassed when the theater's lawyer persuaded me that it would be good public relations to take out an option to produce on Broadway the play his nephew had written, *An Actuary's Adventures.*

I kept looking for the union gnome to find out what the heck had happened, but I couldn't find him, and no one knew who he was.

When I finally finished, I headed out down the hall to the stage door.

Laura, Sidney, and Joel were waiting for me. They were soggy and smudged and smoldering--with anger.

Laura looked at me, a drop of water trailing some mascara down on her outer cheek. She turned a laser-beam stare on me.

"Harry. Tomorrow. Ten o'clock. Conference Room."

I was in more trouble.

Chapter 7

"Harry, we quit," Laura proclaimed.

Oh crap!

I looked around the table to see if she spoke for all of those assembled. They had the same look as when I'd last seen them yesterday. Only drier. The hysteria in the pit of my stomach leaped up. My life was getting complicated.

Again.

"Laura, darling," I pleaded, "what's wrong?"

"Harry, we had a small village as our union crew yesterday. They never got the notice about the crew size." Laura attacked the subject. "I had the requisition all set and in the outbox weeks ago."

"Laura, these are Broadway stage hands! They never listen to anyone." I supplied a lame excuse.

"I specifically put those color choices into the server to be emailed to the scene shop," Joel said. "They claim they never got them." He pouted down into his latte, which he ordered from one particular coffee house.

"You probably got their email address wrong," I stated.

"Harry, I was replying to their email," Joel said.

"You know, I never trusted that new version of Windows!" I pounded my fist down on the table.

"Harry, our version of Windows is so old, it's written in Latin," Laura stated.

"And that's why Rome collapsed!" I launched another lame excuse.

"Aw, man, none of the stuff is working," Sidney said. "The only reason why the set piece wasn't thrown out of the theater was because the thing arrived too damned late for anyone to check for the flame-proofing certificate."

"You see, it helped us to be late on delivery," I said. I had a whole herd of lame excuses limping around the room.

"Harry," Laura reached over and grabbed me on the arm with both hands. She was starting to get angry, and I didn't want that. She leaned forward and brought a searchlight-like stare boring into my eyes. "We've already got a whole lot of clients who are misinforming us; we can't misinform ourselves. You've got to fix things."

A siren wailed down below in the street, a normal sound in New York. Its clarion call confirmed that I had an emergency exploding around me and needed to get on this problem, fast. As owner and operator of a small business, my unofficial but actual job title is: President and Janitor. I was reverting to the latter and listening to what my bosses had to tell me. "What's the fix?" I asked.

"You've got to get one of those things for this office," Laura stated firmly.

"One of those things?" I probed.

"Yes."

"What things?"

"You know," she said, waving her hand around vaguely. "What are they called? Oh yeah, a Traffic Manager." She implied the initial capitals in her tone of voice. Like all of us in the biz, she had a PowerPoint Title Case accent.

"A Traffic Manager?" I'd heard about such things, but had

never met one in the flesh.

"Yes."

"You want to add someone to the staff? But we've always been a group," I protested. "The Fab Four. We can't mess with our chemistry."

"Harry, we're the Frustrated Four, right now," Laura said.

"We're the Frantic Four, trying to catch up," Joel complained.

"We're the Fucked-up Four, with all this confusion," Sidney pointed out.

Laura bore her gaze into me. "Harry, a Traffic Manager."

"You bet!" I enthused. "I'll get right on it." I paused and looked around at the faces surrounding me. "By the way, what does a Traffic Manager do?"

"Circulates all of these messages to the right people on the network," Joel announced.

"Gets the jobs flowing smoothly through the office," Laura proclaimed.

"Gets all the gear trucking to the right place at the right time," Sidney pronounced.

I stared at them. When you have people ready to quit, you don't tell them they just gave you three different answers. "Is that what a Traffic Manager does?"

"Yes!" they affirmed together.

I smiled and nodded. The faces in front of me were quite resolved. I decisively slammed my hand down on the table. "I'll get right on it."

I would, but it wouldn't be easy. I have problems trying to hire people because of this dog & pony business I'm in.

And the industry is so crazy I've even housed dogs and ponies in my offices. The good news: the dogs were housebroken; the bad: the ponies weren't.

My major problem is that I conduct my business in accordance with the poorly defined rules of Corporate America. Instructions are confusing, deadlines are suggestions, but budgets have to be adhered to, even though requirements have gone up exponentially. I'm forced to be the only sane person navigating through the corporate world. I glue a smile on my face and breeze through in controlled-hysteria mode.

I keep trying to figure out how I got started in this business. Memories are vague, I seem to recall a seaside bar and some spiked rum. Now here I am, a few years later, with my only skills being how to finesse my way through this bizarre industry.

So, I had to find this thing called a Traffic Manager. Time to see Ruthie, my headhunter, and beg and implore; the usual.

It was lunchtime, but I couldn't wait for that to pass. Had to ambush her. That was easy; I knew Ruthie would be at Percy's.

Percy's Bar is a typical New York place. The menu features a fusion Irish/Jewish cuisine: corned beef, pastrami, and ham sandwiches. The clientele of the place is a rich mixture of New Yorkers, the ones treading on or over the lines separating neurotic and psychotic. You don't sit at Percy's bar unless you sport a fully developed attitude, and you never go there on St. Patrick's Day without battle armor.

I dashed into Percy's and spotted Ruthie sitting in her usual booth in the back. She was having her pre-lunch martini. She counterbalanced that with a post-lunch martini. They bracketed her lunch which *was* a martini.

I walked up to her. "Hi, Ruthie."

"Zayt mir moykhl, Ich ken eich?"

"Ruthie, please, you gotta help me."

She dropped her head down into her hands. "Harry, *bubelah,* whatever it is, it won't work."

"Why not?"

"Whenever you call me, I interview bunches of people, a lot of them qualified, but every time I tell them what business you're in, they change their minds."

"What do you mean?"

"They come up with some cockamamie excuse. I had three prospects the last time. One decided to become a professional daredevil. Another said she was going in for something a little less dangerous: nuclear waste removal. The last one decided to devote her life to curing the common hangnail."

She raised her index finger up in the air. "Actually, there was a fourth, someone perfectly suited for your business. But something came up."

"What?"

"The Governor didn't grant him a stay of execution." She leaned back and looked at me. "Harry, what're you doing in this *facocta* business? Look at you! You're a nice young man. Got alla your hair.--You're not Jewish, but some things can't be helped.--What're you coming to me for?"

"Ruthie, I'm trying to find a Traffic Manager."

"Good luck."

"By the way, what does a Traffic Manager do?"

"In your business? Keeps the homicidal psychotics away from the benign ones."

"You can't find anyone?"

"Harry," Ruthie said, "I can't do magic."

"Don't talk about that crap!" I bellowed out.

My memory's a little vague on what happened next. Someone may have thrown a chair across the room. That someone may have been me. Then, for some reason, Bruno, Percy's bouncer, felt it necessary to tackle me and sit on my chest for several minutes until I calmed down. The details escape me about what happened afterwards, but I may have been forced to buy a round of drinks for the bar to quiet everyone else down.

Let me explain about my outburst.

I don't like talk about "magic." It reminds me of Mirabel, my ex-wife. When we met, I was young, and coming off the effects of some spiked rum. I fell for her, hard, then reality set in. Mirabel said she was a witch; she should have looked earlier in the alphabet for the initial letter for that word. It didn't take long for our relationship to go from magical to martial. I finally got out: our marriage was dissolved, and I'm in hock to keep her living lavishly off my alimony checks. So, I equate magic with Mirabel. Therefore, I don't even like to hear the word *magic*. There's no such thing as magic.

After calm had been restored in the restaurant, Percy and Bruno felt compelled to escort me out of the premises. I went willingly. If I'd been foolish enough to reject departure, Bruno would have set me out on the sidewalk with my limbs rearranged.

"Percy, what does a Traffic Manager do?" I asked. Maybe he knew.

"Makes sure all of your deliveries arrive on time," he said.

"Naw," Bruno said, "that's the guy what makes all the traffic lights work." That was a large sentence for Bruno. Usually he conversed by means of the tattoos on his knuckles.

I left Percy's mulling the fact that I was looking to hire someone with a cryptic job description.

Was Ruthie right, that I needed magic? The very thought of it started getting me angry again.

Chapter 8

When I got back to my office, somebody was already there, seated behind my desk. She was tiny: hard to gauge her height while sitting, but I guessed she wasn't more than five feet tall. She was very slender, her weight about ninety pounds. Her skin was almost blue black with small and narrow features. She also had vivid, sparkling green eyes. And all of this was topped by an abundant Afro.

With the thin body leading up to that 'fro, she looked like a dandelion just gone to seed. Only in black.

"I've come about the Traffic Manager's job," she said. Her demeanor was bright and cheerful. Not just perky, but a quantum leap past.

How had she heard about the job? "Who sent you?"

"The Ruth Henson Agency."

That meant that Ruthie had either been lying, drunk, or forgetful, and I'd seen her be all three, sometimes together. But why hadn't she told me she had a candidate?

"And you know how to handle office traffic?" I did an inner wince as I'd just come up with the world's stupidest question.

"Oh, yes."

"Where have you worked?"

"All sorts of places." If I'd asked a stupid question, she deserved to give me a stupid answer.

"So you know how to manage traffic, don't you?" I asked.

"Oh, yes," she replied.

The tone of her voice told me she was lying.

"Tell you what. I've been having problems with this computer. It's really slowing down." I suddenly glanced up at her. "That's Traffic Management, isn't it?"

"Uh-huh." Same tone of voice as before.

"Could you take a look at it, see if you can find what's wrong?"

She idly traced her fingertips across the CPU and said, "Oh, yes, I can tell it's having problems."

"You can?"

She looked up at me in alarm, then continued, "Yes, I'm very familiar with this miniature."

"Miniature?"

"Yes."

"You mean 'model?'"

"Oh, yes, that," she said. "Anyway, I know a lot about it."

"Okay," I said, "since you're sitting there, why don't you see what you can do?"

She turned to the computer, and flashed her hands quickly over the keyboard. The screen jumped into something resembling Command Prompt mode.

It's bad manners to peer over anyone's shoulder when they're sitting at a computer, so I do it all the time. She typed the following:

Was that font installed in my computer?

She hit the Enter key, and the display jumped back to its original mode. She got up out of my chair and beamed at me.

"That should do it."

"Okay, let me see how it works," I said. I'd check out her computer flash-and-trash maneuver. "I'm having trouble getting a video to download from a client's site." They hadn't compressed the file, so it was huge. I also think part of the link to the site included two tin cans and a string. I sat down in my chair, went to the site for the file, and clicked to download it--and it instantly said "complete." I gave her a wan smile and said, "That looks pretty good. Let me just check to see if it's there."

It was, all 200 Megs of it.

I changed my smile from wan to winning and said, "Well, you certainly speeded that up!" Something clicked in the back of my mind. "How rude of me! I never got your name, Ms...?"

"Peasblossom."

Quaint.

"Yes, Ms. Peasblossom. I'd say with that little display, you got yourself a job! Let me show you where you'll be working."

I led her back to the office I'd prepared a week ago. Okay, even before everyone blew up at me in this morning's meeting, I'd known something had to be done, so I'd set up this room. Then I tried to fix things myself. I didn't get very far improving the system. I did get more proficient at some computer games.

As we passed their individual offices walking down the hall, I filled Ms. Peasblossom in on the rest of the staff. "Laura's my producer, she's very tall, fashionably dressed. I don't know what I'd do without her. Joel's the designer. His tastes are impeccable. When you have a chance, take a look at his office; it's gorgeous. Sidney is the technical director; he's an unreconstructed Roadie. Knows how to party; knows more about technical theater than anyone else."

We'd reached the office. "This is where you'll work. There's a server in here; you can give it the network name of Traffic, or whatever you want. We've all done that with our computers.

Mine is called Sauron. Laura's is named Red Sonja; Joel's is Titania; Sidney's got Jamison; and the printer is Grumpy."

"Who's Jamison?" she asked.

"He's an ancient Irish god of libation."

She gave out a musical giggle. "No, he's not, or I would have met him!"

I stared at her for a minute, trying to figure out what she'd just said, then decided not to go there. I retreated to my office to let her acclimate herself.

How could she know an Irish god?

Chapter 9

The following morning I dropped in on Ms. Peasblossom to see how she waas acclimating herself.

Her office had accumulated a number of plants.

"Well, someone seems to have a green thumb!" I said. My voice had taken on a hearty tone. Her bubbling personality was affecting the way I acted. I'd better be careful. If I started to effuse all over the place, nobody would recognize me. "Are you settling in?"

"Yes, I'm getting the drape of things."

"Drape?--Oh, you mean hang?"

"That, too."

"That's wonderful," I said. I strolled away. My sardonic inner voice was chiding me about being much too cheerful. Not good for business.

I settled down behind my desk. My phone rang; it was the aide from my lawyer's office. He was here to see Sidney about a Worker's Comp case. He thought he'd pick up the signed contract on an upcoming project from me while he was here. I pulled the thing out of my inbox and told him it would be on my desk.

My inbox is one of the more frightening environments in this world. I've let it sit there and settle over the years, kind of like a compost heap. Somewhere close to the bottom are the

Incorporation forms that should have been vacuum sealed in a safe-deposit box ages ago. Below that level there are new ecologies forming. My fingers fell across an old proposal that a client had rejected. I started to leaf through it for a moment, rather like mooning over the picture of a girl you never dated. I reached the conclusion it was a dead issue. In a sudden outburst of tidiness and environmental awareness I scooped the proposal off the top of my desk and headed toward the paper shredder.

The shredder was in the Conference Room, largely because the trash barrel was also there. Okay, my Conference Room also has the coffeemaker, refrigerator, sink, microwave, dishwasher, and the Conference Table is topped with white Formica in a boomerang pattern.

I stuck the papers into the mouth of the shredder. Nothing happened. I pulled back and pushed in again. Once more, nothing. I did the usual idiot check of verifying that the plug was in the wall and the power switch was on. Having satisfied myself that I must have fixed the thing by doing nothing, I again offered the document up for sacrifice. The machine just sat there, like it was sulking.

I needed help. Was that part of a Traffic Manager's duties? I started to step into the hall to find her, when Ms. Peasblossom walked in. "He's right here," she said over her shoulder.

The legal aide followed her into the room. "This is all I could find on your desk," he said, holding up the defunct proposal.

I looked in my hands; I held the signed contract. I'd picked it up by mistake.

We exchanged documents, and he went on his way. "Ms. Peasblossom, I can't seem to get this to work." I pointed at the machine.

"You mean the pulper?"

"Shredder?"

"Yes, that. Give it a try now."

"Now?"

"Yes."

I obligingly stuck the old proposal into the mouth of the shredder.

Which ate it up.

"Well" she chirped, "isn't it nice having a shredder that knows what it should and shouldn't shred?" She bounced out of the room, as I tried to figure out what was going on.

Chapter 10

First thing the following morning I steered myself toward Ms. Peasblossom's office to see how she'd settled in.

"Will you look at all these plants?" I enthused. Damn! Couldn't I do anything around her but bubble?

"Yes, they're growing wonderfully," she gushed back.

I furrowed my inner brow. The few plants I'd seen in there yesterday couldn't have grown that much. I was beginning to smell something fishy--well, at least I would have, had the air not been laced with oxygen from all those plants.

"By the way, that was quite a feat you pulled the other day with my computer. That command you typed in, was that COBOL?"

Her face lit up. "Why, yes. Do you know Kobold?"

"Did you just put a *d* at the end of that word?" I pasted a bright smile across my face.

"Yes, don't you?"

"Uh, no." I decided she was just confusing words again. I changed the subject. "Did you manage to get Eric and Emily out of Denver? The Weather Channel said there was about three feet of snow there."

"Yes," she chirped.

"You see, now *that's* Traffic!" I said, and escaped from that final *d* she'd used.

When I got back to my office, the phone rang.

"Dude! That was awesome!"

It was Eric. He's at home on top of a surf board, scuba-diving, climbing a mountain, or skydiving. All of these accomplished with the additional handicap of toting a video camera. He is one of the best camera operators in the world. Mixed among the clutter of his place you can find Emmys and Oscars, sharing space with empty vitamin drink containers.

"Let me talk to him!" It was Emily's voice as she tried to gain control of the speakerphone.

"Man, I've never done anything like that," Eric continued.

What in the world could there he that Eric had never have done?

"Hello, Harry," Emily cut in on the phone with her precise English accent. "We made it to Seattle just fine. We're setting up for the shoot in the conference room now."

"How did you get there?" I asked.

"That new person you have, Ms. Peasblossom? She arranged transportation."

"Awesome, man!" Eric's voice in the background.

"He doesn't want to hear about these things!" Emily was trying to get Eric to shut up, something that didn't come easily.

"You got a flight out of Denver?" I asked.

"Uh--yes," Emily replied. I recognized that tone of voice; she was lying.

"I heard no flights could get out. Too much snow."

"Well, we used a--uh--a private carrier Ms. Peasblossom had arranged."

"Yeah, man," Eric hooted out.

"Why are you on a speakerphone? Can't you get cell service

at company headquarters?" I asked.

"I--I don't have my cell phone anymore. I'll have to buy a new one," Emily responded.

"Did the old one break?"

"No, I had to throw it away. I couldn't take it on that--private carrier."

"Couldn't you just turn it off?" I asked.

"No, man, it gave the pilot a headache," Eric chimed in.

"Darling, I'm absolutely parched. Could you please go see if they have a bottle of spring water here?" Emily was imploring him to get the hell out of there.

"Sure, babe."

"What's this private carrier Ms. Peasblossom got for you?" I asked.

"Well, darling, what does it matter what it was? It could have been a bus with a bunch of chickens flying about. We're here, and that's what's important."

I knew that tone. In our business it said: I've exhausted the number of lies I can tell about this subject, so let's get on another one where I can invent different lies.

I mulled that one for a moment. Emily knew my feelings about the M-word. It sounded like she was trying to avoid it. We let the conversation turn to the logistics of the shoot they were setting up. At the end I said, "Tell me something. What's Ms. Peasblossom supposed to do? What's her job?"

"As Traffic Manager? She's supposed to schedule people to be at the right place and the right time."

"No she's not, Dude." Eric was back. "She's supposed to keep cars from driving through your location shoot."

We quickly outlined the info I needed for the shoot and concluded our conversation.

When I hung up, I sat for a moment brooding over what I'd just heard.

What experience could be so unique it had Eric all fired up? And why was Emily tap-dancing around their means of transportation?

And why did everyone always come up with a different definition of a Traffic Manager's duties?

Unpredictable things were starting to happen around my new employee. That didn't make me happy. If I want unpredictability, I've got clients for that.

I knew one thing I had to do: find out what the hell a Traffic Manager did.

I logged onto Monster.com. If anyone knew what a Traffic Manager was, it'd be the people who were looking for one. I read all the job descriptions.

Every damn one of them was different.

Chapter 11

The day was coming to an end. Days in my place can be anywhere from two to twenty-four hours, sometimes more. It was after seven o'clock, and I was in reception when Laura came bursting back into the office, hysterical.

"They can't do this to me! The bastards can't do this to me!"

"What? What's the problem?" I asked.

"They picked up too soon at the FedEx box."

"Are you sure?"

"Of course I'm sure."

Laura can sometimes have a tenuous relationship with Father Time. It would have been useless for me to try to discover what level of "sure" she was.

"I have to get this off tonight." She waved a package in the air.

"Can we call for a pickup?"

"It's too late. If they came in half an hour, the thing wouldn't make the plane."

"What else can we do?" I knew the answer to that question; it had lots of dollar signs attached to it.

The elevator dinged outside in the hall.

"Is there any way we can email this thing?" I asked

hopefully.

The front door opened and a FedEx guy came in. “Came for the pickup.”

Laura stared at him, open-mouthed, handed over the package. “How did you know to come here?”

“I've had this scheduled since this morning,” he said. “My Traffic Manager set it up.” He turned and left the office with the package.

Ms. Peasblossom stepped into the reception area. “Everything okay?” She smiled.

“Yes,” Laura said.

“Things are moving?” she perked.

“Yes,” I answered.

“Good!” She bounced back into her office, leaving Laura and me staring at each other. Anger was beginning to boil its way up from my gut.

This seemed a lot like magic.

And it wasn't just Mirabel's fake stuff. Ms. Peasblossom was managing to do something, and I couldn't explain what the hell it was.

Chapter 12

The following day, when I stopped into my Traffic Manager's office, I found a riot of plants. They were everywhere.

"Well, you certainly like plants, don't you!" You know, I once won the Mr. Obvious of the Year award?

I advanced into the room, surrounded by greenery. It seemed to be everywhere. As I continued to advance, it felt like I'd moved much further than the limits of her physical office. Logic dictated that I was standing ten flights up over Sixteenth Street. The foliage formed a seemingly endless tunnel. Ms. Peasblossom must have had one of those nature tapes running, with birds and forest creatures chittering away from the greenery. The fidelity of her sound system was great; the animals seemed real.

I escaped back to her desk. I was intimidated. I think one of the plants was trying to reach a branch toward me.

"I'm glad you like it," she chirped. Her cheeriness was beginning to grate. After all, I'm a creature of set, nasty ways.

"Just so long as it helps you."

"I'm exploring ways to speed things up."

"That's great!" She was doing it again, making me more enthusiastic. I had to escape to my office to restore my usual caustic demeanor.

I settled down behind my desk with a cup of coffee, turned on my computer, and pulled up my agenda to see what was on for today.

It was a foolish move. My real-life agenda attacked me from the outside world, shoving its way past the computer. Joel came into my office, wide-eyed, clutching papers to his chest. He sat down in front of me and wordlessly handed the papers over to me, acting like he was offering the Holy Grail.

It was a proof of a print piece that he'd been working on. It started with a large, calligraphic initial letter. "Joel, you've outdone yourself! This looks so damn good it's like illuminated text. I mean the leaf looks like real gold. Did Repro Depot get some new printer that can generate colors like this?"

"I didn't send it out to Repro Depot," he said, still staring at me.

"Oh, you've got some new house? Well if this is a sample of their work, they're keepers."

"I didn't send this out," the wide-eyed stare continued.

"Huh?"

"I did this on Grumpy."

It was my turn to switch over to a wide-eyed stare back at Joel.

Grumpy was a black-and-white printer.

Joel suddenly burst out, breaking the silence, "Harry, that little lady, the new one, I asked her about it, and she said it was okay, she'd fixed Grumpy." Joel suddenly leaned in toward me, imploring, "Harry, can I keep her? Can she stay forever and ever and ever?"

I raised a calming hand. "Joel, I'm sure there's a logical explanation for all of this. Let's go take a look to see what's happened."

We got up and headed out into the hall. We practically ran

into Sidney, coming the other way. "Aw for Chrissake!" he growled.

A Sidney "aw for Chrissake!" demands looking into, so I pulled Joel with me, and we followed the technical director into his office. He was already punching a number into the phone.

"What's the trouble?" I asked.

"They delivered the sofa for the demo room. I told them we had a very narrow doorway, I gave them the specific measurements, and they assured me it'd fit. Now we can't get the damned thing through." Fitting things through doorways was a technical director's stock in trade.

Sidney began to shout and swear over the phone at the furniture company. I turned to Joel to launch myself back into his problem when there was a crash of shattering glass from Laura's office, followed immediately by a long wail from my producer. She came running out of her office, continuing the wail, and rushed up to me in tears.

"Harry, my award!" she moaned.

Laura had an award, a glass thing. It had some name for "Industry Achievement," but I think it was for working the most consecutive hours. We have a ritual in our business. Some organization holds an awards banquet once a year. This is how it works: if you pay your membership dues, they nominate you for an award; if you buy a table for ten at the banquet, you win the award. Laura absolutely loved that damned thing.

She was blubbering on. "I went to dust it, and it's on that display case that we fixed up with duct tape, and the thing wobbled, and it fell, and it broke, and I'll never be able to put it back together."

"Now, now, I'm sure it's not that bad." I was lying. Judging from the sound I'd heard coming out of her office, I wouldn't dare walk into that place barefoot for a year. "Why don't we go and take a look at it and see what we can salvage out of it." Glass dust.

We started to head out the door of Sidney's office, when we ran into the sofa delivery guy. "Hey, buddy, you want to sign for this?"

"What do you mean, sign?" Sidney asked as he slammed down the phone. "We can't get the sofa through the door."

"Oh, yeah, we solved that problem," the guy replied.

"Huh?"

"The little black lady with the Afro, she took us the other way."

"Other way?"

"The back hallway. Hey, let me tell you about that place," he said as he leaned in confidentially. "First off, you need to replace all the blown-out bulbs back there. That place is dark. Then, once you got some light, I'd send in the exterminators. You not only got a bug problem, you got animals. I heard 'em."

"Let me see the damned sofa," Sidney said and led us into the demo room.

It was there sure enough. Sidney even satisfied himself by testing out its sitting capability. With his brow knit in bewilderment, he signed the receipt.

On to the next problem. "Okay, Laura, let's go check out your damage."

We headed back down the hall to Laura's room to look at her award--

--which was back in place on the display case, looking whole and hearty. Not only that, but the case had lost the duct tape that had been the better part of its structure and stood there strong and secure.

Standing next to it was Ms. Peasblossom. "Hi! I heard the thing fall in here and wanted to see what I could do. It wasn't bad. There was one tiny chip out of it, but I managed to glue it back on."

"And what about the display case?" I pointed.

"That was a little wobbly, but I tightened some pins on it, and it's now solid as a rock."

"Pins? You mean screws?" Sidney asked.

"Oh yes! Those things."

Sidney was staring intently at the case. He was trying to figure out where the cabinetmaker managed any joins in its structure. He softly voiced approval. "Neat!" It was no longer the trashy little refugee from Goodwill it had been. The wood grain turned corners, like it was one solid piece.

There were a lot of extraordinary things happening in our office, and I didn't like it one bit.

"That--" I pointed at the display case as my temper began to surge, "--I know what that is, and that's--not--Traffic!" I sputtered out. "You should be doing Traffic!" This was too much like that word beginning with *M*. I changed gears. I turned to the other three, a smile that was both frozen and manic painted on my face. "I think we should have a quick production meeting in my office to discuss the project we're working on."

"What project?" Joel asked.

"That thing!" I said.

"What thing?" Joel persisted.

I glared at him as I flashed my eyes over to Peasblossom and back. "You know," I squeezed out.

"Oh, *that* thing."

We went back to my office, securely shutting the door. I sat down at my desk and leveled a look at everyone else. I wasn't happy about Ms. Peasblossom, and everyone knew it. They, on the other hand, liked what they'd seen.

Joel still clutched the printout to his chest. "Can I keep her?" he implored.

"She brought my award back to life," Laura said.

"How the hell'd she get that sofa in here?" Sidney asked.

"Now listen, guys," I reined my emotions back and tried to reason with them, "I know she can do some really extraordinary things, but let's not go overboard here. I've got enough of a problem with phony--M-stuff--from my Mirabel days. Now there's some truly weird shit happening, and you're ready to go along with it?"

"Personally, I love it," Sidney said. "But what the hell, I spend my evenings taking stuff that makes the world turn weird." A thought struck him. "Man, she could really cut down on my entertainment expenses."

"Guys, let's not go down that road," I said. "Does it occur to you that we could be dealing with some dark, occult thing here? I mean this could be some kind of weird witchcraft shit."

"I don't think so," Laura said.

"You don't?"

"I don't think she's a witch."

"Why?"

"Well, not exactly, anyway. I was talking to her, and I was standing over her." And Laura's so tall, when she stands over you, she really stands *over* you. "I got a view looking through her Afro, and I could see down into it. There was something there."

"Something?"

"Yes." She was reluctant to continue.

"Okay," I said, beaming encouragement at her, "would you like to tell us what this something was?"

"Things." She did not display good elaboration skills.

"Better than something that isn't there. What were they?"

"Things on the top of her forehead."

"Gooood?" I gestured her to continue.

"They could have been antennae."

"Aw, for Chrissake, Laura, don't start giving me that

magical, mystical Mirabel bullshit. Things like that don't just happen."

Joel held up his illuminated print job. "Things like this don't just happen."

"I'm sure she's very technically adroit." I was rushing off to bask in the sun on the banks of Denial.

"Harry," Joel managed to squeeze the word out through his lips. "When Peasblossom told me Grumpy had printed this, I went to look at him. There were little voices coming from inside his cabinet."

"Oh, come on, Joel! 'There are Fairies in the bottom of my printer?' It was probably just some little animals."

"Anything like the ones that live in the hallway?" Sidney asked. "The hallway she took the sofa guy through?"

"When's the last time you believed anything a truck driver told you?" I countered.

"I can believe there's not another hallway in this building, and that the sofa couldn't fit through the door," Sidney reasoned. "If she can do what I think she can, we'll avoid all sorts of shit, like the incident with the dogs and the ponies."

I winced at the memory.

"Harry, she healed my award," Laura said.

"She didn't heal anything!" I shouted. "She can't do any of those things! I will not be dragged back into Mirabel's world again! I can't have her around! Tell Peasblossom to..."

"Did you want to talk to me?" she bubbled as she came in the door.

"YES!" I shouted that out. It made me even more pissed off to know she'd anticipated my words.

"Yes." I pulled myself back into proper office manners. "I think we need to talk. As you know I was taking you on as Traffic Manager to see how you would work out..." I paused to consider my next words. The other three glared at me.

Then my computer dinged, announcing a new email. I did the usual Pavlovian thing and swung my eyes around to check the message. It was from Wendell Simmons, my client at Lambert Industries, my biggest account. I leaned into the screen as I caught the Subject line.

PROPOSAL DUE TOMORROW!

"Shit! That bastard's done it again!" Proposals run to about twenty pages of creative, budgets, and scheduling. We'd need a week to get one together.

The panic in my voice brought the other three around behind me to look at the message. I opened it.

> Harry:
>
> So sorry! They suddenly dropped this in my lap.
> Proposal due tomorrow, August 25th, at 10am, on the following: 5-day meeting on the big island of Hawaii at the Hilo Kensington, Molokai Ballroom, October 16-20. Attendance of 500. Theme of the meeting: Planning the Future.

Something very strange caught my eye. The message was dated Wednesday, August 24, at 4:03 pm.

Sidney pointed at that last information on the screen and said, "What the hell's this? Today's the 10th."

I leaned back from my desk and exchanged a glance with Laura, Sidney, and Joel. We had the same thought on our minds: if that date was true, I was getting an email from the future. The four of us checked today's date with glances at various watches and cell phones. The calendar on the lower right-hand corner of my computer screen confirmed the date of the 10th. Up in the middle of the screen was the contradictory date on Wendell's message.

In contrast to the frowns the four of us shared, Ms. Peasblossom smiled serenely. I stared suspiciously at her as I picked up my phone and dialed Wendell.

"Hi, Wendell, it's Harry," I said in my most casual voice. "Just calling to find out if there's anything brewing over there that we could get a jump start on." I knew a project this big would not have come up at the last minute.

"No, Harry, it's as quiet as a tomb around here. You can be assured you'd be the first one I'd call if I heard anything going down."

"Okay, buddy, let me know if there's any way I can be of assistance to you," I gushed back.

"You bet," he said, and we hung up.

I slowly raised my gaze up to Peasblossom.

She beamed back at me. "Is that message one of those Traffic things I should take care of?" she asked.

I scowled and returned my gaze to the computer. I wasn't giving in to her! I whipped out a Reply to the email.

> Wendell,
>
> Would it be at all possible to give me a bit of breathing room by letting me submit sometime a little later in the day? As it is, we'll have to pull an all-nighter to get this thing out.

I clicked Send.

My message went out dated the 24th at 4:05 pm.

I rechecked my computer's date and time settings. They showed the morning of the 10th.

A reply came back immediately. It showed 4:50 pm on the

24th. I noted that it was nearly an hour after my response and just before the end of the business day.

> Harry,
>
> I'm sorry, buddy, but I have to give Purchasing my budget by noon tomorrow.
> By the way, you know how they are about open bidding! I needed a competitive proposal, so I also sent an RFP to Gordon Montbatten over at Metro. He said he could get it done on time.

That double bastard! Translate "noon tomorrow" to mean he didn't need a budget until the middle of the next week. Well, the middle of *that* next week! And what's he doing getting a bid from Metro? They're my biggest and worst competitors.

At that point, Sidney got off a call he'd made on his cell phone. "I just talked to Lenny Kanaka at the Kensington. He told me Wendell's department booked about 600 rooms for those dates back in May."

I was pissed off. I was pissed off at Wendell for not letting me know about this project sooner. I was pissed off at him for going to that sleaze Gordon Montbatten for a competitive bid. I was pissed off because I was finding out information through magic, and I hate magic! And there was magic happening in my office! I wheeled around toward my Traffic Manager, ready to fire her. My anger shriveled up when I saw what was in front of me.

Sidney's phone call had moved him over to the center of my office. He was standing behind Peasblossom. As a matter of fact, all three of them were grouped around her. Earlier they'd surrounded me, but they had all migrated to form a protective barrier around the Traffic Manager. I had the distinct impression that they had taken sides, and it wasn't mine.

"Well," Sidney said, "at least we've got lots of time to put together this proposal. I think I'll give a call to suppliers and start getting budget figures. I'll also have to figure out how to *Traffic* all the gear to Hawaii." He gave Peasblossom a pat on her shoulders and left my office, pointing his index finger at me with the thumb extended upward.

"I'd better go check on the availability of freelancers for that time," Laura said. "We'll have to *Traffic* them onto the job." She smiled at the Traffic Manager and headed out the door, trailing a steely glance toward me.

"I can just see it!" Joel enthused as he spread his arms wide. "In the tropical paradise of Hawaii! I'll fill the place with exotic plants. I'll *really,*" the last word was directed at me, though he leaned over Peasblossom, "need some help with plants. I'll have to *Traffic* them in." He turned his significant glance back to Peasblossom, then glided out the door.

The three of them had left me alone with my Traffic Manager.

Now was the time to get rid of her.

"You want to get rid of me."

Damn it! She'd done it again. But I wasn't going to let her steer the conversation. I was going to take charge.

"Listen..." I started.

"This is all about Mirabel." Not a question, a statement.

And she'd done it again, dammit!

"How do you know about her?" I asked.

"I have ways." She smiled.

"Did Mirabel send you?"

"Goodness, no!" she tittered. "Mirabel can't talk to us!"

I purposely avoided that "us" she'd just said. I narrowed my eyes as I spoke to her. "Then why are you here?"

"She can't talk to us," she leveled her gaze at me, "but *you* can."

I frowned as I tried to absorb what she'd just told me. I can talk to the--whatever--but Mirabel can't! This won't do! I decided to get the conversation back to where I wanted it. "Listen..."

"Can I relax?" she asked.

"Huh?" Damn! She'd caught me off guard again!

"Can I relax?" she repeated.

"You can always relax around me," I lied.

She didn't touch her hair. She didn't reach up and comb or brush it or do a thing, but her Afro shrank. It retreated to short curls, revealing the antennae at the front of her head along with the points at the top of her ears. The hair also turned green. I couldn't help but notice there were a couple of other things that she did. One of them was to suffuse a very strong perfume. It smelled like a flower store, only without the refrigeration. It permeated to every point in the room. My office had never smelled this good. Certainly not since the ponies. Her clothes had also changed to something that looked like a bunch of leaves gathered around her body.

I continued to stare at her. "Well, that answers the first question I was going to ask, so I'll move on to the next one. What do you mean I can talk to you? Who's the 'you' you're referring to?"

"All of us in my home. We knew you needed help."

"And you got sent to help me. You're helping the guy who hates magic," I tapped my chest, "*with* magic."

"That's right."

I leaned back in my chair. "Well, I don't want it!"

"You've got to get rid of her." Did she just steer the conversation again?

"Who?" I asked,

"Mirabel."

"I got rid of her." I folded my arms across my chest.

"No, you didn't. You keep dragging her around after you by holding onto your hatred of magic. Magic doesn't mean Mirabel, and Mirabel doesn't mean magic."

I pouted down at the floor. "I still hate magic."

"Did you hate getting that email ahead of time?"

"Well, no but..."

"Did you hate the print job Grumpy did?"

"I'll admit that was nice..."

"Then what's the problem?"

"I don't believe in--" I waved my hand around aimlessly. I couldn't face the end of the sentence.

"What?"

"--you!"

"But I'm right here," she said.

"Don't try to confuse me with facts! You *can't* be here."

"Why?"

"Because Mirabel says you *are*!"

Peasblossom's laughter tinkled across the room. "Mirabel says things that aren't true. She said she could do magic, and she couldn't. That's why you had to leave her." She turned her gaze on me. "The problem is, you left her, but you didn't get rid of her."

"I divorced her. She's out of my life."

"No she isn't. She's still here."

And suddenly I realized she was. That bitch had sunk her claws so deep into me that I was still dragging her around after me.

"Let me help you," Peasblossom said.

"Huh?"

"Let me help you get rid of her."

"How?"

"Just watch."

Now in Mirabel's world, Peasblossom would have started incanting, waving her hands around, and throwing unspeakable ingredients into a cauldron. But she didn't do that. She didn't do much of anything but look at me for a moment, then turn away.

I waited. "That's it?" I finally asked.

"Yes."

"What a fake! I'm supposed to feel some immense purge happening. I should see all sorts of kaleidoscopic colors, and my blood should be surging through my veins. How can this be magic?"

Her response was one, slow, wait-for-it nod.

"Wait a minute! That's it! I feel *nothing*. There's no longer that knot in my stomach. My nerves aren't stretched out like bowstrings. I'm--I'm--*relaxing*."

She gave a satisfied smile.

"Shit! This won't do! I can't possibly function in my business being a calm, even-keeled tower of strength. I need those nice, familiar neuroses short-circuiting my brain. My business will fail within a year."

"Don't worry," she said. "Just think about the proposal you've got to prepare."

"What? That's no problem. It just needs a budget--Omigod, a budget! They're going to fight me every inch of the way, trying to pare down the cost, then blame me about the quality."

"Feeling better?"

I looked up at her, bright-eyed. "Yes! Yes. There's good, old-fashioned hysteria coursing through my brain."

"You might think about getting along with magic. It could become a part of your life."

"You think so? You'll be able to do other things like this?" I began to open up to it a little.

"Within limits."

I contemplated. "We'll be able to do a proper proposal for Wendell, even though he doesn't deserve it."

"Yes."

"Wait a minute! I remember something!"

"What?"

I raised an accusing finger up at her. "You people don't just help. You always make a deal, don't you? You expect something in return. There's always a tradeoff."

"Yup, yup," somebody said from a chair over in the corner. The chair had been empty a minute ago. "We do expect some'at in return."

It was the little union gnome guy! He'd just appeared out of nowhere.

Chapter 13

There were bunches of qestions I had to ask this guy. Why was he here? How did he get here? What came out was, "Did you cause that fire at the theater?"

"Nope."

"You didn't?" It sure looked that way.

"Th'explosion caused the fire," he stated.

"Did you cause the explosion?"

In response, the little man got down out of the chair. His legs were so short they didn't reach the floor. He was shorter than Peasblossom. His spindly legs led up to an egg-shaped body. A long, twisty, bulbous nose dominated his face.

He wasn't answering my question. "Did you?" I pursued.

He pursed his lips and looked back at me. "Mebbe."

"Why did you do that?" I asked.

"It prevented worse things," he answered.

"What worse things?"

"Hard t'explain," he said.

I wasn't getting anywhere with this line of conversation. Had to move on to the next order of business. "How did you get here?"

"Always been here," he replied.

"What do you mean?"

"Always been here. Couldn't be there, 'cause I've always been here. *There* is over there some'ere." He waved vaguely.

I was getting frustrated. Best to stay logical. "When did you arrive in this room?" I was ultra-concise in my wording, or else this guy might wind up telling me that Who was playing first base.

"About three widgins ago."

And I Don't Know was on third base!

"Widgins?" I asked.

"Yup."

"I guess it'd take a while for you to explain how long one of those things is," I said.

"Quite a few more widgins." He nodded.

"Okay. Now that we haven't settled that issue, maybe we should move on to see what else we can't settle. Why are you here?"

"Because I'm not there," he responded.

I stared at him for a moment, then turned to Peasblossom. "Do I need an interpreter?"

"He has a very logical mind," she replied.

"You call that logical?" I was getting no help from her. Was she so petty as to resent the fact that I'd been about to fire her? I swung back to my new guest and said very slowly, "Is - there - a - reason - why - you - came - here?"

"Yup. Yup."

I waited. He did nothing but pull out an absolutely filthy-looking pipe and begin to stuff tobacco into it.

I put on a pre-school teacher's tone of voice. "Do you want to share that reason?"

"Yup. You wanted me."

That piece of illogic hit me like a bucket of water thrown on a sheet of oil. It didn't stick. "I think I made a mistake. I couldn't possibly have wanted you."

"Yup, you did. You wanted to make a deal with me."

"No way I would've wanted to deal with you. The negotiations would have taken too many widgins."

"More like wodgins."

"There, you see, I don't have that much time." I hoped I'd concluded the conversation.

"But you said we'd want some'at, and you were right."

"Oh sure, I know how those deals work. You'd want something like my first born. But I don't have a first born. I don't have a--wait a minute!" I jumped up out of my chair. "Okay, you people want to make a deal? You want something in return? I've got something to give you: my ex-wife! Okay! Take her, and we've got a deal!" I bounced my fist on the desktop like a gavel.

"Don't want her," he replied.

"But she's into that magic shi--the stuff that you do. She'd be a great match."

"No, don't rightly think she'd fit in," he said.

"I told you she couldn't talk to us," Peasblossom interjected.

The little guy smacked his lips and gazed at Peasblossom. "Now, let me see, if you agree to take her..."

"*Agree* to take her?" I pounced on his words. I sensed something here.

"Well--uh, yup, uh--that's right."

"Is there something wrong with her?" I smelled a bargaining point.

"Nothing you'd much mind."

Yeah there was something there, but I didn't know what it was. It was going to take me far too many widgins or wodgins to get this out of him. I had to streamline the negotiations. I swung around to Peasblossom. "What is it?"

She looked down at the floor and muttered, "My people have been trying to find a place for me."

"For you?"

"Yes." For once her brimming confidence faded away. Hesitancy came into her voice. "I'm not exactly like everyone else back home. You know how I was able to do things with your computer, and the shredder, and Grumpy?"

"Yes?"

"Most of my people don't do that. As a matter of fact, they have an allergy to iron. My people don't like your machines, don't want to have anything to do with them. But I do. I'm able to work with them, and because of that, my people laugh at me."

"They laugh at you?"

"Yes."

I slowly sat back down, stared at her and started ticking things off on my fingers. "You can work with computers. You have no problems with machines. Your people make fun of your ability." I paused, looking at her. "You're an elf nerd?"

She nodded the slightest bit of assent.

I swung my gaze back around to the little man, mustered up all the negotiation outrage I could, pointed at Peasblossom, and said, "Damaged goods!"

"Yeh be thinking that?" he asked.

"Of course," I replied.

He turned to Peasblossom. "What were that thing he got what referred to the Far Isles?"

"An email," she replied.

"Yup," he said, as he turned back to me. "That there scream mail, did it not serve you well?"

I pursed my lips and looked up at the ceiling, feigning

indifference. "It might have."

"We don't have to do them things." Whoops! There went my no-concede clause.

"Let's just suppose that I could use *little* services like that," I mentally hefted my negotiation stance.

"Yup. Yup. We could do that, but you've got to agree to help us." He was staring off, trying to be casual, but I could tell this was the crux of what he was getting at.

"You need help?"

"Yup."

"On what?"

He pursed his lips. Since they had started out already pursed, this was more like shoulder-bagging them. "Troubles," he said.

I paused, waiting for him to fill something in. When he stolidly sat there puffing on his pipe, I ventured, "You know, I'm a little vague on this 'Troubles' thing. Could you do the favor of filling me in on it?"

"There be some of your people--," a pause, "--and some of our people what are causing Troubles."

"Okay," I spread my hands and laid them down on the desktop, "so we've outlined the cast of characters, but we still haven't straightened out this pesky little 'Troubles' issue."

"Yup."

"I thought you might like to fill some of us--oh, maybe--*all* of us in on the details of that item." I let my gaze fall on Peasblossom.

"It be Troubles." He puffed on his pipe, laying down an actual smoke screen to accompany his verbal one.

I brought the palms of my hands together and rubbed them. "I think that in your--uh--business this 'Trouble' thing seems to be a term of art that I don't fully understand." I was on familiar ground. My language had lapsed into Corporatese.

"Hard to explain it t'you."

"All right, then, let's set that issue aside, and let's get to the question of how often I may have to take care of this thing."

"Every few wodgins."

Great! Not only couldn't I nail down the 'Trouble' issue, I needed to know the rate of exchange between elf and Earth time. But, ignorance never slowed me down in negotiations. "That's way too often!"

"We could maybe let it stretch a little longer."

"I should think so."

"Yup, then it's settled." And he disappeared.

"What? What's settled?" I jumped up from my chair and raced over to the place where he'd been and stared at empty floor. I turned to Peasblossom. "Where'd he go?"

"Back."

"Back where?"

"Home."

"Why did he go back there?"

"Because you'd settled the deal."

"What deal?"

"The one you talked about."

"We didn't talk about anything! We talked about some things called wodgins and widgins and some goddamned 'Trouble.' That's it."

"That's right." She beamed agreement at me.

I beamed back in sarcasm. "I knew that was *right*. However, I don't know what the hell it *is* that's right."

"Don't worry, you'll find out."

"That's what scares me." I closed my eyes to calm myself. "Okay, let me figure this one out. We just made a deal?"

"Yes."

"By the way, who is this guy?" I indicated the recently-vacated spot in my office.

"He's someone very important."

"He's a big deal in the elf world?"

"Yes."

"And what's his name?"

"You could call him Corgus."

"Okay, I'll call him Corgus, in lieu of several other names I'd like to call him." I wandered back to my desk chair and sat down. "So my buddy, Corgus, and me, we made a deal. I don't know what the hell the deal is, but I think it involves some widgins and wodgins, which are also things I don't know anything about."

I put the tip of my index finger to my mouth and contemplated for a minute. "You know what? I'm used to this. I'm making a deal I don't know anything about with someone who isn't clear on what's going down either. That's corporate life!"

I took that same index finger and pointed it at Peasblossom. "Dealing with Fairyland is just like dealing with Corporate Land. I should get along fine."

"I guess things are under control here," she said, all composed. She started to leave, secure that she still had her job.

That brought me back to the moment. "Uh, one thing, Ms. Peasblossom, I think it would help the others if you put your hair back the way it was." Oh, yes, I was lying! I was back in control!

"Oh, okay," she said, and the Afro grew back into place.

"One other thing," I called her back as she turned toward the door. She faced me again. "The clothes. It'd be a good idea to put the clothes back."

"Good!" she enthused. "I like them. You can keep changing them, depending on how you feel." Proper business attire reappeared on her body. I wondered if anyone would notice that it was a different outfit.

She opened the door. "I'll just go out and make sure the traffic is moving in the office. You know, I've got some friends in Hawaii. I bet I can get some really great fairy lights for Joel." She started to leave.

"Wait a minute." She stopped. "I've got a piece of magic you can do for me first," I said.

"What's that?"

"Find out what the hell a Traffic Manager does."

Chapter 14

The following day I decided to head to Peasblossom's office to get some more info. She was seated at her desk in her office, with all the plants curling and cooing around her. A tunnel of greenery burrowed off into the space above Sixteenth Street. I tried not to look into it.

I sat down in the chair in her office. "You might find this hard to believe, but there are a few holes in the conversation with this Corgus dude that I'd like straightened out."

"Yes?" she said.

"There's that word he used--Trouble? I can imagine all sorts of degrees of Trouble, ranging from a Little Bit of Trouble all the way to Big-Time Trouble. Then there's different flavors, like Trouble with a 90-pound guy all the way to Trouble with someone who's the size of a jumbo jet."

"There's Trouble with the first kind, the 90-pound guy," she said.

"Oh, good!"

"But there is something else," she responded.

"What's that?"

He's major wizard of the occult arts."

I closed my eyes, then re-opened them. "Uh, Peasblossom, that's a different variation on the flavor thing."

"Oh."

"But on the other hand, you should be able to handle that. After all, you can do some pretty mean magic yourself," I said.

"Not really."

"Why not?" I blinked. She usually tried her best to be helpful.

"Because I'm LAPH-ing," she said, all seriousness.

I saw her expression, but plowed on. "Okay, but could you get serious for a minute and take care of this guy?"

"I am serious."

"Then why are you laughing?"

"I don't understand. LAPH-ing is very serious."

I stared at her for a moment. "Okay. Are you doing this serious laughing thing right now?"

"Of course."

"You'll find this funny, but I failed to notice it. Maybe you'd better explain it to me."

"It's something that we do, my friends and me back home."

"Your elf nerd friends?"

"Yes. All of us who can work with machines. We're called the Drawbacks."

"You all laugh together?"

"Oh, no, we don't do it together."

"You laugh separately."

"That's right."

"Can you describe this laughing-in-different-rooms thing you do?"

"Yes, L-A-P-H." She spelled it out.

"L-A-P-H," I repeated dully.

"Yes. Live Action Playing Human. We pretend that we're human and can only do what humans do. That's why I came here to be your Traffic Manager. All the other Drawbacks really envy my title. I get extra points if I can go back and describe what my duties are."

"Good luck on that part," I said. "Let's get back to this killer wizard. Why can't you counteract his magic with your own?"

"Because I'm LAPH-ing."

I leaned back in my chair. "Let's just assume I haven't memorized the rules of LAPH-ing. You used magic to get me the email ahead of time. Isn't that magic?"

"Yes, but only minor magic."

"And you can do that while LAPH-ing?"

"Yes."

"And whatever you might need for this evil wizard, you can't do that?"

"No."

"Why not?"

"It's kind of involved. Corgus could best explain that."

I raised an eyebrow. "*He* could explain that? I didn't understand a word he said before. How could he manage to make these things clear to me?"

"Oh, he couldn't make things clear, but he could explain them."

I stared at her for a moment. "Now you're beginning to sound like him. Okay, so when can I expect to hear from this evil wizard?"

"I don't know."

"Figures," I said with a nod.

"But I'm pretty sure you'll get some sort of warning."

"Yeah. I'll turn into a frog and that'll be my signal."

"Something like that," she replied.

I was beginning to get a migraine. I got up and headed back toward my office. "Let me know if you see me suddenly nailing flies across the room with my tongue."

"I'll be on the watchtower."

"Huh? Oh, you mean lookout."

"Yes. That."

On my way back to the office, I realized I had just discovered something else a Traffic Manager does.

LAPH.

Chapter 15

I was seated in my office when Laura, Sidney, and Joel came barging in and arranged themselves in chairs in front of me.

"Harry, this is an intervention," Laura announced with puritanical righteousness.

"Oh really?" I replied, taking them all in. "Funny, but I don't recall taking bunches of drugs. Of course there's a reason for that: I don't take any."

"No, this is about something else," Laura said.

"Okay, what?"

"We think you're heading down a path that will only lead to trouble," she continued.

"What path is that?"

"You should know that it's inadvisable to have an affair with one of your employees." She pursed her lips in disapproval.

Since the roaring majority of my employees were sitting in front of me, and I wasn't having an affair with any of them, I tried to figure out what Laura was talking about. Then it struck me. "You don't mean Peasblossom."

"I most certainly do," Laura said with an I-am-only-here-to-help-you tone of voice.

"What do you mean?"

"The other day we left you alone with her in your office, and we were under the impression you were going to fire her. The next thing we know, she re-emerges from your office, *wearing a different outfit,* and she is now an employee in good standing. Harry, you know that you don't want to carry on affairs with members of your own staff."

She was right. Never mix business with pleasure. "Oh, I see what it looks like. Well, how do I explain this?" My gaze drifted around the room. "She spilled something on her dress, however she had another outfit with her. Yes, she did change her clothes, but I discreetly turned my back. It was all very proper."

"Nothing happened?" Laura leaned in accusingly.

"Absolutely not." I clasped my hands together in front of me and formulated my words. "Let me explain something else. I think you'll admit that Peasblossom is a little different from the rest of us."

"Yeah, there's something strange about her," Sidney said.

"She's a nice person, and all of that," I continued, "but I can honestly say that she doesn't attract me at all, in a physical way."

"You know, he's right. I've got to admit that I've noticed no sexual vibe coming off her," Sidney said. "And I'm good at sexual vibes. I can find them in a toaster."

Laura swung her gaze from Sidney around to Joel for confirmation.

He glanced around the room, gave a small shrug and said, "Don't ask *me*."

Laura turned back to me. "Harry, nothing happened?"

"I can assure you, Laura, I have a strictly professional relationship with her." If she only knew. I didn't even LAPH with Peasblossom.

"Well, I'm glad of it," she begrudged.

Sidney and Joel appeared to accept what I said. I could tell that Laura still entertained a small doubt.

#

I decided to spend the evening at Percy's bar counting my blessings. So far those blessings totaled half a dozen peanuts in the bowl in front of me. I had also counted a glass of scotch in front of me, but it had come and gone about half a dozen times.

I contemplated a problem I was facing with my company. If you're a graduate of the Wharton School of Business you might talk about how you are experiencing an adverse cash flow event. Since I did not matriculate at that esteemed institution, I was not experiencing one of those events. I was broke. Especially after all of the costs I'd incurred on the Patten Products fiasco. The other wonderful thing about clients like Wendell is that they not only expect you to deliver on a moment's notice, they take a few geologic eras to pay your invoices. I was waiting for several companies that were overdue on my bills. I really needed that Hawaii job.

I decided to head back to the restroom after having spent several hours at the bar. When I stepped out of the men's room, I was faced with a choice. It was time for me to leave, and I reasoned that it was really more direct to head out Percy's back door to get to my place. Me and my adverse cash flow may have forgotten about the tab I'd been running during my stay at the bar.

The back door exited to the alley in the rear. I was halfway to the street when I was suddenly grabbed from behind and a very sharp knife was put to my throat. The blade pressed against my jugular vein. I wanted to swallow, but had no room to do that.

Part 2

...taking on Responsibility

Chapter 16

The person holding the knife to my throat hissed out, "He wants to see you."

"And words just can't describe how eager I am to see him." Whoever the hell "he" was. I tried to keep my voice from quavering while I did my best to maintain the conversation, rather than lape into *anything* physical. "But I know just how meticulous 'he' is."

"You do?" His voice registered surprise.

"Absolutely," I assured, propelling the conversation forward. "And I know how distressed 'he' would be if I arrived not properly dressed."

"Properly dressed?" That's right, sweetheart, keep talking.

"Yes, you know, if I arrived doing something like bleeding profusely from the neck. I'm sure that would upset him a lot."

"You think so?" A new note had come into his voice. It seemed like he was more confused by something else, not so much my talking.

"You bet. I mean I'd probably make a real mess of the rug, for openers, and you know how much he paid for that." I continued. "Don't you think it might be an absolutely swell idea for you to take that knife--oh--just a little way away from my neck? I mean just to make sure we don't get all messy?" In the meantime, hysteria was doing wind sprints up and down my spine, bursting to come out.

"I'm supposed to hold onto you," he said, sounding like his mind was somewhere else. He seemed to be waiting for something.

"And you can bet that I'll be as still as a rock for you," I assured him.

"I dunno. I gotta hold on to you. But I already gave him the signal and nothing's happened."

Signal? What signal? "That means that you've got to hold back a little bit, stand down from high alert." I continued to babble on.

Then I heard a crunch.

This crunch was exactly the sound of someone being firmly koshed on the head.

I stood there knowing I'd brought it on. I went too far trying to talk this guy out of something, and he grew tired of it and had thumped me to shut me up.

However, that very act of standing there thinking brought home the point that I was still conscious. Not only that, my assailant was feeling the pull of gravity as his arm fell away form my throat and he slid down my back to crumple on the ground behind me. I turned around to find myself face to face with Bruno.

"Hi, Mr. Chatham, Percy wanted me to follow you out. Lucky I did. That guy didn't look friendly. So I banged him."

"Bruno, you're right. His manners weren't the best. Who is this guy? Do you recognize him?"

We turned to regard our recumbent friend. We didn't have a long time to take a look as he suddenly vanished. He disappeared off the pavement. That was strange, but strange things had started happening in my life since I'd taken on my new employee.

I couldn't help wondering what would have happened if he'd still had his grasp on me when he disappeared. Would I have gone with him to meet the "he" he talked about?

I turned to look at Bruno. There were questions flitting across both of our faces.

Then I pulled myself back to the current moment. Bruno had been sent to escort me out past my current bar tab. I had to figure some way to divert his attention, not a difficult task in his case. "You know, Bruno," I said, "I'll bet Percy sent you out here to make certain I got out of the alley safely. Why don't you walk with me to the street?"

"Sure, Mr. Chatham." One thing you had to say about Bruno: he lived in the moment. He couldn't remember the previous one.

When we got to the street, I said, "Bruno I really appreciate you helping me like this. When you get back inside, why don't you give yourself a nice drink, something you really like? You can just put it on my tab."

If I had An adverse cash flow, Percy had to be affected.

Chapter 17

I dashed toward my office the following morning. I'd spent the previous night circling through my apartment, checking all the locks on the doors and windows. Although I wasn't sure what good that would do. If some dude could disappear off the pavement, it only made sense that he could *appear*, right in the middle of my bedroom, where I was sleeping. Therefore, I lay there all night, wide awake, staring at the ceiling.

I raced down the sidewalk, totally focused on getting to the office to confer with Peasblossom.

And then, as I crossed a street, I ccaught the eye of someone crossing heading in the opposite direction. I careened past her, but our eyes had locked, and we both turned back, short of the curb, and stared at each other.

I began to lose myself in her eyes. They were large and green with gold flecks. I was engulfed and floated into them. They were both milky and syrupy, and I didn't care about the conflicting texture because I was just gliding away into them entirely lost in their delights as I...

"Get the fuck out of the way, will ya?" a truck driver bellowed, trying to turn the corner. "Unlike you, I gotta be somewhere today."

We both leaped to the curb closest to us, on opposite sides of the street. The driver gunned the truck between us.

When the truck had cleared, she was gone. I dashed across the street to see if I could find her, in the course of which I was cursed out in Farsi by a cab driver. When I got to the opposite corner, there was no trace of her. I darted around in the crowd, looking frantically. I asked several of the people if they'd seen her and got the standard New York answer: "Who gives a crap?"

The sidewalk seemed to have swallowed her up. After hanging around for about ten minutes, not going anywhere, I finally gave up and continued toward the office, trying to figure out who the girl was, and how I could possibly see her again in the multitude of streets in New York City.

#

When I got in the building I bolted into Peasblossom's office and told her about my experience in the alley the previous night.

"They weren't fair," she said, righteously.

"You know, when he was holding that knife to my throat, I wasn't thinking whether it was fair or unfair. My thoughts were more focused on the live/die thing. What do you mean, unfair?" I exploded.

"They shouldn't use disappearing magic if they're LAPH-ing."

"The 'laughing' you just said. You're not talking about the ha-ha thing? You're talking about an elf pretending to be a bus driver?"

"Yes."

"Without using the kind of logic our friend Corgus employs, could you explain that to me?"

"Disappearing is too high a level of magic to be used when you're LAPH-ing."

"It's too serious to be a LAPH-ing matter?" I never let a good pun pass.

"Yes. And they shouldn't have done that before you were introduced."

"If holding a knife to my throat is only the pre-introduction, I'd be happy to skip the rest of the formalities."

"But they really shouldn't do it." She was quite outraged.

"I'll be sure to get the Fairyland Miss Manners on their case."

"They wouldn't let *me* do anything like that," she said.

"They wouldn't?"

"Not if I'm obeying the rules of LAPH-ing."

"Do me a favor. If someone's holding a knife to my throat--cheat!"

Chapter 18

I was back in Percy's the following night, seated in a booth. It had been a banner day. I'd received payment on a job we'd done six months ago, so I'd managed to take care of a number of outstanding items, which included making up a few weeks of payroll. I'd also made a decent-enough dent in my tab at the bar to once more become a customer in good standing. Even so, Percy had stationed Bruno near the rear exit in case I decided to once more make a hasty departure.

I was mulling several things. What did this Corgus guy mean when he said there were "Troubles" that I had to cope with? I was also wondering how I might devise to once again meet the young lady with the delightful green eyes.

I kept my attention on my drink and the table in front of me, ignoring the other patrons in the restaurant. Not a bad practice. Percy's is a New York bar. You don't want to make eye contact with most people in the place.

So I wasn't aware of this guy until he suddenly thrust himself in next to me in the booth and said, "Yes!" He wasn't agreeing with anything, just making an affirmative exclamation. "The conversation we're about to have has such a top-rated classification, you're going to have to forget about it the minute we're finished talking."

I leaned back and regarded the guy. "Tell you what. I'll

forget about this conversation *before* we've even had it." There are a number of Percy's clientele you don't ever want to interact with. They're too adroit at handling both sides of a dialogue all by themselves.

"You are called upon to serve your country in a time of national crisis." The guy just barreled on. He had to be one of Percy's regulars.

"Which particular national crisis is this one? Politicians keep coming up with a crisis *du jour*. I don't know how many of them I can fit into my schedule."

"We have reason to believe that you are at a nexus of operations that make your company's services critical to national security."

"Yeah, and I'm also at a nexus of I-don't-have-enough money."

"Your government needs you." He sounded like a recruiting poster.

This gave me pause. "Wait a minute." I held up a traffic-stop hand while I thought about what he'd just said. "Let me get my mind around that one." Something began to percolate in my brain.

"Does that mean that my company has become a defense contractor?"

Jackpot! Those people spent money like they could print more the following day--which was actually true. An awful lot of me wanted to believe that this guy was for real.

I took a closer look at him. He was small, not taller than five six, and wiry with a middle-age pot belly. He had an intense look on his face, and he had a bulbous nose that looked a bit familiar. I couldn't place where I'd seen one like that before. He also operated at an intensity that was just this side of hysteria.

"Yes! I think you might just qualify for that. Let me see..." He began to rummage around in the briefcase he'd brought. It was the first time I'd ever seen an armor-plated attaché case. He produced a telephone-book-sized stack of papers and plunked them down on the table. "Fill these out and you'll be able to qualify as an official government vendor."

My mental eyes crossed at the thought of that much paperwork. "So what is this nexus I'm in the middle of?" And does it pay very well, like enough to get me out of hock?

"Ah! Sorry, you do not have the proper security clearance for that."

"I don't have clearance for the nexus I'm in the middle of?"

"Yes! Far too classified for you to know about."

"Okay." I was trying to reason with the guy. Then a thought struck me. "Wait a minute. Does this have anything to do with the dude who put a knife to my throat the other night?"

"Someone tried to force you with a deadly weapon?"

"Yes."

For the first time, this guy leaned back and relaxed, as a smile crossed his face. "Ah! Wonderful!"

"What? Considering it was my neck, I don't think it was that wonderful. As a matter of fact, on a scale of one to ten, with one being Awful and ten being Wonderful, this rates a minus 15."

"That means events are developing as we had forecast."

"It would've been swell if you'd given me that forecast. I could have dressed properly that day."

"Hm!" He paused to reflect. "Means you qualify for hazardous duty pay."

"That's good?"

"Yes!" He reached back into Fort Briefcase and produced another telephone-book's-worth of papers. He slammed them down on top of the first group. "Fill these out, and you get your classification right away."

"Oh swell!" I said.

He leaped up from the table. "Ah! Must report this right

away." He turned to leave, then spun back and pointed a finger at me. "You must forget everything we've talked about."

"What? Where're you going?"

"Yes! Yes!" He dashed off toward the door.

"Wait a minute. Who do I give these papers to?"

He wheeled back to my table, and put a business card down. It contained one thing: a phone number. "Call this," he commanded, then spun around and headed out the door.

Another thought sprang into my mind. "Do you have anything to do with that Corgus guy who showed up in my office?" I shouted at his retreating figure.

He paid me no mind, just fluttered his hand dismissively over his shoulder and zipped out Percy's door.

So two people had suddenly appeared in my life, both of whom knew a lot about some strange happenings going on. However neither one of them was terribly clear on exactly what these happenings were. What was going on? Things were popping into my life, and I didn't know why.

I had a number of questions. What were Corgus's "Troubles?" What was this "nexus" this government guy talked about? Was I in any danger?

More importantly, was I getting some more business?

Chapter 19

The next morning I arrived at the office out of breath from toting all of those government forms the guy had given me at Percy's. I'd also spent a lot of time looking for a pair of green eyes with gold flecks. I dropped the forms down on Peasblossom's desk.

"Ms. Peasblossom, I want you to call the number on this card and see if all of these papers are legit." I gave her the card with the lone phone number on it. "Talk to them. See if we could really become a government vendor. If so, you'll have to fill out all these government forms."

"All of them?" she asked. Her eyes lit up with delight.

"Yeah. I'm sorry, but we can probably make a lot of money if we connect with the government."

"That's wonderful!" she burst out. "I get to plow through blue ribbon."

"Blue ribbon?" I asked.

"Yes."

I pondered. "Oh, you mean red tape?"

"Yes, that too."

"Is this one of those LAPH-ing things?" I asked.

"Yes. I'll get lots of points for this." She snatched up the top page and began scanning her way down it.

"You may have a few questions about them," I started...

She didn't listen to me as her eyes drank up the pages in front of her. I'd totally lost her.

I left and did the rounds through everyone else's office, checking on their progress on the proposal for Wendell.

After that, I went to my office, and turned on my computer to see if there was anything else I needed to focus on.

My computer had just booted up when my office door swung open and Peasblossom came bouncing in, carrying the reams of government forms. "I checked with the people at that telephone number."

"Those are real government forms?" I asked. A trickle of greed began to make its way down the back of my mind.

"Mm-hmm." She nodded her head, smiling.

I was going to ask her if she was sure, but I remembered that she could make emails appear weeks in advance. "Then could you please fill out those forms?"

"They're all finished," she said, plunking the pile down.

I couldn't believe her. I riffled through the pages and saw they were all filled. I got to the final page, checked the signature block and saw:

I shuffled the papers back together and said, "I think you may need to do the signature block in English. Why don't you just cover over this one with Wite-Out and do it again?"

Her eyes widened in delight. "I get to use Wite-Out?" She sounded like she was having a religious experience. "Do you know how many points that is?"

She did an elf dance out my office door.

Chapter 20

We were getting the proposal ready for Lambert. It was Tuesday, a couple of days before it was due. At about two o'clock Sidney came into my office.

"The fix is in." He slumped down in the chair in front of my desk.

"What do you mean?" I asked him.

"I just had lunch over at O'Dwyer's with Danny Haskins." Danny is the Technical Director for Metro, my big competition run by that sleaze, Gordon Montbatten. There's an insiders relationship among all of the TDs in the business. They share information they've accumulated, free-lancers, things like that. "He told me that they're already putting together the proposal for Lambert. They've been working on it since the 11th."

"Dammit! That's two weeks before we got it. Or, it's two weeks before we would have gotten it--or whatever." Tenses were becoming difficult. Or did I mean tense is becoming difficult?

"What do you think this is all about?" Sidney asked.

"Wendell's looking to give the job to Montbatten," I said. "He must have done something for him."

"You think he bribed him?" Sidney asked.

"No, it was probably something more innocent than that, like Gordon convinced Wendell he was intelligent."

Sidney locked eyes with me for a moment, then gave an assenting nod. "You're probably right."

"Actually," I replied, "anyone who can make Wendell think he's smart almost deserves the job."

Sidney leaned back in his chair and scratched his beer belly. "What's with this Montbatten dude?"

I shrugged. "How should I know? It's not like I'm crazy paranoid about him and hired a private investigator to find out all the dirt about him."

Sidney leveled a gaze on me that oozed the familiarity of someone who'd worked with me for several years. "And what did the PI find out?"

I pouted toward a corner of the room at his response. "That was a lucky guess."

"I probably would've done something like that myself," he replied. Then he looked up into the far distance. "No, my reaction would have been to administer truth serum to him."

"Truth serum?"

He turned back to look at me. "Yeah, something over 150 proof. Anyway what's the scoop on him?"

"Gordon Montbatten was born Giggy Makowski in General Hospital in Yonkers, NY," I explained.

"The town does have something to speak for it."

"What?"

"A racetrack."

"True. Anyway, Young Giggy matriculated high school in his home town and headed off to a small college upstate."

Sidney raised a finger in the air and took up the narrative. "And he settled down to a humble career as a school teacher in Syracuse."

"Nooooo."

He wiggled his hand in the air in an erasing gesture. "Okay, okay--" he raised an index finger in the air "--he formed a world-famous acid rock band and became a notorious sex machine."

"Sorry, but you're getting colder," I said with a shake of my head.

"Something's got to explain the English accent," Sidney said.

"Not to mention the change of name."

Sidney started to say something, but I held up a traffic-stop hand and continued. "I know what you're going to ask, and no, there is not a pocket of Britannia in a little valley somewhere in the Adirondacks."

"That *was* my next guess." Sidney thought for a moment. "But there's a lot of mountaintops up north. Was he struck by lightning on one of them?"

"The story will just have to remain hidden in legend," I said.

"Was that when he smarmed his way in as an account rep with Bizmedia?" Sidney asked.

"Yep, and stole all of their clients to open up Metro, where his record has remained consistent. He keeps getting business through means that are both remarkable and mysterious."

"What are we going to do about this latest development with the proposal?" Sidney brought the conversation back to our current predicament.

I rested my chin down on one hand, and contemplated the problem. There had to be a way around this.

Suddenly, inspiration struck. I slapped my hand down on my desktop as I reached a decision. "This is Traffic! It needs to be Managed."

Was I beginning to rely on her?

Time for action. I parted with Sidney and dashed down the hall to Peasblossom's office. I bolted in so fast I nearly became romantically involved with one of the plants in there.

I breathlessly explained the problem to her, and finished, panting.

She sat stone still in thought.

I ran out of patience and said, "Well?"

She focused her gaze on the desktop in front of her.

Finally she raised her head and said one thing: "Mustardseed."

"I'm standing here waiting for you to solve my problem, and all you can do is make out your shopping list?"

She glanced up at me as though I'd brought her back from a distant world, and said, "Let me work on it."

I was about to ask her what she was going to do, but realized a simple fact: I wouldn't understand.

I reluctantly left her alone in her office, but I hung around, waiting to see what she came up with. I went to get a cup of coffee. I riffled through the incoming mail. I glanced at my email Inbox. I got another cup of coffee. I approached her door, then turned around before going in. I checked the date and time on my computer. I headed toward the Conference Room to get more coffee but noticed my hands were already shaking from caffeine overdose. I looked around for something to do. My eyes fell on the inbox on my desk, with its vast, unexplored depths. I started to think about cleaning the thing out. My God! I was getting desperate.

I couldn't wait anymore. I dashed into her office to find out how she was doing, renewing my old flame with the plant in there. As a matter of fact it seemed to be reaching out a limb toward me as I backed off.

Peasblossom was gone. She couldn't have left the office. I would have seen her. There was no place she could have gone, except into the tunnel of greenery that stretched out from her office over Sixteenth Street and into some strange dimension.

Chapter 21

I sat in my office. I'd been sitting there for quite awhile. The realization struck that I was just hanging around waiting for Peasblossom to reappear and tell me what to do about the proposal for Wendell. It was time for me to do something. My brow furrowed as I tried to figure out exactly what. Then the idea hit me. I'd get together with the rest of my staff to review their progress on the proposal. I realized it was the same as rearranging the deck chairs on the *Titanic,* but it was the only thing I knew how to do, so I was going to do it as well as I could.

I checked the design with Joel.

"I thought I'd push the tropical aspect of the locale," he said, spreading some sketches out in front of me. "Rent a bunch of potted plants and trees to spread around the ballroom--make them the foreground of the surroundings. The room's got a floral wallpaper that I'd use as the background."

"Any chance we could save on the budget by just using the wallpaper by itself?" That's the kind of question the corporate types would ask me that I'd have to be ready to answer.

Joel's lips pursed in a frown of displeasure. "Harry, you can never expect art out of a wallpaper company."

"You've got a point there."

"You know, I got the idea for this from Peasblossom's office, with all those plants in there. I mean they almost look like they continue on outside the limits of her office. Let's be sure to take her on site. I'm sure she'll be invaluable to me."

I didn't have the heart to tell Joel that I didn't think any of us were going, that Gordon had the inside track. "Sure, I'll have Laura put her in the budget."

"I've got to admit Peasblossom's done wonders for you," he continued. "You're not exploding every time you hear the M-word." Joel glanced back over his shoulder to make sure no one else was around, then leaned in confidentially. "Don't tell the others, but I think there's something *special* about her. I mean the way she was able to upgrade Grumpy to a color printer. And she just seems to be--*lucky*."

I put on my best fake-confident smile. "Hiring a Traffic Manager seems to have been a good idea."

Joel was all wide-eyed. "Yes."

I rose from my desk to conclude the meeting. "Okay, let's do our best on this proposal."

#

I decided I needed a cup of coffee after the meeting with Joel.

On my way, I checked in Peasblossom's office.

She wasn't there.

#

I crosschecked the technical specs with Sidney.

"I contacted some of my down and dirty sources around Lambert," he said. Sidney's sources were undoubtedly both down and quite dirty. "I've got one big problem. It seems the fucking beancounters over there have poked their noses into the shipping costs for this meeting. They've come up with one of their usual genius plans."

"What's that?"

"Well, we're flying the gear into Honolulu, but they've vetoed the costs of air cargo to Hilo."

"What else is there?" I asked.

"Everything's being transferred to a barge, and it's going to be towed to Hilo. The boys in Finance figure they'll save a bundle consolidating all shipping costs for everyone supporting the meeting."

"Wouldn't they prefer to have everything towed by oxen?" I asked.

"Watch it!" Sidney exclaimed as he held up a halting hand. "They might hear that."

"Okay, put their numbers in for the budget proposal. We'll see if there's any way we can wiggle out of it down the road."

"There's one benefit. I'm going to use the barges to launch the fireworks out over the water on banquet night. I've got Sparkle Plenty to handle that. They've got all the proper licenses for Hawaii."

"Fireworks always work. Since Sparkle Plenty's there, let's also do some indoor pyrotechnics in the ballroom for the main meeting."

"Yeah." Sidney paused like there was something on his mind. He rubbed the palm of his hand across his lips, then leaned in confidentially. "I've been thinking, Harry, that new girl? Do you notice how she's able to do a number of near-impossible things?"

"Yes." I waited for him to continue.

He glanced to the left and right, "Don't mention it to Laura and Joel, but I think she's got some special talents. You might want to take her out on this show."

"That's a good idea. You know, I think she's working out in the job, Sidney."

"Yeah, yeah. Me too."

#

I definitely needed to go to the bathroom. Definitely. On my way I happened to glance into Peasblossom's office.

Where the hell was she?

I went back to my office. Okay, so maybe I didn't have to go to the bathroom.

#

"...And a couple of roadies to do the heavy lifting," Laura sat in my office, reading off the list of on-site crew.

"And the drug consumption," I added.

"Yeah, that too."

"Okay that covers the requirements for airline tickets and hotel rooms. Did you talk to Sidney about the costs for Sparkle Plenty to do the fireworks?"

"That's included."

"Good."

Laura paused, and frowned as she tried to frame some words. "I was wondering if we could squeeze Peasblossom into the travel budget."

"You think we might need some traffic managed in Hawaii?" I asked.

"Not just that. She may prove handy if we have some sort of crisis. She managed that remarkable repair on my award. You know how we always need something done onsite that can't be handled just by duct tape."

"She'd be handy for something like that?"

"I know Joel and Sidney wouldn't think so, but I just have an intuition about her, it's a gender thing. I think she's capable of far more than we might suspect."

"If you think she'd be a good addition, put her in," I gave an affirming wave of my hand.

"Okay."

I tapped my index finger to my lips, in contemplation. "I

think the important thing will have to be the creative treatment on this proposal. Why don't we figure we'll get together tomorrow afternoon to work on it," I said. "We've got to put a lot of love into it. It's got to absolutely sizzle."

Laura scooped up her laptop and left.

I sat alone in my office and drummed my fingers on the arm of my chair. I peered out my door.

I would not, I definitely would not, go looking for Peasblossom. I stared at her office door down the hall. I walked over to my office window to make sure that Sixteenth Street was still down there. I went back to my desk and ran my fingers over the piles of papers scattered on it. I checked through my desk drawers to see if someone had left bags of gold inside. I looked up at my door. I finally bolted and ran and leaped inside her office.

No sign of her.

I returned to my office and sank my head in my hands as I tried to figure out what the hell was happening in my life. Could I manage to escape what it was becoming? Would I ever again see the Traffic Manager I desperately needed, who had disappeared after something called Mustardseed?

Chapter 22

From Tuesday afternoon on, I didn't see Peasblossom. I hoped she was going to figure out some way to level the playing field between me and Gordon Montbatten.

I'd worked well into Wednesday putting as much love as I could muster into the Creative section of the proposal for Lambert. I hoped the old charm would work its usual magi—uh—good things for me.

I messengered the proposal at half past nine on Thursday morning and fretted all through the rest of the day, wondering when I'd hear a response. It wouldn't be a good one unless Peasblossom could fix things by getting some mustard seed from the forest tunnel in her office.

#

I needed a drink. Things had been much too tense for me during the week. I needed the quiet insanity that was the ambience of Percy's.

I was in my usual booth, contemplating an amber liquid when somebody settled down next to me. His clothes cost enough to buy Percy's in and of themselves. He had a bright, confident air about him.

"Hi there, fella," he said.

My first thought was that someone who wore that much

money on his body had a company that seriously needed my firm's services. The fact that I didn't know who he was didn't deter me in the least. I put on my most winning smile. "Good to see you," I replied, extending my hand.

"Really?" he replied as he beamed confidently at me. "That's *just* what I thought. I did a short-term projection and found that a bilateral merger would bring better outcomes than open competition."

This guy spoke a wicked Corporatese. I realized I'd have to break out the simultaneous Corporate-to-English translation.

"There's nothing better than having a little face-to-face," I said. If I kept him talking, he might slip in a verb or two that I'd understand.

"I launched a feeler for a personal interface, but you didn't positively respond," he said.

Translation: he wanted to see me. The ever-so-bright smile on my face froze as my brain worked overtime trying to figure out when he'd tried to contact me. I formulated an answer. "My administrative assistant has been out ill this week, and I'm afraid the temp covering the job hasn't been properly vetting my messages. You know how hard it is to get good help these days."

"Market research told me that your buying patterns included certain down-market liquid retail outlets," he continued, leaning back and pontificating in my general direction. "I sent a customer rep by to give you a cold call."

I nailed the smile on my face while I dove into the back of my mind and started fiendishly cutting and pasting ideas and expressions he was spouting, trying to put them together into some comprehensible order. I caught one thing I understood. "Customer rep, huh?"

"Yes, I thought I might find that your core values are aligned with mine and that I could form a strategic relationship with you for a win-win outcome."

Partial translation: he was trying to get together with me. There were some ciphers he used that weren't in the official Corporate-to-English dictionary. “What could be better?” I asked. I realized the grin was beginning to melt off my face. I should feel completely at home with this guy. Why didn't I?

“Absolutely,” he said. “However, my rep used hard-edged sell techniques with you.”

Wait a minute! I was beginning to put two and two together. I hit the rewind button in my mind and played back what he'd been saying, using the simultaneous translation. He'd sent some people to [down-market liquid retail outlet] = Percy's, to bring me to see him? They had [used hard-edged sell techniques] = been too persuasive? Words came trickling back into my brain: “He wants to see you.” I didn't pay close attention to those words because a knife was pressed to my throat. This was the “he” that the guy had been referring to.

“You sent that guy?” I was beginning to moderate the greed I'd manifested when I'd seen the cut of his clothes.

“That's right.” He straightened his shoulders. “You know, sometimes one's marketing approach can be a little too hard-sell. Now that I see you, I know I only need to appeal to you as one business *associate,*” he raised an eyebrow toward me, “to another.”

Translation: he was offering me a piece of the action. I could smell that that included a lot of money--maybe even more money than I was making in the dog & pony business.

Why wasn't I leaping at the chance?

I had to give him some sort of answer. “I've got to say that I was a little put off by the tone of your messenger.”

“Let's talk some specifics.” He leaned in confidentially. “You have contacts, contacts in all sorts of places. You are connected in places where I need to have representation.”

“I am? I have?” I was lobbing out a lot of questions I damn well knew I'd need some answers to. Like what the hell were these places I had connections with?

"That's right, and now that I've met you, I can tell it's better to work *with* you than try a hostile takeover." He leaned back with a small smile on his face. He never let his gaze wander from me. That concentrated stare was one of two things: either a salesman who wanted to maintain eye contact with the prospect, or someone who was clinically obsessive.

"I agree. The impression I got was there was a fair amount of hostility coming from your representative." And his knife.

"Exactly." He jabbed an affirming index finger in my direction. "And I want to make things up to you by sweetening the pot. I think I should increase my offer."

"Are you increasing today's offer, or the previous one?" I probed.

He squared up and stared even more deeply at me. "I could do both."

And then I realized what it was about this guy that bothered me. Underneath his fashionable exterior--underneath his smooth presentation--underneath his expensive clothing--this guy was batshit crazy!

Through many evenings spent at Percy's, I'd learned how to handle crazies. The very first rule: always agree with them. The second rule: get the hell away from them.

"I think I need to take a bit of time to consider how I want to respond to your offer. I should manifest the parameters of our agreement in cogent, reasonable, logical terms," I said.

He held his hand in a palm-towards-me benediction. "Take some time thinking this through. However, I can't wait long; I'm in a hurry. I have to move forward on my venture either with you or--without you."

I got the distinct impression just how "without" me he intended to be. I also knew that he might be with me for the present, but he'd come to the conclusion at some later date that he could muddle on "without" me.

"Just give me a couple days," I said.

He stood up and nodded reassuringly at me. "You bet. I know you have to structure your response in terms that are agreeable to you." He paused as he started to depart. "Just don't test my patience." He gave a little nod with his head and strolled out the door.

Now what?

I suddenly felt that there was a whole bunch of people who had their sights set on me, and I didn't even know why. Peasblossom was bringing into my office things having to do with the M-word. Corgus wanted me for help with "Troubles." The little CIA guy wanted me to help with something that was too classified for me to know about. And I was just trying to get a show for Lambert despite having the cards stacked against me.

Did the Lambert job have anything to do with all of this?

Would I ever see that girl with the green eyes again?

I didn't know. I didn't know anything.

I take that back. I did know one thing. I knew I needed another drink.

Chapter 23

First thing Friday morning I barreled into my Traffic Manager's office. I shrieked in anguish when she wasn't there. Once I calmed down, I decided to see if there was anything useful I could do. I checked to see if the plants needed watering. Considering they moved around when my back was turned, I wasn't sure if they required a heartier meal, maybe a virgin sacrifice. I was safe there; I'd lost those eligibility requirements a number of years ago. However, the way my sex life had gone lately, I might re-qualify through the statute of limitations.

I was in a frenzy. I stormed back into my office, fired up my computer, and paced around the room. I paused for the usual discipline of checking my emails. I found a message from Wendell, addressed to both Gordon and me. The Subject line was:

Good News!

As I opened up the message I wondered what the hell could be the good news for both of us.

Dear Gordon and Harry,

Purchasing has turned things around faster than I thought. I already have approval on the budgets for the show in Hawaii. Why don't the two of you drop by my office at 11:00 this morning so I can announce the results?
I'm very excited to start Planning the Future!

Wendell

I was dead.

I knew Wendell didn't have to turn in the budget to Purchasing until some time later next week, which meant he'd already made up his mind. Budget approval was just a formality. Since he'd told Montbatten ahead of time about the proposal, he was set to give him the show. I'm sure it was Gordon's idea to drag me over to the office so he could gloat in front of me when he got the job. I was getting a public execution.

I glanced at the clock. I barely had time to throw on the spare jacket and tie I kept in the office and make it over to Lambert at 11:00. I wondered where the hell Peasblossom was. She was probably searching for mustard seed in a Burpee's catalog.

#

I was dashing down the sidewalk over to Lambert, intent on getting to the meeting on time.

I suddenly stopped.

The green eyes were there again. I saw her across the avenue, between all of the buses and trucks that were rumbling their way uptown. I did a death-defying act leaping across ill-defined lanes of traffic to make my way over to try to catch her. When I got to the other side, she had disappeared. I ineffectually ran up and down the avenue, hoping that she'd turn up, but she wasn't there.

I had an appointment. I couldn't wait any longer. I dashed off to Lambert, my mind still on the green-eyed girl. I wondered if I should hire a detective to try to find this girl. That'd be easy: find a green-eyed girl in a city of eight million.

I arrived at Lambert just in time. (Rule of the business world: always be on time to a client, who will always be late his/herself.) When I got to Wendell's office Gordon Montbatten was already there with a big smile painted across his face. If I had any doubts about him having the inside track on this job, I only had to see the smug grin he sported. He wanted me there to watch me twist in the wind. He was dressed to the nines, wearing a three-piece suit with all the trimmings. He was very metrosexual, and wore one of those colognes that was meant to be sweet and fresh; it smelled like a disposable diaper.

Wendell greeted me. "Harry, I worried that you weren't going to make it yourself."

Doesn't the convicted always show up for his hanging?

"I've met your charming associate," Wendell continued. He indicated the other side of the room from Gordon, and I turned to see Peasblossom sitting there.

Chapter 24

"Well, Ms. Peasblossom," I said, "I'm glad to see you could make it here." I was all cordiality even though my impulse was to scream things like where the hell had she been.

"Yes," Wendell said, "she was the first to arrive."

"Harold, how have you been, old chap," Gordon intoned at me. I didn't know whether he used the Queen's English or the Bronx's; he rumbled his faux accent around like a verbal display case. He reached out in greeting. It was like shaking hands with tofu.

"Gordon," I said. Since I was at the client's, I had to be on good behavior. The single word was the limit of civility I could muster.

"Now that we're all here, let's get down to business," Wendell said as he settled behind his desk. Gordon and I took the seats in front, while Peasblossom remained seated on the sofa behind us. Gordon was oozing confidence. I kept a straight face in front of Wendell. He wasn't a bad person; he was just one of those species native to the corporate environment: an incompetent. Today he seemed a bit more on edge. He was nervous about something. "As you well know, this meeting in Hawaii is very important to our company. Mr. Lambert has specifically told me that..."

His speech was interrupted by a brief knock on the door--a ceremonial two raps--followed immediately by the door opening. Someone entered, acting as though he owned the place, which proved to be true, since Charlie Lambert came strolling into the room. Lambert Industries started out in Charlie's garage, and he still owned a majority of the company's stock. Being the founder and inspiration for the company, Charlie was a genius, and a natural, normal guy, which meant he stood out in stark contrast with all the corporate types who were his employees.

When Charlie saw me, he smiled and offered his hand. "Hi there, Harry. What a coincidence you should be here." He held up the papers he was carrying. "You've done it again, Harry. I read your creative treatment, and it's exactly the thing we need for the Hawaii meeting." He swung around to Wendell. "Wendell, I'm really glad you sent a copy of this up to me. Harry's bound to do a great job on this meeting."

Wendell was stunned, struggling to figure out what to say. He managed to mumble, "Yes," the one word that can take you a long way in the corporate world.

"I'm sorry, I don't think we've met." Charlie had just noticed Gordon. It was a little hard to see him since he'd managed to shrink down in the past ten seconds. There were small beads of sweat on his upper lip, I'm sure there were wet spots on his shirt, and his disposable-diaper cologne had gone from new to used.

Wendell hastily made the introductions for both Gordon, who needed a changing table, and Peasblossom. Wendell didn't know what else to do since Charlie had obviously wandered in and altered his plans. He tried to do some damage control. "I figured Harry would be so busy with the main meeting, I'd have Gordon handle the breakout sessions."

"Good." Charlie turned to Gordon. "Just make sure you do whatever Harry tells you to do. He's got to handle the whole message."

The things I wanted to tell Gordon to do were anatomically impossible.

"You can be sure, Mr. Lambert," Gordon said grandiosely, "this will be the most important thing on my shed-yule." That's how he pronounced it: *shedule*. Giggy Makowski said *shedule* ever since he was a *sholar* at that *shool* in *Shenectady*.

Charlie left pretty quickly after that. The rest of us settled down to the usual corporate procedures: taking a long time discussing irrelevant matters and never accomplishing anything concrete.

To say the mood in Wendell's office was strained is an understatement. Gordon's usual attitude was generally remote, as he always maintained a snobbish aloofness. He was even stonier this time. I could tell that he was really pissed at having lost this job, which made him monosyllabic. The expression on his face looked like he was smelling farts.

For my part, I was wondering what the hell was going on with Peasblossom. She had a look on her face like she was the cat that had swallowed the canary--or maybe the canary that had swallowed the mustardseed. I knew she had something to do with my getting the job, but that didn't keep me from being pissed off that she hadn't kept me in the loop on what was happening. Instead, she'd disappeared the last half of the week and only shown up at Wendell's office this morning.

I did know one thing for a fact: I hadn't sent over a second copy of the proposal for Charlie Lambert.

But what else had happened to win me the job?

Chapter 25

Outside the building, I stopped in the middle of the sidewalk and faced off with Peasblossom. "Would you like to tell me what happened?"

"I used Mustardseed." She said confidently.

"Wonderful! And why didn't you use some arrowroot, and caraway, and sweet potato? They'd make a great garden."

"They were all busy," she said matter-of-factly.

"Huh?"

"Besides I only needed Mustardseed. He knew what to do."

"He? You mean he's not something out of *Better Homes and Gardens*? He's one of your friends?"

"Yes. He's a Drawback," she said, referring to her elf nerd group. "He's the envy of all of us other LAPH-ers."

I glanced around at the buildings surrounding us. "What amazing things does he do that has you all green with envy?"

"He works in a mail room," she said, her voice filled with reverence. "Do you know how many points he gets for that?"

"He's got to be all sorts of thrilled. So what kind of special spell did he weave down in the mail room?" I resumed walking downtown.

"He made his way into Lambert's Receiving Department,

intercepted your delivery, copied it, and sent it up to Mr. Lambert's office."

"And that was supposed to work?" I queried.

She averted her eyes, reluctant to say the next thing. "I just knew it would," she stammered.

"I'm glad you were so confident. I wasn't. I was holding onto the vaguest hope that it would go over."

"You didn't have to because there was something else."

"What?"

"There was an Attraction Spell on the proposal."

"You put it there?"

"No."

"Mustardseed did?"

"No."

"Who did, then?"

"It came out of your office that way."

"How could it? You weren't even there when we printed out the final version. Did the little critters in Grumpy do it?"

"No." She worked her mouth, trying to form the words. "You did it."

I stopped dead in the middle of Park Avenue, not happy with the direction the conversation was taking. I glared straight down at the sidewalk. "What do you mean?"

"There's another reason why I came to work for you," she said, averting her eyes.

"What's that?"

"It's the reason Corgus sent me."

"He sent you? Why?"

"So you could get used to it."

"Get used to what?"

She brought her gaze up to me. "You're magic."

Chapter 26

I didn't say another word as I stormed back to our building.

When we arrived, I went charging down the hall toward my office, waving Peasblossom along with me. Halfway down, Laura intercepted me. "Harry, can you approve this budget for me?"

I stopped dead, pouting as hard as I could. "Laura, can't you see I'm angry?"

She rolled her eyes toward the ceiling and announced to the rest of the office, "Hey, everybody, you'd better watch out. Harry's angry." Sidney and Joel groaned.

"Somebody else has to handle it," Sidney shouted out. "I'm much too busy."

"Don't expect me to do it." Joel's voice tumbled out of his office door. "Groveling to get him to stop would absolutely *ruin* my pants."

I stood there, tapping my foot, while they heaped abuse on me. I had to cope with this annoyance, plus I wanted to get Peasblossom to my office to find out what the hell this whole new M-word thing was.

Laura turned back to me. "Harry, can I use a Get Out of Rage Card to cover this?"

I tried to raise a lofty calm. "As president of this company, I should be treated with more respect."

"Harry, don't be silly," Laura said. "You know you get absolutely every last bit of respect you deserve." There was lots of extra meaning poured into that last word.

I turned to the Traffic Manager and said to her through gritted teeth, "Peasblossom, why don't we go into my office, and we'll discuss that last thing you said to me." We started to leave; I stopped and addressed her again, with a backward glance at the other three. "Perhaps you can try to show a little bit of respect for the head of this company while we're there?" I gave Laura a haughty look, then walked into my office with as much dignity as I could muster. It would have been better if I hadn't tripped over my own feet on the way.

I sent a gracious smile back to the other three as I shut the door after us, then wheeled on Peasblossom and screamed, "What the hell do you mean I'm magic?"

"I knew you'd be upset," Peasblossom said.

"Me? Upset? Nonsense." I shrieked.

"You were making such good progress getting over Mirabel. I didn't want to mention magic for a while."

"You don't have to worry about Mirabel. I'm completely over that toad-kissing, incense-sniffing, alimony-sucking bitch. Can't you see that?"

She stared at me, wide-eyed. "You're right. It's really evident." Damn! Was she learning irony?

"So why don't you tell me about my being magic?" I said as I flung myself back into the chair behind my desk.

"It's all four of you."

"Who?"

"Laura, Sidney, Joel, and you. You have an interaction with each other," she explained.

"Sure. We work together," I affirmed.

"It's more than that."

"How?"

“You form a bond of magic. It's an energy. You can sin together.”

I squinted for a moment, concentrating on decoding her meaning. Then it dawned on me. I should have recognized the word after all these years of working in corporate world. “We have a Magical Synergy?”

“Yes, that's it,” she replied brightly.

“How come I've never seen it happen? Why haven't I been able to turn Gordon Montbatten into a toad?” I paused as I considered my words. “Wait a minute. He already is.”

“Your synergy isn't fully realized.”

“Uh-huh.” I stared at her in non-comprehension. “You know, I think I may have been absent from school the day they covered that fully-realized-synergy thing. Could you fill me in?”

“You only have a potential. You need something that will fully articulate it: a catalyst.”

“And where do I find this catalyst?” I asked.

“Right here. It's me.”

“You?”

“Yup, yup,” came from the chair. I wheeled around and saw Corgus sitting there.

Chapter 27

"I'm taking that damned chair to Goodwill tomorrow." I said, pointing at the little man's seat.

"Be that the way ye treat company?" Corgus arched an eyebrow at me.

"Oh, golly, excuse me. Where are my manners? Come in, come in.--Oh, wait a minute, you're *already* in! Well, how are things? How have you been? Who's on first? Is I Don't Know still on third? And how many widgins or wodgins will pass before you get the hell out of here?"

"Ye be a bit testy."

"Glad you noticed!"

"I think he's got something important to say," Peasblossom said as she studied Corgus.

"First time ever," I said.

Corgus glanced at me and pursed his lips. Then he looked up at the ceiling as he reflected. "Could be," he admitted.

"Well, try to say it at a slightly faster speed than you normally use," I said.

"It works this way." Corgus said, as he got down from the seat, reached into his tobacco pouch, and began to fill his pipe with shredded roofing tar. "If the beast be large, it must bear a heavier burden." Corgus looked up at me solemnly on delivering this message.

I stared at him in utter disbelief. “Well, I'm sure glad you explained things to me. That makes everything crystal clear.” I swung around to Peasblossom. “What the hell does that mean?”

“It means that if we gain in power, we will attract more attention.”

There was a puff of black, acrid smoke from the corner of the room, and someone new appeared and said, “Most certainly.”

Chapter 28

Our new visitor surveyed us. He was trying his best to look imposing, but a lack of conviction made it a losing battle. The sleeves on his robe kept drooping down over his hands, like he'd bought the outfit a size too large, hoping he'd grow into it. He surveyed the room with a sneer that looked, well--practiced.

"My dear friend, Corgus, don't tell me that you are on the losing side once again," he sneered.

"Which side be that?" Corgus drawled. He didn't look daunted by our new arrival either.

"Any one that is not mine," the little guy replied.

"Could be." Corgus gave a sage nod and puffed on his pipe.

"Excuse me," I said. "I think I started out having a private conversation with my employee a few minutes ago in, what is--if memory serves me correctly--my own office. Now, I'm seeing a whole bunch of people here that I don't recall inviting." I'd just endured getting no respect from my employees out in the hall. Now I was getting no respect from people I hardly knew. "Here's an idea: why don't you all get out of here?"

The vertically challenged intruder looked me up and down. "Are you the Chatham creature who thinks he can thwart my plan?"

"The last name's right, but I don't recall being in the

thwarting business," I replied.

He drew himself up to his full height. "You will learn not to cross me."

"Hey, I've got a great idea," I said. "You want me to not cross you? How would it be if I never saw you again? That'd be putting me *way* out of crossing range."

"Perhaps you don't understand who you are facing. I am a wizard of the first order soon to be the supreme leader of my world and this one."

"Oh, yeah? I'll have you know I'm--" I groped for the rest of the sentence, "--Hertz #1 Club." I maintained a defiant look while giving myself an internal slap on the forehead.

Rather than landing like a dud, my words seemed to impress. "You won't be able to hurt me," he replied.

Peasblossom grabbed onto my arm, trying to restrain me. "You'd better be careful. He's a really powerful wizard."

I shrugged her off and continued. "Not only that, I've got backup here. You've not only got to contend with me, but I've got a big mocka from Fairy World here to handle you." I swung around to Corgus's chair to indicate the chief elf.

The chair was empty.

I swung around to Peasblossom. "Where'd he go?"

"He has cowered before my wrath," the little guy proclaimed. "I shall have to deal with him at another time. In the meantime," he turned toward me, "I will take care of you, Chatham."

Peasblossom was trying her best to drag me toward my desk. I was still stuck on Corgus, and kept complaining to her as she propelled me away. "Where the hell'd he go? He's supposed to be some big time magic guy, isn't he?"

"Yes, yes," she chattered as she continued to shove me. Meanwhile, Wiz-Inna-Box was beginning to mutter some strange things that either meant he was starting some sort of spell or else he had one helluva frog in his throat. All the words were made with consonants that were formed somewhere in the recesses of his sinuses.

Peasblossom managed to drag me behind the desk, and grab my hands to press them down on my computer's CPU. Wizlet's hand began to glow with a green fire, and he raised his index finger, pointing it toward me. At that instant, something sprang up from my monitor and hung in the middle of the air in front of me, pulsing. It was the same color as a computer's Blue Screen of Death. It had a transparent look, like a piece of blue glass suspended in midair, only glass doesn't ripple. A green fireball grew at the tip of the guy's index finger, then lanced out and rocketed toward me--

--and was deflected by my Blue Protector, as it veered off at an angle and through the back of my chair. When the percussive slap of the impact had died off, an androgynous voice boomed out of my computer speakers. *"Access has been denied. You are not authorized to enter this domain."*

That only induced the little guy to send out another round of greenfire--that was again deflected away to explode against the far wall of my office.

"You have an invalid user name or password," the computer declared.

The little wizard was getting pissed. He launched several more salvos that only accomplished more explosive office redecoration.

"Please consult your System Administrator to correct this problem." The computer had assumed a very bossy voice.

The Wiz shrieked with rage and raised a finger in the air with a B-movie villain pose. "You may have escaped me this time, but I will return." There was another explosion, and the backfires out of several buses surrounded this guy, and he was gone.

There was the briefest moment of silence before my office

door burst open and Laura, Sidney, and Joel came crashing in.

"What the hell was that?" Sidney asked. He glanced around at the destruction in the room. "Harry! Not again!"

"My god, what stinks?" Joel asked.

"Harry, what happened?" Laura looked accusingly at me.

I was wondering the same thing myself. I knew that whatever *had* happened involved some things that were out of the ordinary. I remembered the reason I had originally come into the office was to find out what Peasblossom meant when she had said I was magic. Did I just demonstrate what she was talking about?

I turned to answer Laura's question, mustering up all the humility I could manage. "I think that I have just defeated the forces of evil with potent magic."

The three of them groaned and rolled their eyes to the ceiling.

"Harry, babe, how many times have I told you to leave the special effects to my guys?" Sidney complained. "They have licenses for operating fireworks."

"And don't include your chemistry set in your experiments," Joel said with a sniff. "This place smells hideous."

"Peasblossom," Laura had turned to the Traffic Manager, "you have to monitor what our fearless leader attempts during his play time. He's not careful about toying with fire."

"Don't you guys understand?" I asked. "There was this mean little guy who kept trying to fry me with these balls of green flame. That was after Corgus left..."

"Corgus?" Laura asked.

"Yes. He's kind of the head elf," I replied.

"Peasblossom," Laura continued to stare at me as she addressed the Traffic Manager. "Did the two of you come here by way of Percy's?"

"No," she stated, as briefly as possible. Why was she

clamming up?

"Okay," Sidney said. "Where does this little green man named Corpus come from?"

"It's Corgus, and he usually appears in that chair."

"Harry, I've changed my mind." Laura said, with a bright smile on her face. "Maybe you should *go* to Percy's? You've been a little stressed pushing through this proposal. You need to kick back and relax."

I turned to Peasblossom. "Tell them. Tell them all about it."

For the first time ever, my Traffic Manager remained quiet. Laura started pushing me toward the door.

"Well, I get dibs on redecorating this office," Joel said. He regarded my desk chair. It had a big hole in it right where my head would normally sit. "I always thought this was a hideous color."

"Good," I said as I wheeled back around. "And get rid of *that* thing." I pointed at the chair where Corgus normally appeared.

"Don't be silly," Joel replied. "That's the only decent piece in here. I'm going to make it the center of attention."

Laura continued ushering me out the door. She brought Peasblossom along to be my babysitter.

"No, no! Burn that damned chair," I entreated over my shoulder. "Don't give him anywhere to go."

"That's right, Harry," Laura assured. "You go to Percy's and we'll get rid of all the little green men."

I stared around at my employees, as they shooed me out the door.

I'd just found out I was magic, and no one believed me.

Chapter 29

I was sitting in Percy's with Peasblossom. She'd totally embarrassed me by ordering a Shirley Temple with a double shot of umbrella. I compensated by drinking scotches.

"Okay, I think this goes back to the fact that I didn't understand the full meaning of Trouble when Corgus told me about it." I leaned in toward her. "I mean, did you see that hole in my desk chair? That shot was aimed straight at me."

"Yes."

I stared around the bar. "I wasn't told the whole truth about what I was getting into. I figured I'd just be involved in some business dealings. People would *argue* with me, and I could talk them around to my point of view."

"Yes."

I turned back to Peasblossom. "I mean I can reason with people--even *corporate* people, who are the most unreasonable in the world."

"Yes."

"Could you stop agreeing with me?" I finally blurted out. "Why don't you tell me there's some way I can get around this?"

She pursed her lips and reflected. "I don't think there is." The innocent way she stated the case made it even more damning.

"You mean I gotta face up to this little wizard guy--by the way, what is his name?"

"The Evil Mage Zorch."

"Oh come on! Does he really have that name?"

"He picked it out himself."

I pursed my lips and stared into a corner. "Okay, if I am able to do magic, how do I go about using the stuff? How do I turn it on?"

"I don't know."

"What do you mean?" I snapped at her. "You're supposed to be helping with the stuff."

"Magic just happens. It's not like--what is that thing you have?--physics," she explained. "There aren't any rules. Sometimes it happens, sometimes it doesn't."

"Sometimes?" I tried to coax some cohesion out of her.

"Yes."

"I can't just raise a finger and turn people at the bar into frogs?" I waved at Percy's patrons.

"No. That's not the way magic works," she said.

"How does it work?"

"Usually it happens when you're in a high emotional state, but that doesn't necessarily trigger it."

"In other words, it comes and goes when it damn well pleases?" I asked.

"Yes."

"Okay, let me try something different. I've met you. I've met Zorch. I've met Corgus--although he'd probably decide I hadn't spent enough widgins with him for that. Do a lot of other people know you folks?"

"Oh no! That would be very bad!" she said.

"Why's that?"

"Because we need to keep ourselves secret from your people," she said. "That's our most solemn oath."

"What's the reason?" I asked.

"Because too many of your people are like The Evil Mage Zorch."

"We do magic?" I asked.

"No, you try to eat electricity."

"You mean we're power hungry?"

"Yes."

"Yes!"

Was there an echo in Percy's? No, the second "yes" had come from my friend from the government with the Metallica briefcase. He slid into the booth next to Peasblossom.

"Received the intelligence reports," he continued. "Hear you successfully withstood an attack from the enemy."

"That's the enemy?" I pointed back in the general direction of my office. "That's not what I bargained for. I was under the impression I just had to deal with some balky Purchasing Agents, maybe negotiate a pithy contract. I didn't think someone would be hurling explosive fireballs at me."

"Aha!" the little guy exclaimed. "They were firing at you? Excellent!"

"What do you mean 'Excellent'? Explosions heading my way is not a lifestyle I would call excellent."

"Means security may be tightening up," he said with an affirmative nod of his head.

"How about my security? Can we tighten up on that? Like *really* tight?" Could he think in my terms?

"Have to keep communications open," he said. He scribbled on a scrap of paper. "Here's a telephone number. If you have to reach me, call this number and ask for July."

I stared down at the number scrawled on the paper. "This is

your office?"

"Yes, yes. Secure connection."

"Yeah, good, can't have anyone spying on us," I said. "It could put me in danger. Like that might send some guy hurling green fireballs at me."

The guy was digging into his briefcase. He obviously hadn't gotten my hint. "Action under enemy fire. Includes a hazardous duty bonus." He pulled something out and handed it to me. It was a cigar box. Oh great! At best they were Havanas that I could impress some clients with. I looked inside. My expression changed. It was filled with green pieces of paper, a lot of them, printed by the government. They all came with the number 1,000 on them. I looked at the guy.

"You pay in cash?"

"Yes, always pay in cash."

"And quick, too," I said appreciatively. I stared lovingly at the money. I began to think that those green fireballs hadn't been all *that* big. I looked at the money again. I'd always felt my desk chair had been pretty flimsy. Wouldn't take much of a fireball to knock a hole in that rickety thing. I was beginning to mellow. I'd also had a few scotches, which helped. That, and pictures of Grover Cleveland. I looked into the cigar box to check on all of his portraits in there. This money was going to put a serious dent in my accounts payable. "It's always a pleasure doing business with..." I dragged my concentration away from the contents of the cigar box and turned back to the little guy, but he was gone. "Where'd he go?" I asked Peasblossom. "Did he disappear in a cloud of bus exhaust?"

"No. He just got up and left," she said.

"It must have happened while I was admiring all the portraiture in the cigar box." I considered for a minute. "Did he say when he was coming back?"

"No."

"Did he say he'd bring another cigar box when he did

return?"

"No."

"Do you think I should send him a thank-you card?" I was really beginning to mellow under the scotch and the boost in my receivables.

"That might be a good idea." I knew she was humoring me, but in my mood, I didn't care.

"Would you look up his address?" I asked. "That's traffic management, isn't it?"

"Yes."

"You know," I hugged the cigar box to my chest, "I should probably put this someplace safe. After all, I work very hard to make my money. I have to stand up to green fireballs."

"That's right."

"Let's go back to the office. I'll put it in the safe until I can deposit it in the bank."

"That's a good idea."

On the way out of Percy's, I used one of those Grover Cleveland portraits to take my tab into the ethereal heights of a credit balance, while also lavishly tipping the bartender and the waitress.

I stumbled out of Percy's with Peasblossom and headed down the street the few blocks to the office. I was pleasantly buzzed with my new fortune.

"Just keep walking," the voice behind me said. I felt something cold and metallic press into the back of my skull. It didn't seem friendly.

Chapter 30

I should have had Bruno come with us when we left the bar with all that money.

"I made sure your large friend was occupied inside the bar," the guy behind me must have been reading my mind. We walked toward the office.

It was an emergency. I immediately flipped over into lying mode. "You may think you're safe, but you're not. This young lady next to me may be small, but she's a gold belt in karate."

"What's that?" Peasblossom asked.

The guy behind us sniggered. I squeezed my eyes shut. Maybe I should have said platinum.

"I couldn't help but notice that cigar box you got back in the bar," he said. "Why don't you hand that over to me since you'll have no use for it? That'll be a little exgtra perk for this job." My stomach sank. I gave him my collection of Cleveland portraits. His hand was in his pocket where I assumed he held the gun. His type always carried around things like that.

"Mister, what were your orders?" Peasblossom suddenly asked him.

"I'm supposed to take care of your friend here," he replied.

"Your instructions didn't include me, did they?" Was she up to something?

"No, but it'll be a little hard not to include you. You're what they call an eyewitness. Besides, I'm sure I'll get a few extra dollars 'cause you're probably on their list."

"I notice you're taking that money for yourself," she continued. "I could show you a lot more, if you'll let me go. It's special money."

"Where's that?" he asked.

"In the office. We were heading there now. It's just a couple of blocks away."

"That's as good a place as any for me to take care of him."

We continued toward the office as I tried to figure out what she was up to. I was painfully aware of how little money there was around that office. What was this "special money" she was talking about? Was it some sort of weird elf currency?

We entered the building and went up the elevator. When we got upstairs, I unlocked the offices.

"Where's this other money?" the guy asked Peasblossom.

"In my office," she replied.

When we turned in there, she steered me toward her desk. "That's it. Face the desk, away from me," the guy instructed us from behind our backs. He was standing across the office, somewhere close to all of the plants. "The money?" he demanded of Peasblossom.

"It's in my desk drawer," she said. I could see her next to me, pulling out her keys. That was interesting. None of her desk drawers had locks.

Come to think of it, I never gave her any keys.

The guy behind me started talking. "You know, sweetheart, I didn't quite tell you the truth. I'm afraid I'm going to have to do you in, too. It's what we in the business call a clean job. But I'll be nice to you. I'll make it quick. And I'll have some nice fun with you before I..."

He stopped talking. I looked over at Peasblossom, who had

relaxed and given up any pretense of opening her desk drawers. I decided to take a look behind me.

There was no one else in the office. The spot where the guy had been standing was empty.

The plants behind the spot were swaying, settling down from being agitated. I peeked around them to see if the guy was on the far side of the office. But he wasn't there. He'd disappeared.

Almost. There was something on the floor where he'd been standing. I went over and picked it up. It was half a thousand-dollar bill. The raw edge at its middle was steaming and slowly disappearing as something quite toxic ate it away. I dropped it on the floor before it dissolved me.

"What happened?" I asked Peasblossom.

"Echinacea got to him."

"What's that? Some sort of rare elf disease that makes you disappear into thin air?"

"No, that's her." Peasblossom indicated the plant standing near the spot where I'd last seen the guy. The plant she pointed at was the one I'd almost had the romantic incident with the other day.

"Her? Do plants have gender?"

"She does."

"Wait a minute." I glanced over and pointed to where the last bit of the thousand dollar bill was being dissolved away. "What happened to the money?"

"He'd been holding onto it. I guess she swallowed it too."

"All that money? She just swallowed it?"

"Yes."

"Couldn't she have spit it out? I mean isn't money awfully fattening to plants? All that extra greenage?"

"I'm afraid she had to take down the whole package. The guy *and* the money."

“What?” I shrieked. I stood there, clenching my fists. I swung my gaze back and forth between Peasblossom and what was now the biggest asset my company owned: the world's most expensive plant.

Chapter 31

I bolted into Peasblossom's office the first thing the next morning.

"I'm fed up. I agreed to help every few widgins with something that was supposed to be a little bit of Trouble. Ever since, I've had people holding knives to my throat, hurling fireballs at me, and pointing guns at my head. I'm used to working with corporations. They're known for backstabbing, but now people are using actual knives. I have to get out of this thing. Where's Corgus? Can you send him an Elf-gram, telling him to appear in my office so I can quit? I want to get on with my life without all of these people threatening me."

"I can't tell him to come here."

"Why not?"

"That would be bad manners."

"Bad manners?" I shrieked. "What about all these people who are trying to kill me?"

"Aren't they called neck-slicers?"

A pause in the conversation, like a cylinder misfiring. "Yeah--cutthroats. How am I supposed to get rid of them?"

"Excuse me, but where is the head of the company?" Some guy had poked his head into the doorway. He wore a suit and tie and sported a briefcase.

"He died of starvation trying to keep up with his alimony payments," I said. Mirabel usually sent around one of these collection jerks every time I was late paying off her tribute.

"Uh, I see," he replied. "Is there a new head of the company?"

Shit! This could be a possible client. "That would be me, Mr...."

"Thompson. I'm from the IRS."

"...however I just got voted out of the position and demoted to file clerk. The head of the company is a Mr. Gordon Montbatten. He has his offices over at a place called Metro, on 19th Street."

"Are you..." he glanced at a 3x5 card he was holding, "...Mr. Harry Chatham?"

"Yes, he is," Peasblossom replied brightly.

I glared at her. What was she doing lapsing into truth?

"I wonder if I could have a little conversation with you, Mr. Chatham?" he asked.

"My office is at the end of the hall." I started to lead him out, pausing briefly to grit my teeth and glare back at Peasblossom.

When we got into my office, I had to remove the protective plastic from the new chairs Joel had already installed. Once we'd settled, Mr. Thompson asked, "What sort of security do you have in this office?"

"Well, I've got to admit, the economy being how it is, the whole business isn't all that secure." I displayed a broad, we're-sharing-some-business-humor smile on my face.

He stared back at me blankly. "I was talking about surveillance security. Are there any safeguards against bugs?"

"I have the exterminator in once a month," I gushed. I gave an inner wince. Okay, IRS guys make me nervous.

"So that means you have no protections against electronic

espionage?" He quickly reached into the briefcase on his lap and pulled out something that he hung from the corner of my computer monitor. It was a little plastic fir tree that looked like a car deodorizer. "That's a jamming device," he explained.

It even had a pine scent.

"This is a standard procedure," he continued. "Now let me see." He consulted his 3x5 card again. "I have been informed that you are in receipt of some Top Secret funds from an intelligence agency of our government. Is that true?"

"Are you talking about the guy who carries around an armor-plated briefcase?"

"Yes."

"I think he gave me a few dollars, enough to pay for his part of the bar tab." Negotiation time. I was starting low.

He squinted back down at those 3x5 cards. "My records show it was quite a bit more than that."

Screw! "What do your records show?"

"An amount that requires me to do this follow-up visit."

"Why is it required?"

"We at the agency discovered that when that government representative's department spends Top Secret cash there's no paper trail linking the money to the persons in receipt of the cash. Our Director felt that we could be overlooking some taxable income. Therefore I'm assigned to follow up on these transactions."

"And that means?"

"I need you to sign this 1099-TS form to acknowledge the receipt of the monies." He held up a piece of paper.

"What's a 1099-TS Form? I've never heard of it."

"That's a 1099-Top Secret Form."

I swept my eyes to the ceiling. "Of course."

"So if you could please sign this." He leaned over, offering the form.

I hid my hands behind my back, so I wouldn't take the paper. "But I don't have the money," I protested.

"That's understandable. All you have to do is document the expenditure of the funds."

"But somebody took it."

"Who did that?"

"It was this guy who held a pistol to my head..."

"Ah-ah-ah!" Mr. Thompson held up a precautionary hand and glanced furtively over both of his shoulders. "This is getting into classified information, and I can't be sure that I have entirely jammed this office."

"Okay, I gave the money to this--'Top Secret'--guy."

"That's better." He smiled.

"And he and the money got eaten."

"Eaten?" he asked.

"Yeah. By the plant."

Mr. Thompson started to chuckle indulgently. "Well, Mr. Chatham, I see you're trying to use a variation on the old 'the dog ate my homework' gambit."

"But that's what happened." I protested.

He continued to chuckle. "I've got to say your story is going to keep all of the guys back at the office really amused. 'The plant ate my income.' That's really great IRS humor."

"But it actually happened," I protested.

"Well," Mr. Thompson chortled, "I certainly hope you got a receipt from the gentleman before you fed him to the plant." He broke out in more laughter.

"How could I?"

His whole aspect changed in an instant. He turned a very serious face on me and said, "Mr. Chatham, you will sign this 1099-TS form and report this amount on your company's tax return." He thrust the form under my nose. I looked back up at him, hoping he might soften. His stern look was my answer. I complied.

"Remember, failure to report this income and/or pay taxes for it will bring the full force of the Internal Revenue Service down on you. We will seize your company, your bank accounts, your personal property."

"I don't suppose you'd consider taking my ex-wife also, would you?"

"No."

"Worth a try."

He crammed all of the papers into his briefcase, reclaimed his car-deodorizer jammer, and got up to leave. "Goodbye, Mr. Chatham. I hope I don't see you again."

After he'd left, I sat at my desk and pursed my lips in thought. I picked up my phone and punched in a speed dial.

A voice answered on the other end. "Abraham Goldstein, CPA."

"Abe, it's Harry. Tell me something. What would happen if I had--oh, say about six figures worth of expenditures--that I didn't have a receipt for?"

He expelled his breath on the other end of the line. "That's a lot. What expense column would this be under?"

"Plant food."

"Harry, don't do this to me! The reason why I'm able to keep those three letters after my name is because I'm not outlandishly dishonest about my clients' tax returns."

"No chance?"

"Goodbye, Harry." He hung up.

This morning I was all set to get out of this whole Trouble thing. Now I couldn't afford to do it. I had to keep going until I could buy my way out of the hole it'd put me in.

Chapter 32

I had to catch up with the cigar-box guy to try to straighten things out. I found the piece of paper where he'd scribbled the telephone number, and dialed. When someone answered the phone, I said, "July."

The guy on the other end said, "What?"

I said, "July?" I wondered if I had the right number.

"July?"

"Yeah, July."

"Oh! Wait a minute!" I could hear several desk drawers being opened as the guy searched for something. "Yeah, here it is," he muttered to himself. "Call this number." He gave me a new number. "Ask for August."

"What?"

"August, that's what it says here," he replied.

"What it says there?"

"Yeah, some weird little dude came in here, gave me these strange instructions, and paid me with a lot of cash."

"A little guy who talks in shorthand? Gave you the money in a cigar box?"

"That's right. You know him?"

"Of course I know him. Why else would I be calling him

here on this *secure* connection?" I looked up at the ceiling, invoking the heavens to try to send just the least little bit of sanity into my life.

"I've got some advice for you about his cigar-box money," he said. "Report it as income. The guy has some pretty close connections with the IRS."

"That's what I'm finding out."

I hung up with the guy, and dialed the new number.

Most people answer the phone by saying hello, or giving their name. The guy answered with "Yes, yes!"

"This is Harry Chatham. Listen, I need to see you--"

"Wait! Wait! You didn't say the right code name."

I paused and considered. "The right code name?"

"Yes!"

"Why can't I just talk to you?"

"No, no, no!" he burst out. "That would be a non-reliable conversation."

"Wait a minute. I just told you who I am."

"Mmmm," he begrudged.

"I know who you are."

"Not necessarily!" he insisted.

"I see," I said dryly. "I guess you want me to say 'August'?"

"Yes! Yes!" He paused. "Who's calling?"

"I just told you!" I exploded.

"That was during an unclassified part of our conversation."

I squeezed my eyes shut. "Okay, I'm still Harry Chatham. Does that make things official?"

"Yes. Yes."

"By the way, what's the August thing?"

"That's my name."

I wanted to barrel on with this to seek out the logic. I wanted to plow my way through the many reasons why I had called one number to get another number only to find out...

But I stopped. I was toiling with the mindset of a bureaucrat, and I should know better. I took a deep breath and got on with the topic. "I need to see you. There was a guy here from the IRS talking about the money you gave me the other night. Somebody waylaid me, took the money, then the guy and the money got eaten by a plant."

"Got eaten by a plant?" he asked. Now that I'd said it, the story didn't sound plausible even to me.

"Yes."

"Your story made it over from the IRS to our water cooler."

"I'm glad I'm a source of hilarity around government circles. What am I supposed to do?"

"Did you get a receipt from him?"

"You know, while the guy was holding a gun to my head, I wasn't thinking about tight, spic-and-span bookkeeping. I was more involved in a scared-shitless thing."

"Held a gun to your head?" he asked.

"Yes."

"Could get you another payment for hazardous duty. Meet over at Percy's?"

"I haven't had such good luck leaving that place lately. Can we meet somewhere else?"

"The Starbucks on Union Square?"

"Alright." I hung up and pondered the fact that his name was August, Augie for short.

Augie is usually the name of a bookie.

#

I made the rounds of everyone's offices to keep up to date on all ongoing projects, then headed to the Starbucks.

I was crossing Union Square on my way to Starbucks--when

something stopped me dead--I saw the green eyes again. What are the chances that I'd see her so often? There are eight million stories in the naked city, and about another million undocumented. How could I have come across her out on the street on three different occasions? I was determined to get to her, so I bounded across the square--

--Where I ran into a Rainbow Pride demonstration. I tried to make my way through them, but ran into a very tall diva with a prominent Adam's apple and way too much make-up for this time of day. "Hi, darling," he said, "are you here to help us demonstrate?" He looked me up and down. "Or are you here to come out of the closet?"

I had been frantically trying to get around him, but I suddenly stopped. "No, wait a minute! I'm not that way--this way--your way--whatever!"

"It's okay, honey, if you're here to express your solidarity with us, that's just fine, too."

"No, no," I kept jumping around, trying to get past him. "I'm chasing a green-eyed girl who was just here."

He arched his eyebrow. "Is she with us? You really *are* quite the scamp!"

"No, no, she's not with you." I was pushing my way past him.

"Is there a problem here?" The lady who asked the question loomed up in front of me as I squeezed past the diva. She could have served as a defensive tackle on any football team.

"Huh? What?" I had slammed on the brakes and was oozing backward away from the armada who had just presented herself in front of me.

"You got a problem?" she asked.

"There's no problem," I assured her.

"This is a peaceful demonstration." Her tone of voice suggested she was aching for someone to come along and break the peace.

"No, I was just trying to catch up with someone over there," I indicated the direction the green-eyed girl had taken.

"You think we're in your way?" the lady challenged.

"Absolutely not," I said. Then I noticed that she was carrying a KFC bucket with a hastily scribbled sign on it that said, *"Please contribute."*

"As a matter of fact," I continued, "I wanted to contribute to the cause." I pulled out my wad of cash and threw most of it into the bucket, holding back a twenty for myself.

She looked up sharply at me.

I threw the last twenty into the bucket.

I finally burst past the crowd, but the green-eyed girl was gone. I swung my gaze around, doing enough pirouettes to make me dizzy. I couldn't see her. I shrugged my shoulders, gave up, and trudged on to Starbucks.

I settled at a table with a latte, hoping it would offset the scotches of last night. I looked for Augie the CIA guy.

He wasn't the one who arrived.

"Hi there, fella."

It was the smooth-as-silk crazy I'd met in Percy's. The one who'd sent the messenger with the knife, and probably the guy who'd turned into plant food last night.

He opened with, "I've been in tenterhook mode waiting for a go-ahead on a mutually forward modality." Translation: he was waiting for my reply to his "merger" offer.

I countered with, "Completely changing the organization of my company is not an idle decision." I was trying to put him off, hoping he'd go away.

"I've put a very high priority on adding your capabilities to my holdings," he countered. "However, the market is a quickly evolving one. My action plan needs to go forward to remain in sync with the rest of the business world." I didn't know if I wanted to be part of something he called a "holding."

This guy was crazy--crazier than any CEOs I'd met--although some of *them* were pretty damned crazy. I decided to bring up my visitor from the previous evening. "Besides, I'm getting some more visits from your representatives. They have a habit of stressing the hostile in hostile takeover."

"I'm afraid some associates of mine are a little more aggressive in their business practices." He sounded like an indulgent parent describing a misbehaving child.

"They aren't encouraging me to align with you," I countered.

"With you, or without you--the only difference between the two is which one can happen the quickest to let me get on with my business." He stood up from his seat and leaned over the table, giving me that megalomaniacal smile. "I'm giving you this offer because 'with you' is better--but only slightly better. *Faster* is best." He abruptly headed for the door.

Then he sent a farewell notice: the coffee cup in front of me exploded.

Chapter 33

Everybody in Starbucks looked up to see what the commotion was about.

"Whoops!" I said, putting on my most reassuring smile to all of the patrons and brushing drops of latte off my clothes. The minute they saw that, they turned back to their own business and forgot about me. Hey, they were New Yorkers.

Ten seconds hadn't passed from the explosion of the cup before Augie, the CIA guy, dashed up to me.

"No! Our cover's been blown. They must have broken our security system and tapped into our phone conversation."

"Who was that guy?"

"No! Can't tell you that here. Location's been compromised. Here," he scribbled furiously on a piece of paper. "New coded location. Be in effect in fifteen minutes. Call me then."

"Can't you tell me who this guy was?"

He leaned in very close to me. "Code name's Bold Elf."

"Huh?"

"Can't talk now. Contact me using the new coding procedure." He dashed off.

Chapter 34

I got back to the office as quick as I could, grabbed Peasblossom and hustled her into my office.

"Do you know anything about some guy who's got the code name of Bold Elf?"

She wrinkled her brow. "Never heard of him."

"I've run into him a couple of times, and he makes those vulture capitalists down on Wall Street look like angels. He wants to do something like a hostile takeover, only with a double dip of hostile."

"Do you know what he wants?" she asked.

I shrugged. "That's the problem. I have no idea whatsoever. Do you have any ideas?"

"I only know that there are two leaders of these Troubles, one from my world and one from yours. The one from my world is the Evil Mage Zorch."

"The guy who was launching green fireballs at me?"

"Yes."

"And there's somebody who's leading the charge in this world?"

"Yes."

"And what are they trying to do?" I asked.

"Take over both our worlds."

"Yours and mine?"

"Yes."

"What are you doing about it?" I continued prying.

"We have someone who we're relying on to stop their threat."

"What can he do?"

"He has contacts in both worlds, so he can be the spearhead in fighting off their challenge."

"This must be quite the guy."

"We hope so."

"Who is his guy?"

"You."

Part 3

...going on a Trip

Chapter 35

"What do you mean, me?" I asked.

"That's why Corgus talked to you," Peasblossom replied.

"He didn't talk to me. He only babbled about widgins and wodgins, then he disappeared."

"They're very important to him."

"Well, *my life* is very important to me, and these dudes are trying to take it. How do I get in touch with Corgus?"

"You can't."

"Why not?" I asked.

"He just comes and goes--" she started.

"--As he damn well pleases," I concluded. I paced around the office, trying to figure out what I could do to get myself out of this mess. Time to develop an action plan! "Okay, if I can't manage to deal with your Corgus, I'll get in touch with my buddy, Augie, who has those wonderful cigar boxes. He gave me a new code to reach him on this piece of paper." I dove into my seat behind the desk and dialed the number on the piece of paper. A lady answered, I said the password Augie had given me, "June."

The lady gave me the response he'd supplied her with. I squeezed my eyes shut in frustration. Out of force of habit I wrote down the info, whether I needed to or not. I stayed well-mannered with her, despite the hysteria building inside me. I hung up. I drummed my fingers on the desktop and stared at the ceiling.

She'd given me "July," and the same damn number I'd called this morning.

Maybe there was some new routine that I'd go through after this. I dialed the number.

"Hello?" It was the same guy as before.

"July," I said.

"Oh, hi, how are you? Let me give you the codes."

He gave me August and the same phone number as before.

I barreled on, hoping against hope that something had changed. I called the number, and the CIA agent answered. "Yes?"

"Hi, Augie, it's me, Harry," I said.

"The smart dog learns his new commands," he said.

"Augie, what the hell just happened in Starbucks?"

"The one who uses an umbrella will not be rained on," he said in a monotone.

"Augie, who was that guy, and how'd my cup explode?"

"A bird who flies south avoids the cold weather."

"What the hell are you saying?"

There was a sigh from the other end of the telephone. "Don't you know the security password?"

"Security password? When did that happen?"

"Five minutes ago."

"We haven't talked in the last five minutes!" I shouted.

"You didn't check the password website?"

"What's its URL?"

"That's classified."

I looked up and gave Peasblossom a grim smile and launched into a new subject. "How come I'm still calling you on the same phone number?"

"I added another security layer."

"By having me call the lady I said June to?"

"Yes."

"But the last part of the whole thing was--no wait, I'm not going there. Let's reboot this conversation. Hello, Augie."

"The frost is on the pumpkin."

"Would you cut that out?" I bellowed. "Can we just presuppose that I have established my identity with you?"

"That's highly irregular."

"Let's just muddle through anyway. We gotta straighten some things out. Is there anywhere else we could meet?"

"The Dollar Store on 14th Street."

"I'll meet you there. Why don't you bring a cigar box? I think I deserve one after what happened to my latte."

Chapter 36

New York boasts a wide variety of places to shop.

If you want the height of fashion, you go to Fifth Avenue where you can be outfitted with the *haute*-est of *couture*.

If you are more middle class, you go to Herald Square to Macy's.

If you are "none of the above," you go to 14th Street. The street operates with a combination of competitive shopping, snack food poisoning, and open combat training. The Dollar Store is the lowest class of the whole street and you go there only if you're a seasoned New Yorker. A running back would love to have any one of the little old ladies who shop there as a lead blocker.

When I arrived at the store, I saw that Augie was already there by a relatively quiet bin near the back.

The front of the store had the really hot items, and a mob was roiling around the front bins in a feeding frenzy of combat shopping. The store had a permanent medical staff on hand to administer to those who lost out on the bargains. Their first line of treatment was a bunch of syringes filled with sedatives. The patients may have needed treatment for wounds, but they had to be quieted first. They were sore losers.

I edged my way around the riot in the front and headed

back toward Augie. I hoped he had a cigar box for me in his armored briefcase.

"Can we start off by telling me who was the guy who met me at Starbucks?" I said.

"Leader of the group we refer to as Home World."

"And what's the other world."

"That's classified."

"Of course." Time to make my way through Augie's government-style logic. "This guy, this Bold Elf? Is that really his name?"

"That's his code name," Augie replied.

"Does he have any other name, like when he's not on the job? You know, out with the guys for a beer?"

"Understand he's also known as Winfield."

At that moment, a sharp blow to my rib cage knocked the wind out of me. I swung around in an imitation karate stance, ready to protect myself from my attacker. In front of me was a little old gray-haired lady, withdrawing the tip of her umbrella from the pit of my stomach and burrowing between Augie and me to head for a bin in the back of the store.

"Good morning, dear," I said to her.

"Fuck off," she said and flashed me the bird. Born and raised in New York.

I recovered my breath. "Can't you tell me anything about what's happening?" I asked Augie.

"We know there's something being planned for someplace overseas," he replied.

"Overseas? Where? Europe, Asia?"

"We don't know, but our informants feel you have some part in it."

"Who're these informants?" I asked.

"Someone strange. We're not sure." He took great relish in

the secrecy of the whole thing.

Something slammed into my calves and buckled my knees. I grabbed onto the display case in front of me to keep from collapsing. I turned around to find out who or what was there. An old lady was continuing to push her walker forward, having cleared me out of the way. "Can't you move, asshole?" she said.

I scrambled out of the way before she redeployed her cavalry. I turned back to Augie. "Who are these *strange* people?"

"Intelligence hasn't found out yet."

Oh great, I had to rely on military intelligence which is about as reliable as lightning strikes. I shook my head. "Why am I in this thing?"

"Hah! That reminds me." He reached into the vaults of his briefcase and produced another cigar box. My eyes lit up like a child's on Christmas morning. "Latest payment."

I clutched the box to my chest. "Is there any way I can get your friend from the IRS off my back about the first payment? It got taken by a bad guy. Can't we label it as MIA?"

"Can't do anything with the IRS. Not in my chain of command. Have to get a receipt for that money."

"How do I do that?"

"Yes?" His eyes glazed over, and he brought his fingers up to his ear while he listened on an earphone. He stopped and quickly glanced up at me. "Must go."

"What's the problem?"

"That's classified," he said as he dashed out the door.

I stood there, waving my hand after his retreating body, wanting other questions answered.

"Hey, you," another old lady approached me. "You ain't gonna smoke no cigars in here, are you?" She pointed at the box in my hands.

"No."

"Good thing," she said. "The smoke's very caustic. I got delicate fucking lungs, you know." She headed toward a bin of bikini panties.

I wondered what had caused Augie to bolt out of this place. This Bold Elf, or Winfield, dude had been able to find out about our meeting at Starbucks. Was he going to intercept me here at the Dollar Store? I beat a hasty retreat out the door.

I stepped outside and took a look around, making sure there were no dudes ready to hold a gun to my head like the last time I got one of these cigar boxes.

All I could see were the ladies who shopped at the Dollar Store.

Nearly as lethal.

Chapter 37

The Dollar Store wasn't that far from the office; the quickest way back was to walk. I was making my way along 15th Street when a black limo pulled up to the curb beside me. A guy hopped out of the back seat and inserted himself in front of me on the sidewalk. Since he was about the size of a linebacker, maybe two of them, he easily blocked the way. He said, "Would you come with me, please, Mr. Chatham?"

He phrased it as a request, but his attitude and size told me that, of all of the possible answers to his question, "No" was not one of them. A knot began to form in my stomach. If someone wants to see you, they usually call and make an appointment. They don't Godzilla to snatch you off the street.

I looked around on the street to see if someone was ready to intervene.

What was I thinking? This was New York. Nobody was going to get involved. I took the path of least resistance and got in the limo, mindful that the path of least resistance for a lemming is over a cliff.

The guy sat opposite me in the back, keeping a dull, steady stare on me. He had a friend with him, cut from the same mold. Together they would comfortably have made a front four. They wore red blazers that had a logo on the breast pocket featuring a "W." They looked far too competent.

"Where are we going?" I asked the first guy.

"The office." He was very chatty.

The knot in my stomach went down a little bit. We were going to "the office." That sounded civilized enough.

Unless, of course, his office was a Jersey swamp.

I settled back in my seat to take inventory of my situation. I also hid Augie's cigar box further into the recesses of my jacket. We were heading downtown, toward the Wall Street area.

I felt conspicuous sitting there, because the two guys just kept staring at me like I was a specimen lodged in between two pieces of glass in a microscope.

"What'll we do when we get to the office?" I asked the first guy.

"I don't need to know that."

I paused, mostly filling in the length of time that his answer should have taken.

I cast my gaze at the other guy. "Do you know?"

"No."

I christened the two Chuckles and Charming.

I occupied myself with watching the streets passing by, filled with New Yorkers.

The car made its way further into the heart of the financial district. I was surprised when we pulled up in front of the Woolworth Building, one of the oldest and most prestigious skyscrapers in New York.

Chuckles (or maybe it was Charming) said, "Let's go," and motioned me out the car door. We exited onto the sidewalk and into the building, the two of them flanking me. With them forming the wedge, even the most seasoned of New York pedestrians ceded the sidewalk to them.

We went to the elevator bank that serviced the highest floors and rose to the very top. When the elevator opened, I found myself facing a very large and plush reception desk. Dominating the wall behind it was the same logo "W" that the boys sported on their jackets.

The young lady behind the desk was one of those creatures that define the Corporate Receptionist. Her precision-applied make-up and hairdo must have taken at least four hours to put on. Her facial expression was frozen, bearing witness to numerous injections of muscle paralyzer. She also had a very chilly exterior. Her outfit was the same color as the boys' jackets and bore the "W" logo. It looked like a very fancy uniform.

She glanced up at us, and when she saw Chuckles and Charming, swept her gaze away in freeze-dried boredom.

We passed through the doors behind the reception desk and headed down a broad hall toward the inner offices. People walked past, going about their business. All of them wore that same uniform in red with the logo "W" on it. They looked like they used the same tailor as all of the evil minions in a James Bond movie. There was something about these people who passed. They all sported the same vacuous look as the receptionist and my two wide companions.

Then I got it! We were in New York! These people didn't have any expression on their faces. The average New Yorker will never look directly at anybody, but they do it with a real attitude, and it shows on their faces. These people couldn't be New Yorkers. What were they doing in this town? Was it an invasion from Connecticut?

The hallway we'd been walking down was opulently outfitted. The artwork along the walls, if converted to real estate value, could have probably netted you Australia.

We came to a large door at the end of the hall and entered.

I found myself facing Winfield.

Chapter 38

Winfield's office had immense windows that afforded a commanding view looking west from the building, past the Freedom Tower and toward New Jersey. The desk he sat behind was about the size of a hockey rink. The wall sported the "W" logo that everyone else wore. When I first met Winfield at Starbucks, his expensive clothes hinted at the circles he moved in. Now that I'd seen the size of his company, I was beginning to realize how big a player he was in the game. My escorts propelled me into the chair opposite his desk.

"I thought I'd ask you to do an on-site inspection of my facilities to further interface about our proposed merger," he said, leaning back in his chair.

"I've hardly had time to consider your generous offer," I equivocated, aware that his "ask" was more of a "grab."

"At times, my motivational arch outreaches those of my associates," he offered as explanation. "I strike while the iron is still molten rather than just hot."

Great! He was lapsing into self-improvement slogans. "What's on the agenda?" Was he was going to take me on the company picnic to see what a jolly group they were?

"What I'd like to do is use your resources to assist me in a very large takeover," he offered as an explanation.

“What resources? My dog & pony shows? I could whip you out a proposal for one in practically no time.”

He smiled condescendingly. “You hardly realize your company's latent capabilities. I could facilitate your transition into a dynamic operation.”

“Sounds interesting.” Keep him talking.

“But I feel you’re being resistant to giving up control of your operation. However, we have an indoctrination program that we use on many of our new associates,” he said. “I thought it would be good to use it with you. Make you understand the way we operate.”

I definitely didn't like the sound of that. I began to put together “indoctrination program” with the empty stares of the staff I'd seen in the halls, the ones I thought had commuted down from Darien. I began to form a protest when Winfield raised his eyes to Chuckles and Charming and ordered them, “Gentlemen.”

The boys were at my side in an instant and lifted me out of the chair and toward the door. From persuading me off 15th Street, the boys had transitioned to dragging me along on the path they had chosen. I tried to choose my own direction, but my feet were helplessly pedaling in the air.

They swept me out of Winfield's office and took me down the hall the way we'd come. Even though it was obvious I was being manhandled by my two friends, the staff strolled by, oblivious. Maybe the town in Connecticut they came from was called Stepford. I couldn't be sure I wasn't being forcefully relocated to that same municipality.

We veered down a side hall, and the boys shoved me through a door at the end. I looked in front of me and saw The Evil Mage Zorch.

Chapter 39

Where Winfield's office had been light and airy, this room was dark and dank like a dungeon in a castle's cellar. The walls were actually made out of stone. A far corner was covered with a chemistry setup with a retort percolating a viscous purple liquid over a gas burner. Along the wall was a rack of crude-looking instruments, some of them large enough to hold a body. The rest looking like they were meant to tear apart that same body. There was one patch of green, a potted plant close to one corner. It resembled the Echinacea in Peasblossom's office that had swallowed the bad guy the other night. However this plant was grotesque and distorted. It resembled Peasblossom's man-eating plant in the same way that a wolverine resembles a puppy.

I was pushed down into a crude wooden chair in the middle of the room. Zorch did a quick couple of passes with his hands, and straps wrapped themselves around my arms and legs.

"Well, Chatham, now I have you where you can't use your otherworldly devices on me," he said.

He was referring to my Blue Protectors from the other day.

"Do I get to know what's going to happen to me?" Always keep them talking.

"I have devised certain methods to remove resistance from

people who aren't sympathetic to our thinking. You may have noticed that all of the employees in this building are somewhat compliant?" he asked.

"Yeah, I guess you only hire people from Connecticut," I said.

"You're wrong," he sneered triumphantly.

"I am?"

"Yes, they are all from Brooklyn!" he crowed then cackled hysterically.

All those lifeless automatons lived on Flatbush? "You fiend!" I shuddered.

"Yes, Chatham, and I am going to use those methods on you!"

I struggled against the restraints on my arms and legs but couldn't budge them.

Suddenly there was a knock on the door, and someone said, "Messenger!" in a voice that sounded familiar.

"Messenger?" Zorch asked, his brow wrinkling.

"Yes, yes!" said the voice outside the door. The phrasing filled in the blanks and made me realize who it was: Augie, the CIA guy.

At the same time, with everyone ekse's attention focused on the door behind me, I could see the mutant Echinacea over by the corner began to shudder and quiver.

Zorch's face furrowed into doubt then lit up with realization. "Yes, there are some products found in this world that a torture unsuspecting subjects. Perhaps I can use them on you, Chatham."

"What are they?"

"They're fiendishly devious things. They're known as Customer Support Manuals." He turned to the door. "Come in."

Augie entered the room, still carrying his armor-plated

briefcase and wearing a Yankees baseball cap askew on his head--his only concession to a disguise. My attention flashed over to the mutant Echinacea that had gone from quiver to all-out shaking and quaking. Peasblossom suddenly appeared around the side of the plant, fighting her way through into the room.

"You have the delivery?" Zorch asked Augie.

"Yes! Yes! It's right here," Augie said as he opened his briefcase.

Peasblossom had finally won her way past the better part of the plant's foliage. It reached one last branch out and fondled her. Her face contorted in a look of elfin outrage as she swatted back the offending limb.

Augie opened his briefcase and pulled out two tasers, that he leveled at Chuckles and Charming, dropping them in their tracks. He turned toward Zorch and threw his wiry frame into a kung-fu stance. Zorch recovered from his shock at the turn of events and started to wave his hands around, looking like he was going to launch some green fireballs at Augie. Peasblossom crept up behind Zorch, uttered some eldritch phrases that sounded like serious nasal congestion then waved her hands at him. He froze in his tracks.

"Yes! Yes!" Augie applauded her work. Peasblossom flashed her hands toward me, and the restraints lifted from my arms and legs.

"Augie, what are you doing here?" I asked.

"Came to rescue you," he said.

In the meantime Peasblossom had glanced around the room and dashed over to the "device" table. She put on what looked like a pair of heavy-duty blacksmith's gloves, except they had sparkles on them. Not sequins, not glitter, actual sparkles that danced around the surface. She used the gloves to pick up a coil of silver cable. She gingerly carried it over and handed it to Augie. "Use this to tie him up in that chair," she said, indicating Zorch.

He accomplished the task in record time. When he was finished he turned to Peasblossom. "How did you get here?"

"I ensued him," she said.

I quickly translated. "She followed me."

"Very good," he said. He glanced around. "How do we get out of here?"

"I don't think we can go back the way I came," Peasblossom said. "I barely made it here." She glanced over at the plant. I could swear the foliage was glaring at her.

"Get to a window, we could parachute out," Augie suggested.

"Do you have parachutes?" I asked him.

"No, but I could requisition some," he said.

"I don't think we have enough time for the wheels of government to grind along and supply us with the necessary gear," I said.

"What can we do?" Peasblossom asked.

"I've got a great idea," I said.

"What?"

"Let's walk out. The halls are filled with Brooklyn zombies. They won't know anything. They're hexed so they don't think."

"Will it work?" Augie asked.

"If it doesn't, we can always go to Plan Number Two," I said.

"What's that?"

"Run like hell."

Chapter 40

We peered out the door to assess our chances. Things looked pretty good. The Brooklyn zombies were wandering down the hall not paying much attention to anything.

We hazarded our way out into the hall and started heading for the exit. No one paid any attention.

"You see, piece of cake," I said. "When you turn all of your employees into mindless automatons, you get no independent thinking out of them. We can just stroll out of here."

That's when the sirens went off.

An androgynous voice announced that we were loose and rattling around the halls and gave our description, even including Peasblossom's.

It looked like it was time for Plan Two.

The staff walking the halls lifted their vacant gazes up at us and veered in our direction to try to capture us. We were able to rather easily avoid them, mostly because they lacked the independent thought to quickly react to our dodges and evasions. Also, if I knew Winfield, their primary modification was to deliver computer spreadsheets.

We weren't that far from the door to reception, so we were able to do a broken-field run and make our way through to relative safety. After all, we just needed to get past the receptionist.

We slammed the door behind us and wedged a couple of chairs in to barricade it. Then we wheeled around to get to the elevators, and found the Reception Ice Maiden standing there blocking our path.

She looked far more competent than the rest of the staff, undoubtedly trained for some security duty. She was poised there in a low crouch, her arms raised in front of her, ready to keep us from escaping the premises. Her eyes fixed coldly on us, like a predator surveying its prey.

We tried the same thing that had worked for us back in the hall. We all tried to fake our way around her, taking different sides to divert her attention. With inhuman precision and lightning speed, she managed to snatch us up, darting from one side to the other. She got Augie first, then Peasblossom, and finally me. She wrestled us down to the ground, locking the three of us in a steely bear hug. The wind was crushed out of my lungs. Blood stopped flowing to my limbs as her grasp formed a tourniquet around my body. I had one numbing hand free that I weakly reached up toward her face, hoping to break her inhuman defenses. I groped up as pins and needles began to sap the control out of my arm muscles.

I reached up toward her face, hoping to hit her, grab her, anything to make her release her iron grip around us. As I reached for her eyes, my hand totally lost control, falling limply across her face, smearing her eye shadow down over her cheek.

She shrieked in horror, and shot her hands up to face to cover the marred makeup. She cried and moaned like she'd received a gaping, mortal wound, kicking and thrashing around the floor like a short-circuited robot.

The three of us picked ourselves up, and dashed over to the elevators and jabbed the button. Fortunately, there was a car sitting there at the top terminus. We leaped into the car and pounded repeatedly on the first floor and door-close buttons. While we waited the eternity for the doors to close, the inner office doors burst open and the Brooklyn zombies came creeping through. They were joined by Chuckles and Charming, who were still a little uncoordinated from being tased.

The elevator doors finally closed on the scene of the group struggling toward the elevators as the Reception Ice Maiden continued to twitch and shriek on the floor.

We made it to the first floor, dashed out and leaped into a cab, heading toward my office.

I darted worried glances out the back window. Peasblossom stirred next to me, sounding like she was hocking up a super-sized loogey. She turned and flicked her hand toward the back of the cab, and said, "They can't see us now."

I turned to Augie, who was on my other side. "What was that all about?"

"Didn't get news until almost too late," he replied.

"News of what?"

"That they'd try to snatch you," he said.

"When did you get the news?"

"When I left you," he said.

"When you left me? You mean in the Dollar Store?" I asked.

"Yes. Yes. Had to dash off to protect you."

I furrowed my brow. "Augie, you were *with* me in the Dollar Store."

"Yes. Yes."

"Why didn't you just stay there?" I asked.

"Couldn't do that," he said.

"Why not?"

"Department protocols."

The emotional side of my brain wanted to plunge on, get to

the bottom of what the hell he was saying. But the logical part of my brain interjected and told me that this was government talk and I would never be able to get a straight answer out of him.

"Can I expect more of this to happen?" I asked.

"Don't know. They keep changing things. Can't figure out the pattern."

"Do you think they have protocols, same as your department?" I asked.

"Could be."

I slumped down in the seat. Life was getting more involved.

Chapter 41

The car made it back to the office, where Augie took his leave of us. As we headed up into the building I asked Peasblossom, "How *did* you get there?"

"I did that thing you said," she explained.

"Followed me?"

"Yes that!" She smiled blandly.

"How did you get past reception?"

"The same way." Her gaze traveled away from me.

She was lying, but I wasn't about to get the truth out of her. I knew there were secrets that the Fair Folk kept to themselves.

We got upstairs, and Peasblossom peeled off and went to her office. I continued down the hall.

I made my way back to my office and slumped down behind my desk. I considered what had just happened. Things were getting far worse than I had expected. Winfield and Zorch had just tried to mindwipe me, and I'd just barely managed to escape.

I'd treated Winfield as some sort of well-dressed crackpot. However, now that I'd seen the size of his company, I had to alter my estimation of him. His megalomania was much more mega than I had imagined. I was in serious doo-doo.

I tried to think if there was any consolation, which led me to think of Augie's money.

Then I remembered that I'd been carrying around a cigar box with a whole bunch of his money in it when I'd been hauled off the sidewalk downtown. I needlessly groped my hand inside my jacket where it had last been.

It was gone. I must have dropped it when I was wrestling with the Reception Ice Maiden. My temper rose. I could just see the smug little smile on Winfield's face when he found my money.

I then remembered Mr. Thompson from the IRS. He usually chased me down with those 1099 forms. I figured he'd be here already. Maybe Augie told him that he saw it underneath the Ice Maiden as she writhed on the floor, that I never got to keep it.

I looked around the office. He wasn't here. Maybe I was safe.

Chapter 42

I was strolling down the hall with a fresh cup of coffee when I glanced into Laura's office and saw her in deep conversation with Peasblossom. Laura said, "Is it love?"

That made me stop and hover just outside the door to hear the rest.

Peasblossom said, "When you consider the differences, it's not quite the same thing, but it's pretty serious."

"It is?" Laura asked.

"Well when you want to have an offspring by someone, it is pretty serious."

"Have you told Harry about this?" Laura asked.

Me? What's this about me?

"No I haven't yet."

"Well, you'd better. You can't keep this thing a secret," Laura said.

"I need the right moment to talk to him."

"Do it as soon as possible."

"I will."

I could tell the conversation was ending, so I dashed down the hall and scooted into my office before anyone saw me.

What the hell was going on? They were talking about me and "love" and "offspring."

It all began to make sense. That's the reason why Laura came barging into my office with her whole "intervention" thing, accusing me of having an affair with Peasblossom. She must have talked to my Traffic Manager and found out how she felt about me. She'd assumed I'd encouraged it. Nothing of the kind. Peasblossom must have fallen for me, charmed by my roguish good looks.

Laura was right on one point. There should be no hanky-panky in the office. When Peasblossom tries to broach the subject to me, I'll have to set the record straight. As far as her having one of my kids, that was totally out of the question.

I decided to wait until she approached me.

There was a distinctive knock on the door that I recognized as Peasblossom's.

"Come in," I said, bracing myself in my seat.

Peasblossom entered and sat in the chair in front of my desk. She looked at me with her brow all wrinkled. She paused, then she spoke.

"Is it a good or a bad thing to have federal marshals around?"

That's certainly a different way to open a conversation proposing a liaison. I decided to pull together all of my persuasive eloquence and said, "Huh?"

"Federal marshals. Are they good or bad?" she asked.

"They're kind of like police. They're good to have around if you need protection, but they're bad to have around if they're going to arrest you."

"Hmmm." She nodded and considered my answer.

"Would you care to tell me why you're asking me this question?" I probed.

Do you remember that man who was here the other day, Mr.

Thompson?”

“Yes. He's the guy from the IRS.”

“He was by here earlier. He says he's going to send federal marshals around,” she stated very matter-of-factly.

I squeezed my eyes shut as my stomach tied itself into a knot. I returned my gaze back to Peasblossom. “Uh, that would be one of those bad things.”

“Oh, okay, then I guess you should sign this.” She offered over a piece of paper. “Mr. Thompson said that he'd send federal marshals here if you didn't sign this.”

I took the piece of paper. It was a 1099-TS form filled out for the amount of money I’d received from Augie in the Dollar Store.

Dang! I was stuck again. I knew that Mr. Thompson wouldn't accept my “the villain ate my homework story.” I shook my head sadly as I took a pen and signed the form. I handed it back to Peasblossom in resignation.

I looked up at her. “Is there anything else?” I might as well handle her problem sooner rather than later.

She stared at me for a moment in contemplation, then suddenly jerked herself out of the mood with a little shake of her head. “No, nothing,” she said brightly and cavorted out the door in her usual sprightly manner.

I stared up at the closed door. Half of me felt like I should have opened up the topic. The other half of me was relieved to have ducked at least one bullet.

However, the one bullet I hadn't ducked was Mr. Thompson. How could I ever get out of the mess I was in with the IRS?

Chapter 43

We had to keep moving on the meeting in Hawaii, so I made an appointment with Wendell to go to Lambert and get approval on scheduling, design, meeting agenda, and budgets. I was doing my best to distance myself from Peasblossom and her emotional attachment to me, so I left her in the office managing traffic (whatever that is) and took Laura, Joel, and Sidney with me.

The whole meeting in Hawaii involved a lot of different people and departments at Wendell's company, but I wanted to sequester myself with him without any distraction and make decisions on those parts of the meeting that concerned me.

When we got there, Wendell led us to a conference room with a table large enough to seat a fair-sized town. We raised echoes in there. I figured all of the smaller rooms must have been booked.

We settled down with coffees by the door, and I launched into the scheduling. "I think we should fly in on Thursday, the 20th. That'll give us that day to..."

The door burst open and Gordon Montbatten came bustling in. Just what I wanted! My biggest competitor barging into this meeting. "Sorry to be a bit late there, chaps. Had a problem hailing a cab."

I stared at him, trying to figure out what he was doing there. He must have read my thoughts because he continued, talking to Wendell. "I saw on your calendar that you were having this meeting. Thought I'd come by to keep abreast of developments."

There's a wonderful piece of chaos in the business world known as *the calendar*. You have to let everyone access your appointment schedule on their computers. That way they can see where you're going to be and tag along to a meeting you're attending. Not only that, but they can schedule *you* to go to a meeting they feel you need to attend. You wind up having no control over your own time.

"This meeting's only about the general session, Gordon. We're not talking about any of your breakouts." My tone of voice raised a reproving frown from Laura. Was I snarling at my old buddy, Giggy?

"Just wanted to be up on everything, you know." He gave what was meant to be a jovial chuckle. "Might be of assistance in case you get hit by a bus or something."

Laura kicked my shin before I spat out the response that was welling up in my throat. "Okay," I said, icily.

I turned back to Wendell. "So, anyway, I thought we'd fly in on Thursday...."

Some lady came in the door. "Hi, Wendell, I saw you were having this meeting on the conference in Hawaii and thought I should be here to give some input."

Wendell introduced her as Sheila, from Marketing. "I think the menu for the Sunday night banquet is going to be very important," she said.

The door opened again and some guy who looked like a senior in high school came in. I thought he was an intern, however he was followed by his own administrative assistant. "Make a note of that," he said to his admin. The guy duly punched things into the tablet he carried around with him.

Wendell introduced the new guy. He was Brad, Vice President in charge of Strategy. He had to be somebody's nephew.

"We've got to make sure that the strategies for this meeting properly synergize with our core capabilities," Brad intoned. He was using what he'd just learned in CorporateSpeak 101.

The door opened again, and two people came in: Cynthia from Human Resources and Myron from Accounting. Cynthia wanted to make sure that all the hotel rooms had proper *feng shui*; Myron wanted to know what they cost.

The new arrivals joined us at the table.

"So, as I said, I think we should fly in on Thursday, the 20th,.."

The door swung open again. Three people entered, babbling about needing to be involved with the meeting. They were Stephanie, from R & D; Blanche, from International Relations; and Harvey, from Sales.

Stephanie: "How many flip charts are going to be in the breakout sessions?"

Blanche: "Are we going to have translation booths?"

Harvey: "What's stocked in the mini-bars?"

I waved them toward the far end of the table as more people streamed in the door.

People were starting to pull my staff aside to conscript them into their own projects. There was a guy from IT who immediately dominated Sidney's time trying to get him to install the company's onsite network. Sheila from Marketing was trying to get Joel to design special napkins and place cards for the banquet. The guy from sales was hitting on Laura.

He had to be careful; he didn't want to make her angry.

I should explain. Laura is an absolutely lovely young lady--a joy and a delight. However, she is also very devoted to her work. If someone, in any way, blocks her from accomplishing her duties, the Dark Side of her personality comes out.

She gets angry, and when she gets angry, she becomes a force. Whoever puts themselves in her way gets blown over. I've seen her curse out recalcitrant union guys with language that would make a sailor's toes curl. That sales guy had better watch out.

The room was filling up as more and more people filed into our meeting. The chairs had all been taken and it was now strictly SRO. There was even a guy there from Building Maintenance who was checking on the heating.

I'd come here to get my few questions answered and wasn't getting anywhere. Discussion groups kept popping up like little colonies of mold, then dying away and reforming in another corner of the room.

None of the discussions had anything to do with the meeting in Hawaii. Some people were gossiping about in-house romances. One group at the end of the table was forming up a fantasy football league. Sheila was discussing menu items with Gordon by the window.

I decided to give it the old college try and attempt to get answers from Wendell to the questions I'd brought.

"So I was thinking, we MIGHT FLY IN ON THURSDAY...."

My voice suddenly burst out in the silent room as everyone else stopped their conversations to turn and stare, like deer caught in the headlights, at the person who stood at the door, behind me.

Chapter 44

Charlie Lambert settled his scan of the room onto me. Not a hard task. I'd just shouted for his attention.

"Hi, Harry, heard you were here. I wonder if we could have a little chat in my office. There's something I want you to handle for me on the meeting in Hawaii."

All eyes in the room swung over to me, and everyone cursed not having engaged me in a conversation earlier, which would have bucked them up on the Brown Nose List. A few other people in the room scratched their heads wondering what Charlie was talking about with this "meeting in Hawaii" thing.

I stood up, and Laura, Joel, and Sidney shot imploring looks at me to take them along, away from this meeting that had managed to morph its way into some kind of festival. I knew Charlie wanted to talk to me alone, so I gave them a quick shake of the head.

The looks on their faces told me that the company's Christmas bonuses had just jumped up a decimal place.

Out in the hall, Charlie said, "We can't talk here. I've got to take you to my office."

We made idle chatter on the way up to the executive floor. I'd never been to his office before, but I could see his influence on the place. It was littered with electronics. On the wall opposite the desk was a worktable that had enough gear on it to qualify as a fully stocked Radio Shack. His desk was a jumble of file folders, schematics, and computer chips.

Charlie settled into his desk chair and pointed me into the seat opposite him. "I had to get you up here to talk because the security guys have made this a safe room, free from eavesdropping." His office was windowless. "When we get to Hawaii, I'm going to need a special room set up in the hotel for us to have highly sensitive discussions about our latest major R&D project."

"This sounds big." Mental slap of the forehead for coming up with a really stupid comment.

"It is," Charlie replied. "We're groping our way to a brand new source of energy. We're getting a trickle of it right now, but we feel the potential could be boundless. You know what it would mean to this country if we could just tap free energy right out of the air."

"How does it work?"

Charlie grinned wryly. "I'm under a different set of restrictions trying to explain that. They're from my wife. She's designated a number of words as my Lab Coat Vocabulary. I'm not supposed to use those words unless I'm talking to someone who's also wearing a lab coat. Otherwise I'll just confuse them with techno-garble." Charlie could use that vocabulary with his wife. Eleanor was the head of his R&D department. "The experimentation involves quantum mechanics and that thing called dark energy. If I go past that, I'll only get into terminology that'd confuse you."

I smiled. "Yeah, I agree with Eleanor. You've already tested the limits of my scientific knowledge."

He grinned. "Okay. Work with my security guys. We'll need a big electrical supply in the room, and you should also dress up the place so it doesn't look like a laboratory or a warehouse. We've got some government folks coming in for a demo." He paused for a moment, staring down reflectively. "You know, I just felt in my gut it was a good idea to get you involved in this."

We did a wrap on the meeting. On the way back to the conference room, I was wondering what the hell this power source was. What was dark energy? And why did Charlie feel he had to bring me in on this?

Chapter 45

As I approached the conference room, heading back to the meeting downstairs, the door appeared to bulge out from the din in progress inside. People walking down the corridor accelerated and quickly scuttled past, fearful of being sucked up into some black hole of a corporate meeting that had spawned there.

I opened the door, and the roar of the multiple conversations crashed over me. The place was chaos. Even more people were crammed into the room than when I had left.

Sidney was off in a corner on his cell phone, screaming instructions at the display house. Joel had given up on verbal communications, so he held renderings up in front of Wendell, using the thumbs-up/thumbs-down signal to get approval. Laura was staring fiercely at the wall with a gleam of triumph in her eye. The sales guy must have been trying to put some moves on her again, because he was sitting in front of her, rubbing his shin. What that guy had to know was that the shin thing was a shot across the bow. If he continued with his advances, Laura would direct the next kick toward soft tissue.

Brad, the Vice President in charge of Nepotism, was holding court over four other people over by the windows. His admin was collating and binding some reports. The people surrounding him were glassy-eyed from garble overload.

Some guy was giving a PowerPoint presentation, directing it toward another guy who was sitting at the table munching on his brownbag lunch. He religiously kept his gaze away from the presenter, just in case looking at the guy might seem like he was interested.

Three guys over in a corner were practicing some doo-wop singing.

And I glimpsed Corgus sitting in a chair gazing out the window.

What? What was he doing there? I started to dash over to him. I passed behind someone, and when I emerged, Corgus wasn't there anymore. He'd disappeared.

I turned back to the head of the table. Despite the crowd in the room, my chair next to Wendell had been left free, looking like the place set for the Prophet Elijah at a Seder dinner. I must have gathered a certain holy respect from the employees in the room since I had gone off with The Boss.

Somebody, I think it was Sheila from Marketing, suddenly clutched my lapels and said desperately, "We really need to set the proper tone at the Sunday night banquet. The nut cups at each place setting are most important."

I gave a questioning shrug to Laura and Joel, and they shook their heads, indicating they hadn't accomplished a thing in this meeting. I waved like a traffic cop for my staff and Wendell to accompany me out the room.

When I opened the door, several people out in the corridor dove full-length into adjacent offices, afraid of what might emerge from the din in our room.

I shut the door, muffling some of the roar coming from inside. "Look, Wendell, I don't think we can accomplish much in this meeting. You've got to settle a number of internal issues with the people in the room. Why don't I just email you the questions I have, and you can review them in the quiet of your own office?"

Wendell was totally glazed from sensory overload, so he just nodded assent. I grabbed him by the shoulders, turned him around, opened the door, and pushed him back towards his corporate meeting gone viral.

Then the four of us dashed off to safety back to our office.

Chapter 46

I was in my office when the door opened and Peasblossom came in. "We've got to talk," she said as she parked herself in the chair opposite my desk.

I'd been avoiding her ever since I overheard the conversation she had with Laura, but now she'd trapped me. I decided it was time to bring the whole matter to a head. "What do you want?" I'd just have to let the poor kid down gently.

"I'm not sure I know how to phrase this." She looked down at her hands, clasped in her lap. They were cupped around an object. Was she giving me something? She brought her gaze up to me. "You've gotten yourself involved with someone in the office."

Cute. She was referring to herself in the third person. "I got involved with some*one*?"

"Yes. I'm sure it was just an accident. I'm sure you didn't mean to do anything."

"Most certainly. You know," I drove my point home, "it's always a good idea not to play where you work."

"Yes. However, you did set something off, and there are some consequences that you should be aware of."

"*I* set something off?"

She brought her stare back down to her hands in her lap. "Was there a time when you came rushing into my office?"

Several memories popped into my head. "Yes, I guess so. I rush everywhere."

"Did you happen to--bump--into one of the plants in there?"

I couldn't forget the time I nearly unmanned myself. "Bump into the plant? Why I practically..." I stopped and stared at her. "I mean I was just racing along, and there happened to be a branch down at the level of my--" I paused, continuing to stare at Peasblossom. "You mean I?..."

She nodded her head. "Yes, you did."

"Just by bumping?..."

"Yes."

"But that's a plant!"

"Echinacea is a little more than a plant."

"Well, yeah, she did kind of handle that guy with the gun--and the cigar box."

"I wondered why she was so protective of us."

"But how did I--you know--get involved?"

"You pollinated her."

"I couldn't have. Or I didn't mean to. I just bumped into her. It wasn't like we were--dating or anything. I don't date anyone in the office." I was babbling.

"You don't have to be so upset. It isn't like it's that bad." How had she become the one in charge of the conversation?

"How can it not be that bad?"

"It doesn't involve that thing that you men are so afraid of. What is it? Commencement?"

"Huh? Oh, you mean commitment?"

"Yes, that. There's not much you have to worry about there. After all, plants get pollinated every year by different bees."

"Oh, so I can just be proud when I look at this year's

blossoms? Boast about how well they're doing in school?"

"Not quite," she said tentatively.

I stared at her. "There's more?"

"Yes."

"What?"

"You get this," she said as she brought her hands up to the desktop and revealed what she was holding. It looked something like a snow pea pod, except it was a bright magenta with orange streaks.

"I get that?" I asked, staring in bewilderment at the thing she was holding.

"Yes."

"What is it?"

"It's her fruit."

"What am I supposed to do with it? Plant it? Eat it? Or enroll it in nursery school?"

"You just have to carry it with you."

"Why?"

"That's a bit involved. The closest I could come to describing it would be to say that it's something like a--tribal custom."

"But plants don't have tribes."

"That's why it's so hard to describe."

I stared at her for a minute, then took the pod from her hand and put it in my breast pocket. It gave off a remarkable fragrance. "So there's nothing I have to worry about. I mean her father the oak tree isn't going to be chasing after me with a shotgun?"

"No."

"And there's no involved relation thing between me and Echinacea?"

"No, you're just a very good friend. You're the bee who helped to pollinate her."

I stared at her, nodding. "That's great."

"It is. I'm sure she'll turn out to be a good friend." Peasblossom got up and left the office.

I pursed my lips and stared out my window.

I was afraid I had aroused great passions in Peasblossom's elf breast. I thought that my dashing good looks had won her over.

No, it turns out I was just a good bug.

Chapter 47

I'd had it. The whole abduction to Winfield's office and my narrow escape out of there had been enough. I didn't care about Mr. Thompson and the IRS. After all, what could they do to me? I needed to talk to Augie, the CIA guy, to bail out, so I gave him a call at his usual phone number. I got an intercept, and a recorded voice telling me the number had been changed. I then got sucked into a labyrinth of recorded messages requesting that I punch a cabal of phone pad keys. After numerous robotic conversations, I finally got his new number.

I called and Augie answered the phone, "This is the Smart Fit Brassiere Company."

"Augie, this is Harry Chatham."

"And what size do you wear, madam?"

I slumped down in my chair. He was using some new security cover. "Augie, birds fly south in the winter, the frost is on the pumpkin, and this is Harry, and I need to talk to you about this whole mess."

"So, madam, you say you are from the Different Worlds Bookstore, and it's on East 13th Street, and what was the number on 13th?" I recognized that he was going through one of his Security rigmaroles.

I gave him a number between one and a thousand.

He gushed and confirmed a completely different number. Boy, he was sure setting up a smokescreen!

Anyway, he'd given me a meeting spot. The number he'd given me was someplace on 13th Street way over between Avenues C & D.

I felt it might be best to take Peasblossom along with me, so I grabbed her and we headed out the door.

#

On the lower east side of Manhattan, the island bows out at 14th Street, making room for four additional north/south streets east of First Avenue, Avenues A through D, otherwise known as Alphabet City. Originally it was dotted with tenements that featured cheap, shabby coldwater flats. The low rents attracted a lot of artists and writers who moved in and turned the area into the East Village, scooping up some glamour from Greenwich Village to the west of it. Real estate people ripped out rent control and gentrified the neighborhood. Rich people moved in, forcing out the artists and writers who originally gave the place its cachet.

The block where Different Worlds was located was a throwback, it hadn't gone through any of the gentrification process. It featured a row of six-story tenements leaning against each other for support.

The store was also a throwback. It was a plain old bookstore with mostly used, hardcover books lining its shelves. Some of the books looked ancient. Mirabel, my ex-wife, would have loved this store, except for its being in a down-market neighborhood. She wanted her magic squeaky clean with a proper restroom.

I strolled away from Peasblossom, looking around the establishment, and glanced at the checkout counter in the middle.

I saw the green eyes. I stopped dead in my tracks and stared at them.

"May I help you sir?" the voice attached to the eyes spoke to me. The voice was as beautiful as the eyes. The lips that belonged to the eyes and voice were smiling at me.

"Uh--I wanted a book," I stammered out.

"Well, you seem to be in great luck! This just happens to be a bookstore." She raised an index finger into the air. "Although you may have been able to deduce that by reading the sign out front." The smile continued to beam at me.

"That's what I thought when I came in here." I was beginning to pull back from the eyes, and starting to take in the rest of her features, which included those lovely, full, smiling lips, a pert little nose, and blond hair that tumbled down to her shoulders.

"You display marvelous deductive reasoning." She seemed to enjoy that I was stammering like a teenager,. "Were you escorted by an adult when you came here?" She flashed her glance over to Peasblossom, and a shock of recognition shot across her face. She quickly recovered. "Are you babysitting this one?" She asked my Traffic Manager as she pointed a finger in my direction.

"We came here to meet someone," Peasblossom replied.

"Well, welcome to Different Worlds, a bookstore that caters to different worlds. I'm sure you'll enjoy wandering through the shelves and looking at the selection."

At that moment some pushy customer disrupted our conversation by making a ridiculous request to pay for some books. Peasblossom dragged me away from the checkout counter in hopes of restoring some order to my addled brain. I wandered around the store looking at the books on the shelves. As I stared, I began to have a sinking feeling in the pit of my stomach. Lots of the books seemed to be on topics related to the M-word. They reminded me of all of the magic books Mirabel had spread around our place, with one difference. The volumes she bought had been artificially distressed to look old. The books here were actually ancient.

However, I decided the kind of books here didn't matter. This was where this girl worked. What was on the shelves wasn't her choice. I strolled back to the counter.

"Nice store," I said.

"Thank you," she replied.

"How long have you worked here?" I asked.

"Quite a while. I own it."

I frowned and abruptly turned and stomped away. She owned this store! A lady deeply connected with magic was too much like my ex-wife.

Memories of my initial infatuation with Mirabel came rushing back to me as I paced around the store. There was no doubting that I was attracted to the young lady on the front counter, but I had also been taken by Mirabel, and our marriage had been a disaster. I blamed it all on magic and that was the subject of most of the books in this store.

I further explored the tomes on display, paying particular attention to the more exotic ones. This led me to an aisle of shelves that shot off at an architecturally improbable angle from all the rest. These shelves had the majority of the books on the stranger topics. I glanced down the row to where the aisle terminated about twenty feet away. It came to a dead end, with a couple of floor plants filling the terminus of the row. There must have been a wall behind the plants, but I couldn't see clearly, it was too dark. It didn't seem like an area where there would be much air flow, but one of the plants seemed to be blown by a draft. When I looked at it, the plant appeared to shudder.

I made my way back into the main part of the store. I avoided looking at the girl behind the counter. She may have caught my eye--okay, she may have made me fall on my face in front of her, but I just couldn't see getting involved with another lady who had anything to do with magic.

As I returned to the front, Augie walked in the entrance. I dashed up to meet him, keeping my eyes averted from the girl at the front desk. I was absolutely not going to get involved with her.

Did she really have gold flecks in her green eyes?

Damn! I'd just failed the not-looking-at-someone test.

"Augie, I've got to talk to you about what's going down."

"We consider this place secure. Let's talk."

He led me toward the most remote part of the store, which turned out to be the same aisle I'd just left. I didn't feel comfortable back there. Those ancient tomes seemed to be leaning in toward me.

Once out of everyone else's earshot, I said, "Okay, Augie, I'm fed up. It's time to level with me. I want the whole truth. Tell me what the hell is going on in my life. What happened the other day?"

"Yes!" Augie said. "Intelligence has come up with an amazing discovery. There are two elements we are encountering. We met with the second one the other day..." He looked around slowly to make sure we were alone. His gaze fell on Peasblossom. He pointed at her. "Does she have proper security clearance?"

"Oh, yeah, Augie, I made sure of that. As a matter of fact, you'd have a hard time getting into some of the places she's cleared to visit."

He gazed at Peasblossom in open admiration of her implied security status. "Good. The person we met the other day has something to do with this second element."

"Zorch?" I asked.

Augie's face registered shock. The name was new to him. "Yes! That's right! Zilch!"

"No, Zorch," I corrected.

"Yes, that," he replied.

Peasblossom beamed at the word confusion.

"We are trying to discover his base of operations." He leaned in, confidentially. "It's almost a separate world, one where they have--magic."

"No!" I said.

"Yes."

I turned to Peasblossom with as much severity as I could muster. "You must make sure to tell no one about this world."

"I'm sworn to it," she assured.

Augie continued. "Previously his operation has been separate, but now he seems to have joined forces with Bold Elf from this world."

"Now wait a minute, Augie, I'm confused," I said. "Isn't Bold Elf, or Winfield, one of them?"

"No," Augie replied.

"He's from this world?"

"Yes."

"Then why do you call him Bold Elf?"

"That's just his code name," Augie said blankly.

"But isn't the Elf thing in his code name confusing?"

"That's why it's a *code* name."

I stared away in confusion. "So his name is really Winfield?"

"Yes."

"And he's not from that other world?"

"Yes."

"But he exploded my cup at Starbucks."

"He was taught some minor magic by this Zorch, but nothing much."

"Yes," Peasblossom said, "trying to teach him too much magic would be dangerous."

Augie turned his gaze to her. "How do you know that?"

Peasblossom's eyes widened. "Uh--I heard it from my intelligence sources."

"Very good," Augie said. "We must compare notes."

Peasblossom responded by saluting.

"So they're joining forces?" I asked. "What are you doing about it?"

"We have great hope. We have discovered that there is another force that might be able to contact both worlds, and we are employing it to counter their moves."

"And what's that?"

"You."

Chapter 48

"I quit," I declared.

"You can't quit," Augie replied.

"Why not?"

"Because you're already committed to a government contract."

"No, I'm not."

"Yes, you are." Peasblossom's voice piped up from behind me.

I swung around to her. "What do you mean?"

"When I filled out all those government papers for you, it included the 3305-B Form, Termination of Contract Stipulations."

"What does that mean?"

"You're stalled." She shrugged.

"Stalled?" I did a fast translation in my brain. "You mean 'stuck?'"

"Yes, that."

I turned to Augie. "That's all right. I'll just walk away from it."

"You wouldn't want to do that." Augie shook his head.

"Why not?" I asked him.

"You've already accepted advance payment. You'd have to return all of that, including the money you said you lost."

"What happens if I defaulted?"

"How do you look in an orange jump suit?" Augie asked.

"I look fine," I said defiantly.

"--In an orange jump suit for about ten years with a roommate named Bubba who calls you his bitch?"

"You know," Peasblossom said, "those exact words were in the Form 3305-B."

I looked from one to the other. "If you think you can scare me,--" I brought my gaze on Augie; his features were fixed in a hard stare, "--it was a lucky guess."

I turned to Peasblossom. "Why are you helping him?"

"Huh?" She frowned in confusion.

"Signing all of those government forms that have backed me into a corner," I accused.

"You told me to sign those," she said, innocently.

"Who told you to listen to me?"

I turned back to Augie and gathered my thoughts. "Okay, what are these two dudes trying to pull off? What's their target?"

"We're not sure exactly what it is," Augie said. "However, it seems to have something to do with Lambert Industries."

"My client?"

"Yes. They were attempting to win the contract for the meeting in Hawaii. They wanted their toadie to have control over it."

"From the word 'toadie,' I gather you mean my buddy, Gordon Montbatten?"

"Yes, but he was just a front. They have someone else involved, someone on the inside."

"Who's that?"

"We don't know."

I considered. That had to be Wendell. He was the one who was trying to give the job to Gordon. "So, I'm supposed to take on these worldwide baddies, armed solely with a dog & pony production company?"

"Yes. But word has it that you have some other special power to protect you."

This was getting to be too much. I wanted to get out of there, away from this talk. The two of them blocked my way. "Could you excuse me? I think I need some fresh air."

Peasblossom lurched in front of me, blocking my exit. "You've got to do this."

"Remember Mr. Thompson with the IRS," Augie said.

"And Form 3305-B," Peasblossom added.

"You mean the Bubba's Bitch Penalty?"

"Yes."

"You're setting me up in this." I waved my hands in the air.

"Yes!" They sid it together.

I swung my gaze between the two of them. Finally, I threw my hands up in the air. "What's the use? I'm stuck anyway. I've got everybody on my case."

"I suppose," Augie rubbed his chin as he contemplated, "I could help you with the IRS problem. I could bring some pressure to bear to get a Collateral Damage Exemption for your loss."

"That sounds like a great idea," I agreed, mentally noting to find out what one of those things was.

"Unfortunately, I can only use those for suppliers in good standing."

"How do I gain that status?"

"You have to have completed at least one full assignment. Since this is your first one..."

I screwed up my features into a frown of disapproval. He was definitely leaning on me, and I couldn't see a way around it.

Augie dipped down into his metal briefcase and brought out a cigar box. "By the way, I have your latest payment."

I couldn't restrain myself from snatching the thing away from him. "You're like a pusher! These things are addictive."

"Excellent." Augie slammed his briefcase shut. "We will continue to monitor the situation." He started to head out the aisle into the main part of the store. "If you have any further news, be sure to contact me."

"News? What sort of news?" I asked.

"Oh, you know." He waved his hand in the air as he dashed out the front door of the store.

Peasblossom and I stood there, looking at each other, absorbing the things we'd just heard. Then a pair of green eyes with gold flecks managed the impossible task of tapping me on the shoulder. I turned around and looked at them for a moment. They were beautiful.

But then an image of Mirabel flickered before my eyes.

"Come on, Peasblossom," I said. "Let's get back to the office." I headed out the door of Different Worlds Bookstore, drawing a remonstrative look from my Traffic Manager, and a baleful gaze from the green eyes.

Chapter 49

As we walked back toward the office, I tried to put things in order in my mind. "So the CIA thinks I'm the only one to battle with this Winfield and the Evil Mage Zorch?"

"Yes."

"And your people think that I'm it, too?"

"Yes."

"Who decided that?"

"Corgus," she said, with all of the confidence in the world.

"Oh great! I've been selected to fight a couple of arch villains by a guy who can't even make a coherent conversation!"

Peasblossom looked up at me in round-eyed astonishment. "I think Corgus makes a lot of sense."

I waved my arms in denial. "We're not talking about that anymore!" I trudged on in silence, turning my thoughts to something else that was disturbing me.

Peasblossom read my mind. "You should have got her name and phone number," she said.

I pouted down at the sidewalk. Half of me agreed with her. "Did you see the books in the store? They were all about magic."

Peasblossom knew what I was talking about. "I thought I'd got you over Mirabel."

I stopped walking and swung around to her. "Look..."

I would have said more, but a bullet ricocheted off the building right where my head would have been if I hadn't turned.

We wheeled and ran. More shots clattered off the buildings as we ducked and dashed.

Okay, we were on the streets of New York. Bullets flying through the air is a common event there. However, I knew this wasn't the city's normal background ambience. This was one of Winfield's guys. The reason being, this shooter used a silencer. New Yorkers don't use silencers. When a New Yorker fires a gun, he's loud about it, like everything else.

Peasblossom headed toward our building up ahead.

"We shouldn't do that. We could be trapped in there," I said.

"We won't be," she stated.

"What if the elevator's up at another floor?"

"It's waiting for us." She seemed quite sure about it.

The elevator was there. As we careened in, I lurched toward the panel to press the buttons. Peasblossom gave a little nod, and the elevator took off. I knew that we were secure for the moment, but during the ride up I could only imagine what else might go wrong.

We got to the office. I quickly unlocked the door, we dashed inside, and then I re-locked it. I breathed a sigh of relief.

Peasblossom said, "Come on," and headed toward her office.

"We've got the door locked," I said.

"That won't stop him," she replied.

"What are we going to do?"

She dashed into her office, and kept going, right into the tunnel of foliage that seemed to stretch out over 16th Street.

I sucked in my breath and followed.

Chapter 50

I had tried to lie to myself about what seemed to be in the tunnel of greenery in Peasblossom's office. I had chalked it up to an optical illusion. I could no longer lie to myself.

We had gone much further than the limits of her office. Logic told me that we were now far enough to be floating someplace up over Seventeenth Street, but there was still solid ground under my feet. I'd felt a transformation from the air-conditioned office. It was a lot warmer and more humid, pungent with the smell of decaying foliage, and quite dark. Vague light flickered through the thick foliage surrounding us. I couldn't deny it any more. We had traveled into an entirely different world.

"Well, I guess there's no longer any danger..."

She shushed me.

I leaned into her and whispered, "Isn't this where you live?"

She nodded, while keeping a sharp lookout, checking all around her.

"Then shouldn't we be safe?"

She leaned in toward me. "Where do you live?"

"New Yo..." I paused, then nodded. "I get your point."

We were creeping along, making our way through what was

almost a path. Peasblossom was crouching low, peering about her in all directions.

"What in particular should we be worried about?" I asked.

"You could call it an immigrations problem."

"How bad is it?"

"Some of the rules are rather fatal."

I crouched lower than she did.

Up ahead the path skirted a clearing. There was light coming from there. It flickered like firelight, but some of the colors it gave off weren't right: greens and blues and purples. I also heard some sounds coming from the clearing. They resembled chanting, only with voluptuous overtones.

Peasblossom made her way very cautiously past the clearing. When we got about twenty feet beyond it, she turned toward a small hole in the foliage and slipped in.

I followed her through and suddenly found myself at the far end of the back aisle of the Different Worlds Bookstore.

Chapter 51

"How did we get here?" I asked Peasblossom.

"Through a portal." She nodded back toward the potted plants at the end of the aisle in the bookstore.

"You mean that's like the thing you've got back in your office with Echinacea?"

She indicated the plant we'd just passed. "That's Echinacea, also."

"How could that be Echinacea?" I pointed at the plant.

"Runners."

"Plant runners?"

"Yes."

"How? Runners are supposed to get a plant to the sunny spot three feet away. This is blocks away. Did she send a root through the subway?"

"No, she takes the shortcut."

"What shortcut?"

"The same way we just came."

"But we traveled about a hundred yards back there." I jerked my thumb toward the end of the aisle, indicating the world we'd just left. "How could she manage that?"

"She doesn't have to go as far."

"How?"

"She's able to build a shortcut down in the dirt where her roots are."

"What's it called?"

"A wormhole."

I shrugged. "I should have known that." I stared at her for a moment. "Do I want to know any more about this?"

"No."

"I'll take your word for it."

She ushered me toward the main part of the store.

The young lady behind the counter glanced up and a surprised look scampered across her face. "Well, I knew you kept interesting company, but I never expected you to use the back entrance," she said to me.

I sulked. In my head, there was a pitched battle going on between my attraction to her and my mistrust of the M-word.

Peasblossom took the lead. "This is Harry Chatham," She pushed me forward like she was forcing a reluctant kid onstage for a third grade play.

"Hi," I mumbled.

A smile crept across the young lady's full, red lips. "How eloquent!"

"You're now supposed to ask her what her name is," Peasblossom prompted.

My emotions boiled to the surface. I turned back to Peasblossom. "I'm sorry, but I've got real reservations about all this. These shelves are just filled with all sorts of books about magic, and I've had a really bad experience with that stuff."

The young lady leaned over in quite a fetching way, gave me a finger wave, and said, "By the way, my name is Violet Hunter, thank you *soooo* much for asking." She may have been sarcastic, but it was really *cute* sarcasm. "So you don't like magic? Well, as the psychoanalyst would say, at least you've gotten to the point where you can talk about it." She paused and stared at me. "You *can* talk about it, can't you?"

"I was married to someone who said she was a witch. Her name was Mirabel."

Her eyes lit up in recognition. "Mirabel? Oooooh, I've *heard* about her."

"You have?"

"Yes, we bookstore owners talk to each other at conventions. She's infamous. Biggest phony going."

"Well," Peasblossom chirped in, smiling at each of us, "the two of you seem to have a lot in common. I bet it would be a great idea for you to get together to discuss your similarities."

"Shall I sit here and demurely cast my eyes to the floor and wait for you to answer?" Violet asked.

"How about dinner?" Peasblossom asked for me.

"That would be lovely," Violet directed her answer to me, even though Peasblossom had asked the question.

"When would you like to do that?" Peasblossom continued.

"How's tomorrow?" Violet continued to look at me.

"That would be fine," Peasblossom plowed on. "Do you have a particular restaurant you like?"

"I've always liked *Lo Stregone Della Cucina* down on Mulberry Street."

"What time?" Peasblossom.

"Eight?"

"That's good."

"Be sure to put that in your calendar," she said to me.

"Listen, I can talk for myself," I burst out.

"I just put it in his calendar," Peasblossom said.

Violet shot her eyes around to Peasblossom. "You're able to

work the computer from here? You must be one of those elves who like computers, a Drawback?"

"Yes."

"Where are *my* manners? What's your name? Or should I just call you Cyrano, considering you've been doing the wooing for our bashful friend there for the past ten minutes?"

"My name's Peasblossom."

"Oh! I've heard about you. You're involved with..." She swung her gaze back to me. "I think we *do* have to talk." She turned back to Peasblossom. "He *can* talk, can't he?"

"I most certainly can talk. I was just having a hard time getting a word in edgewise with the two of you arranging my life."

"You're right," Violet said. "We've been very rude. Why don't you invite me to dinner yourself?"

I pursed my lips. Experience had taught me to play along. "Would you like to go out to dinner with me tomorrow at eight at--what's the name of the restaurant?"

"It's in your calendar," Peasblossom said.

"Good," I said. "That place."

"How sweet of you to ask," Violet beamed at me, then put on a mock-serious expression. "Although I don't know if I should accept. You haven't exactly displayed an affable personality; you've been downright surly at times. And your attraction toward me mostly emanates from your groin." She paused and considered. "However I choose to regard that as a compliment. I accept, since I'm assuming you have a better side."

I stared at Violet. "Well, whatever comes of it, it should be an interesting evening," I prophesied.

Chapter 52

Peasblossom and I decided fewer people would take pot shots at us if we took a taxi, so we hailed one of the many cabs to be found in New York.

It only took a few minutes to get enough English through to the cab driver to give him the directions to Sixteenth Street.

I leaned back in the cab and ruminated, my emotions coping with a dilemma. I was secretly elated about my pending date with Violet, but the content in her store raised the specter of Mirabel and all the terrible times I had with her. I assumed the latter emotion and frowned down at my feet.

"I think she's very nice," Peasblossom gushed.

I dialed up the level on my frown. No cheery little elf was going to redirect me when I was seriously pouting.

She continued. "You have to get over the magic thing."

I growled. "I keep being reminded of Mirabel."

"It would be better if you faced your demons."

"I'm still not comfortable with magic"

She glanced over at me in the back seat in that perky way of hers. "You should be."

Then she said the damning thing.

"You're part of it now."

Chapter 53

When I got to the office the next morning, everyone was all excited. The front door had obviously been broken open by our friend from the previous night.

One of NYPD's finest was there making a report. I sat down with him to go over the details.

"Well I gotta say, the means of entry was different," he said. "The lock was shot out. Most B&Es use a crowbar. Oh well, as they say, to each his own."

"What does that mean, officer?"

He screwed up his lips and looked up at the ceiling. "That means that your locksmith's bill is going to be even bigger."

"It usually is."

I got an appreciative nod from the officer. "What you got to do, Mr. Chatham, is check to see what is missing and stolen."

A light clicked on in my brain. I stared at the cop. "As a matter of fact, officer, I had quite a large amount of cash in my office that appears to be missing."

"How much?"

I did a quick calculation in my mind as to the amount in the cigar boxes that I'd lost. I then told the cop a number that was about four times that amount.

His eyebrows shot up. "Jeez, that's a lot of money. An awful lot to keep in a place that's as lightly secured as this one." He leveled his gaze at me. "You know, Mr. Chatham, the mayor got a big contribution to his campaign from the insurance people the last time he ran. He's really hot on any insurance fraud that someone might try to commit. He's ordered all of us to investigate and prosecute any and all cases." He looked into a corner of the room, as he scratched behind his ear. "Ya know, I might check again to see if that money isn't in that place where you *very carefully* concealed it. Especially since I met you right at the door this morning, and I haven't seen you look around for anything missing. Why don't I just head back to the precinct, and you go and check that very special hiding place--*again*--and if that money's still missing, give me a call?"

New York police are very diligent about crime prevention. If nothing happens, they don't have to fill out any reports.

I finished with the officer, dropping my claim. I was still behind the eight ball with Mr. Thompson and the IRS.

#

A little later, I checked in with Peasblossom in her office. "What happened to that guy last night?"

"Well, if he got past Echinacea and through the portal, he probably found that place where I wanted you to be very quiet." She nodded her head toward the far end of her office.

"What does that mean?"

"He's probably starting a new life," she said.

"A new life?"

"Yes. They probably considered him a bit hasty, so they decided to teach him patience."

"And that means?"

"He's now a beech tree. Beeches are very patient."

Chapter 54

The calendar in my computer gave me the name and address of the restaurant for my date with Violet. I arrived there at a couple of minutes to eight.

The place was Italian and fairly small, sporting about two dozen tables, with the usual red-checkered tablecloths. The little votive candles in the center were about the only light in the place. It was intimate.

The waiter greeted me at the front. I told him there would be two of us, that I was expecting a young lady.

"Very good. And the name of the lady when she comes?" he asked.

"Uh--Violet Hunter."

"Ah! Violetta! Come with me." He bustled me over to a booth in the back, and flourished a napkin into my lap. If anything, this table was the darkest in the place.

I wasn't given a choice of drink to start off. The implied social behavior by this waiter was to wait for the lady. I did rate a glass of water.

Violet arrived a few minutes later, received much fussing and a kiss on both cheeks from the waiter, and was escorted back to meet me.

"I think Alfredo likes you," she said as she sat in the booth.

"Alfredo?"

"The waiter."

"I didn't realize I needed approval from the service staff."

She smiled at me. "You don't know the half."

At that moment, Alfredo arrived at the table. "Could I see a menu?" I asked.

"No," he replied.

"Oh, okay." His tone of voice said he would broach no argument. "What do I do?"

"Sit back and relax. You don't need a menu when you're with Violetta."

"Okay."

"Would you like some wine?"

"Do I have a choice?"

"No."

"Fine, then I either do or don't want some wine." He absolutely oozed charm while telling me I had to sit still and shut up.

When Alfredo left the table, I turned toward Violet and fell very deeply into green eyes with gold flecks.

After a moment or two passed with me staring, Violet waved her hand in front of my face to distract me and said, "Anyway, I thought it would be a good idea for the two of us to talk things over. I believe we might have a few mutual acquaintances."

"I probably don't want to know most of them," I admitted.

"Why's that?"

"Not if it includes Mirabel."

She leaned back and looked at me. "You were married to her?"

"Yes."

"I've heard a lot of things about her. I understand she can be quite charming when you first meet her, then she'll suddenly turn and become a total harridan."

"That's a fair description, although harridan might be a little light."

"I guess she didn't let you see her evil side until you guys were married."

"And then it was too late. I began to hate everything about her, especially her main interest, magic." It crossed my mind that I was on a first date with Violet and able to easily chat about my ex-wife.

"But you're involved with Peasblossom and some other things." She was displaying knowledge about a lot of things that most people didn't know existed.

"That's right."

"So you don't like the books in my store."

"That's right."

She made little circles with her fingertip on the tablecloth in front of her as she stared, not only at it, but at thing many miles away.

"I guess I should explain a few things about myself," she said.

Chapter 55

Our conversation was interrupted as Alfredo served the wine I didn't order. He was not alone.

"Hey, Violet."

"Hi, Vi."

The two gentlemen who arrived with Alfredo were in their 20s, tall, dark, well-built, extremely respectful, and sported bulges underneath their jackets. Their names were Vito and Vinnie. I wasn't sure which was which.

After the introductions, they managed to disappear into the dark corners of the restaurant where they stood watch.

"I went to high school with Vito and Vinnie's younger sister," Violet explained. "She was a couple of years behind me. One day these two punks tried to press their affections on her. She was only 14 years old and scared stiff. I intervened and demonstrated to her the fine art of lifting your knee. The two gentlemen generously acted as volunteers for the demonstration. I left them lying on the ground, moaning."

Alfredo was laying out some *antipasti* and some warm bread with olive oil. It was all delicious.

"I actually was doing those two punks a favor by cutting things short," Violet continued. "If they had gone any further, they would've been in real trouble. As it was, Vito and Vinnie decided to reinforce my message to the two guys. Nowadays, whenever the two punks walk, their knees whistle."

"So that's why Vito and Vinnie are so protective of you?"

"Yes."

"What happened to their sister?"

"She took over a part of their father's business."

"What part?"

"Brooklyn."

I paused for a moment and glanced around the restaurant as I absorbed that.

Violet continued. "She learned how to lift her knee."

Chapter 56

"So tell me about the company you keep," Violet said.

"Since Mirabel and her divorce lawyer got finished with me? The folks in the soup kitchen."

"Alfredo, your timing is impeccable," she said. He had come out and was serving *minestrone,* ladling it out of a tureen.

After he had finished, Violet said, "Would you like to give me a more serious answer to my last question? I'll let you gloss over the Mirabel thing. What business are you in?"

"I do dog & pony shows." Violet stared at me in non-comprehension. I was used to that. "I stage meetings for major corporations."

The confusion still flickered across Violet's eyes. "I think I'm going to smile broadly as though I understood what you said and wait for life to show me that sort of thing in the flesh," she said. "Tell me about Peasblossom."

"I hired her as Traffic Manager." I looked up at Violet. "Do you know what a Traffic Manager is supposed to do?"

"Everyone I've ever met has described the job differently, but they seem to feel it's some sort of panacea for all their problems. The best I can guess is that they're supposed to do magic."

"She does a great job on that front. She makes machines work like they were never supposed to."

"That group of elves she belongs to who do the LAPH-ing, the Drawbacks, can be good at things like that," she said.

"Anyway, I hired her. At least I thought I hired her, but I'm not too sure about that anymore. For some reason, I've turned into the only contact between our world and hers. Now I've got good guys from both worlds telling me I've got to be some sort of hero. They're equally counterbalanced by bad guys who have me in their sights."

"You don't enjoy that?"

"It's not my idea of an entertaining evening. I find being miscast as a hero very uncomfortable. I just want to get on with my normal, conniving business life."

"How do you know about this group of international villains?"

"That guy I saw in your store? He's some sort of CIA dude. He's been spooning out information to me. I've also been talking to some strange dude Peasblossom knows named Corgus. Do you know about him?"

"I've heard about him. He's a big muckety-muck among the Fair Folk."

"Well, I'm not impressed. The most he's told me is that there's Trouble, and that's about it. How am I supposed to do anything with instructions like that?"

Chapter 57

After we'd finished the soup, Violet excused herself to go to the restroom. I sat there trying to arrange my feelings in a logical order.

No doubting there was a great attraction between the two of us, but there had been a great attraction with Mirabel, and that had been an utter disaster. Obviously Violet was different, but could I trust that difference?

My thoughts were interrupted as someone swooped in and sat in the booth opposite me, in Violet's place.

“Hi there, fella. This is a wonderful restaurant.” It was Winfield. “I hope you're having the osso bucco."

He leaned back. “I've got to say that the due diligence we did on you did not reveal the full inventory of your resources,” he continued. “I'm afraid I underestimated your core capabilities.”

He was doing a great job of spouting The Babble. I decided to counter with the question that always confuses business types: “What do you mean?”

He leaned in toward me. “I mean that I thought I could solve the problem you pose by relying on associates to do the job. I was wrong. It seems I have to take care of you myself.” He locked his psychotic gaze on me with deadly purpose.

"Is there a problem, Mr. Chatham?" It was Vito or Vinnie, I couldn't tell which one. The two of them had suddenly materialized next to our table.

Winfield leaned back in his chair to look up at the two of them. "Gentlemen, Mr. Chatham and I are conducting our own business. I'm sure we'll be able to conclude it without your help."

"Mr. Chatham is in our restaurant," said Vinnie or Vito, I couldn't tell.

"I will be escorting Mr. Chatham out of here in a few minutes," said Winfield.

"Mr. Chatham is here with a special friend of ours, and we do not wish for her to be deprived of his company," said Vino--Vittie!--or Vinito.

"I don't think you have a choice in this matter," said Winfield.

"We always like to make our own choices," said Vinito.

"Gentlemen, if you think you can strong-arm me, you're quite mistaken. I have a number of associates outside who could join us in an instant."

"Not any longer," said Vinito.

Winfield continued to stare at them confidently. They returned his look. Winfield slowly pulled out a phone. He depressed a pager button, and spoke into the mouthpiece, "Martin?"

He waited. The phone was silent. The confidence drained out of Winfield as he read the certainty in Vito's and Vinnie's faces. He slowly turned back to me and said, "Well, it looks like I've fallen short of my due diligence again." A wry smile pushed its way out from the center of his face. "I keep underestimating how many friends you have. I'll have to stop doing that." He stood up from the table and addressed Vito and Vinnie. "I'll take my leave of you gentlemen."

"That would be best," said Vinnie/Vito.

Just as Winfield made his way out the door, and Vito and Vinnie disappeared back into the back corners of the restaurant, Violet returned to the table. "Were you able to entertain yourself while I was gone?"

"Yes."

No sense telling her my life had been threatened while she was in the Necessary.

Chapter 58

Alfredo was dishing out the chicken cacciatore, which I knew was far superior to the osso bucco.

I was enjoying the view now that my original tablemate had returned. I wanted to find out some more. "How did you come to operate your bookstore?"

"It used to be my mother's."

"How long had she had it?"

"She opened it back in the 70s."

"Where is she now?"

"She retired and gave the store to me."

"Where did she go to retire?" I asked.

"With my father."

"I should imagine so," I said. She wasn't giving me lengthy explanations. "He lives in another country?"

"Yes."

Why did I feel she was holding something back? "How did your parents meet?"

"My father came into my mother's store."

"Was there something special he was looking for in her store?"

"Yes, a particular book."

"Uh-huh?" I wasn't so much drawing her out as dragging her along.

She paused, and traced her fork through her linguini. "There was something special about their meeting."

"I'm sure there was."

"Really special."

"Oh?"

"He came in through the back door."

Chapter 59

My stomach clenched. She was talking about the same back door to her store I had used with Peasblossom after a trip through the elf's home world. I leaned back in my chair. "Was he just shortcutting from another part of town?"

"No."

I squeezed my eyes shut. I opened them back up and looked at the ceiling. I finally leaned in to her. "You're half elf?"

"Kind of."

"Isn't that like being kind of pregnant?"

"No. It works a little differently. First off, my father had been human."

"'Had been' human?"

"Yeah." She nodded.

I paused to keep my eyes from crossing. "Do I want to know more about that now, or should we just proceed?"

"I'll try my best to explain it."

"Okay. So your father 'had been' human?"

"Yes, but he lived Over Here for quite a while, and that changed him."

A frown of non-comprehension rearranged my face. "How

did living over here change him?"

"No, I don't mean over here, I mean Over Here."

Snapping my fingers, I said, "Oh, that explains it." It didn't.

"I understand your confusion. That place past the end of the back aisle in my store, the place you came out of?"

"Yes?"

"It's called Over Here."

I paused. I'd stopped consuming cacciatore and was consuming data. "I see."

"Yes. They have a rather direct way of naming things."

I remembered Corgus. "In my experience, I've found them to be anything *but* direct."

"Well, it's direct to them. Anyway, they refer to this place as Over There."

"So the place that's over there is Over Here, and the place over here is Over There?"

"Yes. You just have to look at it from their point of view."

"I don't think I want to." I glanced away from her as I reflected. "But I do know one thing. If I find myself in that place, *that* Over Here, I am sure as hell not asking the locals for directions." I leaned back in my seat. "Why don't we leave that subject and continue with this little-bit-elfin thing."

"There's something in Over Here--" she started.

"--Which is over there," I pointed a finger around vaguely.

"Yes! Now you're getting it!" She beamed encouragement at me.

"I don't think I want to."

"Anyway," she continued, "in that land there's something like a radiation makes you more and more elfin."

"So you're father's human, but he's lived in that place called Over Here for quite a time, therefore he's more elfin than someone who's just visited there a little..." I stopped as I added up two and two. Comprehension began to dawn. "I was just there the other day. Does that mean that I...?"

"Only a little," Violet said as she reached out a calming hand.

I closed my eyes, leaned back, took a deep breath to relax, pulled back to my center, got myself entirely under control, was calm and stable. "What do you mean, 'only a little'!?" I shrieked.

Vito-Vinnie appeared out of nowhere and did a fast check on how things were going. Violet waved them away. She patted me on the hand. "I mean really just the least little bit; something less than a tenth of a percent."

"That's not much, is it?" I hoped.

"Really, it's like a very mild euphoric. It just makes you a tiny bit happier at times." She leaned back and appraised me. "Admittedly, this is not one of those times."

"And you're about five percent elfin?"

"Yes."

"What does that do to you? Do you have points on the ends of your ears?"

"No, they're just a little bit longer and thinner than most people's."

"How about antenna? You got those?"

"There are little ridges up there on my skull."

I shot my hands to my head and accelerated my premature balding by checking every square inch of my scalp. I looked over at Violet. "Do you have a book on phrenology?"

She rolled her eyes to the ceiling. "I'll get you one," she assured.

"What if I feel I'm getting too elfin? Is there something I can do that'll make me more human again? Like go to a hockey game? Or watch reality TV? Something to suck the elf right out of me?"

"Those sound like they'd do the job," she assured.

"You think so?"

"I know so."

"Okay. I think I'll get season's tickets to the Rangers."

"That should keep you well grounded in humanity."

Despite the spate of high spirits" about the elf thing, I couldn't help noticing how I was opening up to this young lady I'd just met. I didn't usually pour out my secrets to someone I hardly knew. I felt safe with her, but did I feel safe with Mirabel?

There was something else buzzing in the back of my brain, demanding to be let out. I pondered how to spill it to her. I had to come up with some subtle way of disclosing it, so I wouldn't shock her. Some roundabout means to introduce the topic and then explore it in greater depths.

"I'm magic," I said.

Violet leaned back and sucked in a deep breath. "Aren't you supposed to say that about me, to try to compliment me on our first date?"

"I'm serious. I am magic."

Violet puckered her lips; she was confused. "A moment ago, you were complaining about becoming a little bit elfin. Now you're saying you've got these powers. That's a bit contradictory."

"No it isn't," I responded. "Turning into an elf means becoming a different creature. Magic is just--a talent I happen to have."

"Like being able to touch your nose with the tip of your tongue?" she asked. "It implies a little bit more than that."

"You're right, and I don't feel comfortable with it. I used to hate the very thought of magic, thanks to my ex-wife."

"You are full of contradictions," she said.

"The magic thing is the reason why they're enlisting me to

oppose this group of baddies."

"I could see where that talent would come in handy."

"And it's not just me," I continued. "Apparently it's the four of us in the office. We form a group."

"You've got a Magical Synergy? That's quite rare. How did it happen?"

"Darned if I know, but apparently it's what they need to stand off these bad dudes. I just don't see how we're going to pull that off."

"I'm sure a way will present itself."

"I'm glad you're sure." I stared off into a corner of the restaurant.

Finally Violet broke the silence. "I think we've managed to forget our meal. We should continue with dinner. Alfredo thinks I'm going to shrink away to nothing if I don't clear my plate. And if there's too much leftover, Mama will come out of the kitchen to personally administer an intravenous of pasta and sauce."

Chapter 60

We were lingering over cappuccino, tiramisu, and anisette. The evening had been--and I didn't want to use the word--enchanting. As she sipped her coffee, Violet peered at me over the rim of her cup with her gold-flecked, five-percent-elfin, green eyes. "This has certainly been a most interesting evening. I'm sure I've told you more than I ever confessed on a first date. It must be that magic charm of yours," she said.

I still winced inwardly at the M-word. "I've got to admit I've said more things tonight than I should have prudently admitted. I think I also told you stuff that's classified, but everything's classified with those damn CIA guys."

A silence fell over us. It was a strangely embarrassed quiet, as we both realized that we had clicked. Despite my Mirabel-induced misgivings, despite her reservations about this guy who hated the very product she sold, we were heading into something, I wasn't sure what, but I found that I was welcoming it.

"Well," she said, "it's getting late, and we both have to go to work tomorrow morning."

"I was wondering," I launched a trial balloon, "since you've already done some things you don't normally do on the first date, if you might want to...."

"Nice try."

"Had to give it a go," I said.

"Once more, I choose to take it as a compliment."

We had finished the coffee, dessert, and drinks. "I guess I'd better ask for the check."

"The check is in the some place as the menus."

Violet was in very good standing with the restaurant. The management appreciated lessons in raising a knee.

We were *salud*-ed our way out of the restaurant by Alfredo and Vito-Vinnie. Mama emerged from the kitchen bringing many hugs and kisses. Since I was Violet's date, Mama cupped my face in her hands and appraised me. Cupped is a nice word. That little old Italian lady had a grip like a longshoreman. She decided I was all right but looked a little thin, and didn't I want something extra to eat, something to take home, to put a little weight on me?

When we left, I was carrying a bag of cannolis.

Chapter 61

The following morning I headed directly to Peasblossom's office. "How come you didn't tell me about that elf-radiation thing?" I demanded.

For once, I had her confused. "What?"

"You took me into that place where I could have turned into an elf right before my very own eyes. You didn't even warn me."

"Oh, you mean Over Here."

"That's right, that place, over there. I could have gotten lost and been over-exposed and turned into an elf."

"I don't think so."

"Oh, you mean it's actually safe?"

"No, but you're not the elf type. With your magic, you might have turned into a mage. On the other hand, you are more the mountain troll type."

"You mean there's more things I could turn into than just an elf?"

"Oh, yes. Lots," she bubbled.

"Lots? *Lots?* You mean like a centaur or something?"

"Oh, that'd be interesting."

"That's another species!"

"Yes." She was far too matter-of-fact about it.

"Listen, we've got to discuss this. Let's go into my office. I want to know just how involved I am in all of this Trouble stuff." I headed out her office door; she followed behind me. I stopped, and she nearly ran into me. "What do you mean 'I'm the mountain troll type'?"

"That's just one of the possibilities."

"Would you stop acting like that's the good news?"

We cascaded into my office. I sat down behind my desk, Peasblossom took the chair opposite.

"How did your date go last night?" she asked.

"Don't try to change the subject. Going to Over Here can have a physical effect on me?"

Before she could answer, an all-too-familiar voice said, "Yup, Yup."

Chapter 62

I dropped my head down and cradled it in my hands. It was my old buddy, Corgus, again. "You know, it's been several days since I last saw you, and the interesting thing is: I didn't mind it at all."

"It be quite a bit more time where I was," Corgus answered.

"Where's this place that has such a favorable rate of exchange on widgins, or is it wodgins?"

"Over Here."

"Are you talking about the Over Here that's over there?" I asked him.

"Yup."

"If the place makes it seem longer since the last time we met, there's lots to be said for it."

He didn't reply, just dug for his smudge pot with a mouthpiece and started to stuff tobacco into it.

"Why are you here? Or at least, what reason are you going to give that's going to wind up being totally incomprehensible to me?"

"The Trouble be worse."

"It couldn't get any worse than the last time you were here. That guy--what's his name, the Evil Mage Zorch?--was launching green fireballs at me, but I guess you didn't see it. It happened right after you took a powder. Plus his friend Winfield hauled me off to his office where they tried to mindwash me."

"That's not all," he said.

"I know that. I've been the target of all sorts of things."

"The Far Isles be a place of magic," he said.

"And you'd better beware," said my other buddy, Zorch, as he reappeared in my office, spewing out his usual cloud of toxic waste.

"You know you owe me a bunch of money for the damage you did to this office the last time you were here," I accused him. "Not only that. You've got my cigar box."

"Don't bother me with your petty desires," he sneered.

"And while you're in this particular world, find your way to an auto parts store and pick up one of those things that look like a pine tree. It's called an air freshener. You could hang it around your neck. It would clear up the stink you leave behind from your mode of transportation."

"You would threaten me with a destructive amulet?" the Zorcher said. "However, I did not come here to challenge you. I bring you a peace offering."

"Bring me real peace by leaving," I said.

"These are our terms," he continued, not bothering with me. "We will not bother with you in this city. Your wards are too strong in your homeland, but," he drew himself up to his full height, which wasn't much, "do not attempt to go to the Far Isles. We will attack you there."

"Yeah? You only think so." I was beginning to get downright cocky. "I'll come after you with my Magic Blue Screen of Death if you're not careful. Not only that, I've taken it easy with you so far. I haven't even used my big-time magic guy, Corgus over here."

I swung my gaze around to where he was sitting in his chair smoking. With a sound like a bubble popping, he disappeared.

I swung around to Peasblossom. "Aw for good cat's sweet sake, he just disappeared again! I thought he was this humongous magic dude who was going to help me fight the forces of evil."

Peasblossom gave an embarrassed shrug.

"Heed my warning, Chatham, do not go to the Far Isles," said Zorch. Then he disappeared in a cloud of diesel exhaust.

I swung back to Peasblossom. "What does all of this mean?"

"Something's going to happen in Hawaii."

Chapter 63

"Unfortunately, my next order of business is to go to Hawaii," I explained to Violet. Since she had shown me *Lo Stregone,* I decided to show her the seamier side of life and asked her to join me at Percy's. She'd looked around the bar and declared the local life forms to be almost as bizarre as those found in that place called Over Here.

She burrowed back into the protection of the booth where we were sitting and suspiciously cast her eyes about. "Are you sure there's not some sort of radiation in here that is the direct opposite of what we've got in Over Here?" she asked. "Am I going up to the bar to watch some reality TV and get into some fistfights?"

"Or I could suggest some other physical activities that you and I could practice," I said.

"Nice try," she said as she gave me a reproving look. "I guess I'm not being affected by these surroudings that much. I'm not foolish enough to fall for that line."

"But you'd be further away from this places evil influences if we went to my place."

"Only to fall under the darker influences of your lascivious urges," she countered.

I gazed away. "Well, I thought it was worth a try."

"Why do't you tell me about this trip you're taking to Hawaii before you're supposed to go to Hawaii?" she asked.

"We have to do a site survey to make sure we can properly mount the meeting," I continued. "We've been to the Kensington Hotel before, but you can never tell what might have happened to the place since."

"What could they change?"

"They're owned by a major corporation. They could have changed anything on a whim," I explained.

"Couldn't you just ask them if anything's changed?"

"Repeating myself: they're owned by a major corporation. It's best to take a look ourselves. There's also a good business reason to go."

"What's that?" she asked.

"It's in the budget."

"Good reason."

"I knew you'd see it my way," I said. "Fortunately, Lenny Kanaka, our contact at the hotel, will be able to cover our butts on most anything. He's well connected with people all over the islands."

"Check to see what sort of 'special people' he might know," she said. "There are portals from Over Here to Over There on the islands. Zorch probably has some friends there, himself, although they'll be a different race."

I paused for a minute to get my *here's* and *there's* in the right places. "You mean the Over Here there is different from the Over Here, here--which, by the way, is Over There, which is here?"

She smiled at me. "Now you're getting it. That was easy, wasn't it?"

"No," I said.

"Yes!"

That last piece of dialogue was not Violet agreeing with me.

It was Augie, the CIA guy, thrusting himself into our booth.

"How do you manage to appear and disappear almost as quickly as magic folk?" I asked him.

"We take special stealth training in a classified location somewhere in Asia"

"Where is it?"

"Don't know. It stealths into and out of its location."

Made as much sense as everything else he said. "You have to go all the way to Asia to learn how to pop up in a New York bar?" I asked.

"It's an ancient oriental art," he replied. He looked at Violet. "Who is this person? Does she have proper clearance?"

I jumped in. "She's my liaison and my primary contact for--" I leaned in confidentially to Augie, he liked that sort of secrecy thing, "--that place called Over Here."

He straightened up, and his eyes popped. "Excellent!"

"Okay, so what's the scoop with you? Have you come to tell me that the Defense Department has released an all-new, powerful weapon to me, so I can use it against all these hoods who are taking pot shots at me?"

"No."

"Okay then, I'll settle for a cigar box." I looked hopefully at his steel briefcase.

"Can't do that," he said.

"What?" Several purchases I had sitting in online shopping carts began to wither on their electronic vines.

"Austerity program in place," he said. "They're auditing our expenditures more closely and making us cut back. I only have this," he said as he pulled an envelope out of his jacket pocket.

I checked inside and was reassured to see portraits of Grover Cleveland in there, just not in the abundance I'd become used to. I consoled myself with the thought that New York had an excellent subway system so maybe I didn't need that

Lamborghini I'd been eying. "Is this all?" I never would have said that a few weeks ago, but one's tastes can change fast.

"I'll requisition more," Augie said. Words I loved to hear. "Intelligence has told us that the focus of the opposition's attention is on something that's going to take place in Hawaii."

"I know. That's what they've been telling me. Do you have any idea what it could be?"

"None. You'll have to tap all possible resources on the islands."

"Well, I've got a guy named Lenny Kanaka at the hotel."

"Can he supply you with the necessary strategic weaponry to use against the opponents?"

"Sure." At least Lenny was able to supply me with troupes of hula dancers and fire swallowers. And I'm pretty sure he also supplied the Roadies with the pharmaceuticals of their choice.

"Yes! Excellent." And he lurched out of the booth and dashed out the door.

Violet stared after him, then turned with an overly bright smile on her face. "Is that your government contact?

"Yes."

She gave an appraising nod of her head. "Do your best to rely on Peasblossom when you're in Hawaii."

Chapter 64

The day arrived for us to travel to Hawaii to do the site scout.

Some bean counter from Lambert Industries had figured out that any group of people traveling on the company expense account had to take the company's car service (with whom they had a discount) to get to the airport. That meant that a car had to start at the crack of bejesus at my place picking up all five of us to take us out to JFK. We were all cheek-to-jowl in an SUV, sucking on coffees to try to get the caffeine in our blood up to proper levels.

The conversation between us didn't rival Noel Coward for its quick wit and rapid-fire exchanges, with the exception of Peasblossom, who was her usual bubbly self. She rhapsodized on the beauty of the sunrise. The rest of us sulked.

When we got to the airport, we stood in the line of sullen passengers waiting to be harassed by equally sullen security people.

In other words, it was morning in New York.

When we got to the gate, we sat around, desperately sucking on new coffee containers, trying to cope with all that sunshine blasting in at us through the overly large terminal windows.

Other employees of Lambert began showing up at the gate,

having fought their way through the security obstacle course. Wendell was there with Gordon Montbatten fawning all over him. Sheila, the gal from Marketing who was so concerned about the banquet, showed up. Myron, the accountant took a seat with the lady from International Relations. Everyone who'd showed up at my aborted meeting over at Lambert started appearing: the sales rep, the IT guy, a couple of the doo-wop singers, and the guy who was doing the PowerPoint presentation, toting a small video projector as his carry-on. They were all going on this site inspection: the one where we were supposed to be setting up technical specifications.

Finally the desk attendant began to prepare for boarding, and Brad, the Vice President of Nepotism, came swooping into the gate area. He had obviously not shared his ride to the airport like everyone else. Although his admin was loping along behind him, taking notes.

When the gate attendant started the boarding with the First Class section, we all stayed seated, since the bean counters would only lay out for economy seats. However, bright little Brad jumped up to board. Apparently accounting had been made aware that he was Related to Someone.

The initial capital letters on an expression are a mark of corporate life. They all operate in PowerPoint's Headline Case. Any word that seems important gets upgraded to an initial cap. Corporate communications often looks like the style of English used when Henry Fielding wrote *Tom Jones*.

We finally got our seats called and were herded along like cattle into coach and settled in for the long flight.

Chapter 65

There's something devilishly fooling about the flight to Hawaii. You think the islands are just a little way past California, but it's again as far. You touch down in LAX for a while, and then make your way across 3,000 miles of ocean, heading for Honolulu.

Laura, Joel, and Sidney had opted to sit together so they could compare their agendas for the meeting the following day. I was seated at a window seat with Peasblossom next to me. The guy from the Sales Department at Lambert was next to her, on the aisle. Early in the flight he must have felt a little cramped and had ventured his hand past the dividing arm of the seat toward Peasblossom. She had stuck out one delicate little forefinger and touched him on the back of his hand. He had immediately recoiled in shock and spent the next three minutes writhing miserably in his seat. He promptly invested in some anesthetic from the refreshment cart and had buried himself in the in-flight movie.

The rest of the Lambert employees were scattered throughout coach class, while Brad, the Vice President of My Daddy's Your Boss, kept sending missives back from first class to his admin to generate some more reports.

I stared out the window at the endless ocean beneath us. As

the flight stretched on, Peasblossom seemed to be more and more on edge; she kept looking around, expecting something to appear out of the plane's air ducts.

"What's the problem?" I asked.

"The Evil Mage Zorch and Winfield warned you not to come out here. I'm sure they're going to do something."

"What can they do? We've seen everyone who's boarded this plane. There was nobody threatening there. And all of us had our body cavities inspected by security. What could be the danger?"

On that cue, the plane lurched.

Part 4

...it's all Relative

Chapter 66

We took a dip down as the engines' steady hum turned into a shrieking whine. Some monstrosity landed on the wing right outside my window. It looked like a praying mantis, but it was really big, almost human sized. The middle pair of legs sported something like hands at the end. The big difference was in the head. It had a mandible, but the rest of it looked human, with a pair of un-faceted eyes that carried a suggestion of dim intelligence behind them.

Several more of the beasts landed on the wing. There must have been just as many on the other side as I heard the gasps from people across the cabin. The creatures scuttled around on the wing, some of them using the sharp edge of their forelimbs to cut away at the surface of the plane. Others scrambled over to the intake of the engine, and began to drool out a thick yellow paste that got sucked into the turbine.

The plane started to sputter and jerk, and rapidly started losing altitude. Bells dinged and warning lights came on.

A flight attendant came on the PA system. "Ladies and gentlemen, we are experiencing a bit of turbulence. The Captain has requested that you return to your seats and fasten your seat belts. We should clear this little patch of air and be....OH, MY GOD!"

She had skillfully grasped the reins and taken command of the mood in the cabin and instigated total pandemonium. People were jumping up and screaming.

I wanted to leap out of my seat and join in the panic, but I was restrained by both my seat belt, that I'd forgotten to unfasten, and Peasblossom, who had grasped me firmly by the wrist.

"You've got to do something," she commanded.

"What? What can I do?" I didn't know what the hell she meant. Suddenly, I felt a warm glow from my wrist where she held me. It radiated out through the rest of my body, the heat growing in temperature. I thought I was turning incandescent. I could feel the radiation escaping from me and spreading out toward the body of the plane, being absorbed into the structure. I felt pulses of power seethe into the plane from my hand on the arm rest.

I looked outside the window, and saw the texture of the wing changing. The smooth, metallic surface mottled and puckered and transformed into evenly spaced irregularities, air currents rippling over this new surface.

Then I recognized what the surface was. The wings had grown a coating of feathers. The structure began to change shape as joints formed, delineating the sections of what was now, obviously, an organic bird's wing.

I scanned the inside of the plane to see if the outside changes were making their way inside. Everything looked the same, a normal plastic plane's interior, except for one little section of the cabin's ceiling that was beginning to look--fleshy.

With the transformation, the course of the plane became jerkier as the wings flapped a couple of times attempting to stabilize the flight. Some of the insectoids were flicked off the wings by this motion, but they quickly flew back and continued attacking the surface. The wings were fully deployed now, the end feathers were spread as the bird/plane tried to gain lift.

Then we heard an enormous sound.

"GRAWK!"

It resounded both outside and through the chassis surrounding the cabin.

I looked out the window and saw something dart backwards from the nose of the plane/bird and snatch up one of the insectoids and gulp it down a beak. There were two more lightening-quick strikes and two more creatures disappeared as the head of the bird pecked off and devoured the pests.

If the front of the plane was turning into an actual bird's head, I couldn't imagine what was happening with the cabin personnel.

Catching the spirit of the flight attendant's not-so-calming announcement, everyone in Coach Class was shrieking and screaming.

The bird head swung away from our side, and I could feel the chassis of the cabin shudder with what felt like similar pecking actions on the other wing. Quickly the head was back and picking off some more of the attackers as their number shrank. The head swung away again and there were more shudders in machine-gun-like rapidity from the other side. It came back to my side, and was picking off the last few, as some stragglers escaped to safety off into the air.

Flight stability was returning, as the surviving insectoids raced for the distance. Suddenly, one larger beast appeared alongside with the Evil Mage Zorch riding on his back. He raised his hand, looking like he was going to fling another green fireball at us, but he motioned with his hand in a slow and circular manner, like he was washing a window. He then turned and flew away.

I immediately began to calm down. Simultaneously, in a kind of slow cross-dissolve, the wings lost their feathers and restored their smooth, metallic surface, and the sound of air rushing around us morphed into the steady hum of jet engines.

The Captain came on the intercom. "Ladies and gentlemen, we seem to have passed through a small patch of turbulence and should have smooth flying the rest of the way. Just as a precaution, why don't you keep your seat belts fastened in case we hit some small pockets ahead? I'll turn off the seat belt sign in a few minutes."

--I relaxed. I was glad we were past that little air pocket. I hated it when the plane bounced around. Some people in the cabin had been upset, but they'd all calmed down now.

"You've got to remember what happened," Peasblossom bored her gaze into mine.

"What? That turbulence? Believe me, I've been through far worse," I said.

"No," she continued, "we were attacked by Zorch and some Preying Mansects. He nearly crashed the plane."

"What?"

"He wasn't successful. He had to put a Forgetfulness Spell on, so no one would remember."

"What are you saying?"

"Zorch just attacked our plane with insectoids."

"We just had turbulence a minute...." I suddenly saw two images in my mind; one flashing over the other. There was what I remembered now, and there was something else that kept erupting out of my sub-conscious. "What?"

"Zorch attacked us," she drove the point home to me. "He was trying to crash this plane into the ocean."

Her words made sense to my sub-conscious. "Okay, if you say so, but how did we escape?"

"You turned the plane into a chicken, and it ate the insectoids."

I stared at her incredulously. "Peasblossom, did you have anything from the beverage cart?"

"You must remember. Concentrate," she implored.

"Okay, let's just assume what you say happened. Why can't I remember it?"

"Zorch lay down a Forgetfulness Spell."

"And I did what?"

"You changed the plane into a chicken."

Suddenly, I remembered. I recalled the sensation of the power flashing through my hand into the plane's chassis. But I wasn't ready to believe my own memories. I shook my head in denial. "It couldn't have happened."

"It's a very natural thing. Humans try to deny that they've seen magic. The spell enhances that reaction."

"Come on, Peasblossom, it didn't happen," I dismissed her.

I felt some strange lump in my jacket pocket that hadn't been there before. I reached in and pulled it out. It was a stone, a gooey one.

"What's that?" I asked.

"It's a gizzard stone," she replied.

I glared at her long and hard. I was angry that she had the temerity to be right.

I put the damned stone in the barf bag.

#

We flew on in silence for a good 20 minutes. I broke the mood by saying, "Why a chicken?"

An embarrassed look flashed across Peasblossom's face. "Why not?"

I had mixed feelings about that answer. I knew she was equivocating, but professionally, I was also very proud about how well she was learning to deceive.

"Why wasn't it some sort of fierce raptor to fight those things off? Why not an eagle?"

"Wild magic, like yours, is hard to predict. It originates from a random instinct within you, so it will take on some very subjective form. It might have expressed itself as a chicken because you were frightened."

I turned away from her and pouted out the window. Frightened indeed! What nonsense!

Scared shitless, maybe, but not frightened.

#

We were into the approach for Honolulu. Something about the previous conversation disturbed me. "Why did Zorch put a Forgetfulness Spell on us?"

"He had to. If everyone on the plane remembered the Preying Mansects, they'd realize there's something more than just their world."

"That's bad?"

"Yes. If everyone here in Over There knew that Over Here was there, it would be very bad for us."

I squeezed my eyes shut until I sorted out the *here's* and *there's* from her last comment. "Okay, and why would it be bad?"

"If the passengers remembered what happened, everyone would start looking for Over Here. We can't have you find us. Zorch couldn't leave a trail; everyone in my home would have turned on him."

"And that's bad?"

"Yes, we have to stay separate from your world."

"I understand." I lied, nodding my head sagely.

I was totally lost.

Chapter 67

We arrived in Honolulu without further incident.

As we filed out of the plane the flight crew was standing by the door doing their usual, "Bye-bye. So long. Goodbye. Bye-bye. Goodbye." As we passed the cabin door, the Captain shifted his weight to one leg and ran his other foot back along the floor as though he was scratching in the dirt with his claw.

#

It was late afternoon locally, which meant six hours later where our bio-rhythms lived, and we still had to travel the last leg, hopping to Hilo on the big island. It had been a long flight, and our nerves were even further frayed from the attack on the plane, the one no one remembered. With an hour to kill at the airport, everyone scattered to different parts of the gate area to amuse themselves.

The guy from Sales, who had slept through the whole attack, headed off to the bar. Everyone else from Lambert was gathered together making plans for tomorrow. The hub of this activity was Brad the Bright who seemed to be locked in a competition with his admin to see which one could text faster on their smart phones.

The five of us gathered in the coffee shop. Joel was digging into his shoulder bag to pull out various cleaning implements and solutions to fix up his pants. Coffee had spilled over them in the turbulence when we were locked in the battle with Zorch. Joel was very distressed that his appearance was less than impeccable.

"It's bad enough that the only thing available on the plane is that hideous airline coffee. Then, to have the stuff spill all over me is past endurance," he said.

I shared a quick glance with Peasblossom. "Is that all it was? Turbulence?" I asked

"Yeah, it just slammed like a sonuvabitch, and then went away practically as fast," Sidney said.

"You didn't notice anything else?"

"Well, I did have a sudden image of what it would be like to soar through the air like a bird--an eagle," Laura said.

I tried suggesting to them the truth: that we'd been attacked by Zorch. They insisted we'd just encountered turbulence.

Suddenly they all felt hungry. All three ordered omelets.

#

Our hop to Hilo was called for boarding, and we all shuffled like zombies onto the plane. The flight itself, took less time than the wait for it. It was a local carrier, which stressed the native culture. We landed, got our luggage, made it to the Kensington, got to our rooms, and collapsed in bed.

#

I woke up at a jet-lagged four in the morning, ten o'clock back in New York. I fired up my laptop and fussed my way through my email, trying to eat up as much time as possible by obsessing over every last detail on my agenda. When I finished, I looked up to see that it was still dark outside. What the hell could I do?

#

"So," Violet said over the telephone, "you're jetlagging, awake in the middle of the night, you don't have anything to do, you're bored out of your mind, so you decided to call me. What a compliment!"

"I was also feeling alone, lying in bed. Would you like to remedy that situation?"

"You certainly aren't wasting any time." She cleared her throat officiously. "No proper young lady would succumb to mere cravings of the flesh in so short a time." She paused for an appropriate moment, then said, "Try a third date."

"What are you doing the morning I return?" I fired back.

"What an offer! Let me see. You'd be coming off a red-eye, grouchy from lack of sleep, unbathed, and scratchy from an overnight's growth of beard. Why do I somehow think there might be something lacking with you as an ardent lover?"

"Give it a try."

"It should be over candle lights and wine, and I don't consider that a proper morning pastime."

"Okay, that night?" I asked.

"You'd better not be yawning, buster."

"I'll nap."

She changed the subject. "So you're on the wonderful island of Hawaii. What exactly are you doing there?"

"We're getting all our ducks in order, so we can roll in for the meeting and not be surprised. I'm also hoping to make contact with someone who can introduce me to the local natives of Over Here." I was proud I was able to use the terminology without getting confused. I could even begin to put the initial capitals into my tone of voice.

"That's a pretty hard job. The Fair Folk aren't easy to locate."

"That's all right. I may know the guy who can put me in touch with the right people."

Chapter 68

The meeting with the hotel staff was set for eight in the morning in the Molokai Ballroom. We knew we'd feel the effects of jetlag, so we scheduled the meeting for the early hour.

It's one thing to see a ballroom when it's in use, when the tables and chairs are laid out, the room is decorated, and the lights are dimmed to a comfortable setting. It's quite different to see it as it was this morning. It looked like an empty packing crate.

The group of Lambert employees was all together, swarming like a hive of bees, ready to get started. I looked at them and wondered if one of them was the mole that Winfield had placed in Lambert. I was pretty sure it was Wendell.

The heads of several hotel departments were there: the Catering Manager, the Banquet Manager, the sales rep, the Setup Manager, and the Convention Manager: Lenny Kanaka.

The name Convention Manager sounds exactly like the all-embracing, umbrella job that it is. These people have to be ready on a moment's notice to satisfy every lame-brained request they get from corporate clients. Audio-visual supplies, theatrical lighting equipment, platforms, staging, hula dancers, fire eaters, dancing waters, balloons, tap dancers, gymnasts, marching bands. The Convention Manager has to have contacts all over the community to solve all sorts of problems, and Lenny Kanaka was one of the best of them. He had often saved my butt tapping resources all around the Pacific Ocean. I'm also quite certain that Lenny aided Sidney in introducing him to the suppliers of all of the local recreational herbage. Sidney, Joel, Laura, Peasblossom, and I all headed to him to re-introduce ourselves and renew our acquaintanceship.

Lenny was in his fifties, about five eight, with a deep understanding residing in his Polynesian eyes. He wore the hotel's Hawaiian shirt uniform.

Sheila from Marketing saw us gathered with Lenny and immediately came rushing up.

"I've got to talk to you right away about the menu for our banquet night," she desperately implored.

Lenny cracked out his professional smile. "Let's take care of that for you." He turned to the group of fellow employees. "Francis, could you come here, please?" One guy separated from the group and came over. "This is Francis, our Banquet Manager; he'll be able to help you." He deftly guided the two of them away from our group, then turned back and cast a sidelong glance at me, gave a slight nod of his head toward Sheila and said under his breath, "Nut cups?"

I kept a straight face, and gave him a small nod of affirmation. He returned an I-thought-so nod.

The rest of the Lambert employees began to spread out like a flurry of fusspots to set about their business, far more efficient than they were in their normal corporate life. Something was at stake here: the sooner they concluded their agenda, the sooner they could get themselves out to the beach. I figured most of them would make it there by ten o'clock.

Lenny got swept away by about half a dozen Lambert folks. An exchange of glances between us said that we'd start our business by about 9:15. Sidney was wandering around the room, checking dimensions and verifying power supplies and audio and computer network connections in the wall. Joel was cruising the room with an enormous wheel of color samples that he was holding up against the wallpaper and the rugs, to check their exact shade. Laura was involved in a conversation with Wendell, explaining to him where the whole presentation would lay out in the room.

I stood there trying to figure what I was going to do next.

"Mr. Chatham?"

I turned to the guy behind me who'd spoken. He was big, with a buzz cut, wore a suit, and had a wire leading up to an ear plug. "Yes?" I said.

"We were told by Mr. Lambert to show you the Harbor Room so you could help with the special demonstration taking place during the meeting."

This had to be that special power-source thingy Charlie had told me about, when he had pulled me out of the meeting with Wendell. "Oh yeah."

"Would this be a convenient time for you to go down to look over the room?"

"There couldn't be a better one. All these bright young corporate people are keeping me from doing any work. I've got about an hour before the migrating impulse hits them."

"Migrating impulse, sir?"

"Yes, the sun gets high enough, and they dash off to the beach."

"Yes, sir," he said in the same monotone. Entry into his organization required surgery to have your sense of humor removed.

We went out into the hall, and down in an elevator. The ballroom we'd been in was on the ground floor. I thought there was nothing much below us except perhaps some laundry rooms and an occasional dungeon.

Exiting the elevator, we entered a little hall that had three doors leading off it: the obligatory pair of restrooms and the Harbor Room.

Inside, a bunch more suits with buzz-cuts and earphones were literally crawling around the place, running sensors over the floor, the ceiling, and the walls, checking for electronic bugs.

I checked the room. It didn't have many distinguishing characteristics from any other hotel meeting room, except it seemed less used than the rest. It appeared they saved the Harbor Room for special occasions.

My buzz-cut friend swiveled his head back to the entrance to the room as someone new entered, and said, "Can I help you sir?" The phrasing of the question was in perfect manners, the tone of it was like the warning bark of a watch dog.

I turned around to see who was there. It was Gordon Montbatten.

Chapter 69

Gordon turned on his best imitation British accent for the guy. "Yes, I'm in charge of the breakout sessions for the meeting, and I thought I'd check out this room."

The guy didn't miss a beat. "Sir, may I please see your Green Card?"

"Oh--uh--actually, I don't have one." Gordon had guessed that he didn't want to lie to this guy.

"Are you in this country illegally, sir?"

"No, no!" He paused. "Actually, I'm a native-born citizen."

"I see. Did you spend a lot of time in England?"

"Well--uh--no." Pause "I've never been to England." Gordon's accent had travelled from the British Isles to somewhere in the mid-Atlantic as he began to transform to the Giggy Makowski he really was. Pretty soon he'd be speaking pure Yonkers.

I heard the slightest susurration from my buzz-cut friend's earphone. "Sir, are you Gordon Montbatten, a/k/a...."

"Yes, I am," Gordon quickly cut in before the cat was not only out of the bag but chasing mice around the room. He was displeased that he'd been identified.

"Mr. Montbatten, you are not cleared to be in this room."

"But I'm supposed to handle all of the breakout sessions for the meeting."

"Sir, I have express instructions from Mr. Lambert that Mr. Chatham, here, is supposed to handle the presentation in this room."

"That's right, Gordon. Charlie talked to me directly about this particular area," I said.

"Well, that's most irregular," Gordon huffed.

"Mr. Montbatten, I'm afraid I have to ask you to leave. You do not have the security clearance to be in this location." His manners were still impeccable. However, you could tell that an answer of "No" to his request immediately qualified you for a precautionary body cavity check.

Gordon began to grumble, but he did it in the direction of the door as he left. He was not being foolish enough to cross my buzz-cut friend. I had the feeling that he and his associates were not the kind of people you trifled with.

I took a quick turn of the room, getting the general feel of the thing. I asked Mr. Buzz-Cut if he knew of any power requirements that might be needed. He put a finger to his ear plug and then gave me the number. For such a small room, it was quite a lot.

"I'm going to send my technical director and designer down later, a Mr. Sidney Friedmann and Mr. Joel Eaton. They'll be checking out the room."

"Yessir, we have them on our list." That list was quite complete about who could and couldn't come in this room. The preparations going on solidified my conviction that the demo in this room was the focus of Winfield's and Zorch's interest.

I was about to wrap up and head back to the rest of the group in the ballroom, when a number of hands went up to earphones, obviously a message. Everyone in the room quickly straightened up and squared their very large shoulders. Hands strayed to ties to make sure they were centered and properly knotted. Clothes were brushed off to clear any possible lint. Everybody stopped what they'd been doing and turned toward the door. They'd obviously received the message that someone was coming who was a high muckety-muck in their organization. They were all alert for who was coming in the door.

The handle of the door clicked, it was pulled back, and in walked Mr. Thompson, the guy from the IRS.

Chapter 70

The minute he saw me, Mr. Thompson beamed and headed over in my direction.

"Mr. Chatham, good to see you again." All the guys in the room were looking at me with great respect. "I've got to say I owe you. Your excuse about the plant eating that money was the story of the month around the department. I got all sorts of drinks bought for me for telling that one."

"I'm glad you liked it. I don't suppose the story was so good you'd like to overlook the missing record of the money's distribution."

He laughed heartily and slapped me on the back. "That's a good one. You know, I'd really like to help you, but the rules on this are quite strict."

"Well, I don't suppose you could put in a good word for me? I mean just in case I can't find that pesky receipt, and the department decides to follow up on this."

"You bet I'll help you. I sure owe you."

"Well, that's great."

"I'll be right there for your sentencing."

"Sentencing?"

"And I'll ask the judge to go real light on you."

"Sentencing?"

"Well, yes, I'm afraid the amount of money is no longer in that area the law refers to as 'petty.'"

"Is there a 'moderate' or even 'modest' area?"

"No, I'm afraid it's either petty or grand."

"What about that thing called a Collateral Damage Exemption?"

"I suppose you could do that, but you'd have to have a record of service to the Agency for quite a while."

"Like if I finished a mission?"

"Yeah, something like that."

He acted like it was real simple. All I had to do was withstand green fireballs, insectoids attacking my plane, and other such lovely stumbling blocks.

And I was painfully aware that I counted as my chief ally Corgus, the guy who disappears every time there's trouble.

Chapter 71

My job iin the Harbor Room was pretty quick. I strolled in a small circle in the center of the place and said, "Yep, this is a room all right." Sidney and Joel had to do the real work.

I rejoined the group back in the ballroom. The swarm of Lambert employees had left by the time I got back. As we strolled outside to check the area where the oceanside banquet would be held, we found where the Lambertines had migrated. They were all in position on the beach, in the bar, or by the pool. I even saw that one guy had set up his projector and was doing his PowerPoint presentation for the wait staff at the poolside bar.

We spent the rest of the day in conference with the hotel staff about various requirements for the meeting, either together or separately. Many times we had to walk other people through their meetings: Wendell with the meal and banquet requirements, Gordon Montbatten with the in-house AV department. He was totally superfluous; we should have just handled the breakouts ourselves.

Someone must have pushed real hard to include him on this job.

#

As the afternoon began to wane, it was a time for me to

address what I referred to as my Special Needs. I had to find some of the Fair Folk in Hawaii.

I was walking the route from the beachfront area to the hotel's loading dock with Lenny and Peasblossom.

Hotels always maintain a glitzy front for the guests. However, somewhere off to the side, or in the back, they've got their practical facilities, not meant for public viewing. It's like a Hollywood diva hiding her growing backside. Of course the loading dock was one of those places. We were on a remote side of the hotel that held a lot of shrubbery to disguise the workings of the establishment.

In addition to the loading dock, the landscaping shed was back here. Peasblossom stared at some rocks that were piled up.

"What are those rocks?" she asked.

"They're just used for curbing and edging," Lenny said.

"But there's something special about them," she replied.

Lenny brought a piercing gaze up to her. "As a matter of fact, they are kind of special. They're lava rocks and are called Pele's Children. Pele's the goddess of volcanoes. They say if you take one of those rocks away from the island, it angers Pele and you get bad luck. You don't want to get Pele angry. She's famous for her temper."

Peasblossom stared down at the ground. Something was going through her head.

I figured it was time to start pumping Lenny for info.

"Hey, Lenny, while we're on the subject--I know this is going to sound funny, coming from me--but I wondered if you could help with a little project I'm working on."

"You bet," he replied.

"Ouch!"

We both glanced at Peasblossom, who had lagged behind us in her ruminations. She was now rubbing her ankle.

"Something wrong?" I asked.

"I guess I got bitten by a bug," she replied. The wind off the ocean picked up, and the shrub beside her rustled. She shot a piercing stare down at it.

We resumed walking. "Anyway, Lenny, like I was saying, this project has me doing some things I've never done before, an area unique to me. You know how I used to react about anything to do with magic?" I followed that up with a self-conscious chuckle.

"Yeah, Harry. No one could even say the word *magic* around you." Lenny gave me that look that said he recognized I was holding some things back, but he'd wait until I was ready to tell him.

"Ow!" Peasblossom exclaimed, holding a hand to the back of her neck. A pebble bounced down on the sidewalk next to her.

"Another bug?"

"I guess so," she replied, although her lips were pressed together as though she was extremely peeved. She darted her eyes over the vine climbing the tree next to her. The breeze rippled the leaves, making the shadows dance behind it.

It's funny, but as the leaves rustled, the sound seemed to condense into the words, "We bonk bigtime elf one."

I peered down a bit more closely into the foliage, but I couldn't make anything out past the flickering shadows. I dismissed what I'd heard as my imagination.

"Anyway, Lenny, there's this project we've got coming up for another presentation we're doing over on Kauai where we're going to be using the mythology of the islands as the theme for the meeting. I was wondering if you knew anyone who could give me some background on the different mythical characters that are part of the culture." I found I was talking to Lenny over the head of Peasblossom who had pushed her way between the two of us as we walked down the sidewalk. She kept checking around, this way and that, looking for something.

"You want to know all about the people of the hills?" Lenny inquired.

"Yeah."

We stopped on the pavement alongside the loading docks. Lenny looked steadily at me. "You need to talk to the kahuna."

"Isn't that like some big-time boss man?"

"Boss or chief, or chiefess, you could say."

"Yeah?"

"But the kahuna is mostly the shaman."

"Okay."

Lenny stared out toward the ocean for a minute. Then he turned back to me. "Will you be in your room at seven o'clock tonight?"

"Sure."

"The kahuna will come by to see you then." He turned to Peasblossom. "You should be there, too."

Why had he decided that? "Lenny, you truly are amazing. You almost re-define the job of Convention Manager."

Lenny looked up at me with a wry smile on his face. "You don't know the half of it, man."

Chapter 72

"So what kind of person is this kahuna supposed to be?" I asked Violet over the phone. It was about an hour before the appointment.

Yes, it was the second time I'd called Violet that day.

"Is it going to be someone with a bone lanced through his nose?" I continued. "Or will he be wearing a demon mask?"

"It's probably going to be a normal, modern person. Anyone with connections to Over Here is going to move forward with the times, not be locked in the past. That includes both the shaman and the Fair Folk. Look at Peasblossom. She knows more about computers than you do."

"She's different," I said.

"Yes, she is. She's had so much exposure to Over There that she's probably about five percent human. She's like the reverse of me."

"She's becoming more human?" I asked.

"Yes."

"You think she could go all the way and develop into a football fan?"

"No, I still hold out hope for her. However, her exposure is why she's a Drawback."

"How does being five percent elf alter you?"

"I have heightened senses. I can see things that most normal people can't detect. Things like your good side."

"I'm the way I am because my experiences have exposed me to the Dark Side. I work with corporate America."

"And you live in New York," she said.

"You've got a point there."

"Anyway, you've got to be prepared to work with this kahuna. The Over Here creatures you meet can be pretty weird."

"If you think I can't relate with strange beasties, may I re-open the subjects of corporate America and New York City?"

#

When I'm at a hotel on a job, I have lots of meetings in my room, so I always get a suite so visitors aren't forced to sit on the beds. Peasblossom showed up at my suite at about ten of seven to meet the kahuna.

"First thing I want to know, what was happening to you when we were heading to the loading dock?" I asked her.

"There was something, or there were some-*things*, that were attacking me."

"I couldn't see anything."

"They were small and hard to see, but they were little sprites who kept throwing things at me or pinching me."

"Where were they?" I asked.

"They were in the bushes and vines. You can't pick them out because they are black and hide in the shadows."

"You seemed a little riled by them."

"Yes, I was quite urinated." She pouted.

Pause for translation. "Oh! Pissed!"

"Yes that too."

"I heard something that sounded like the leaves talking."

"That was them."

"Are we going to continue getting assaulted by these little things?" I asked.

"Yup. Yup." Came from behind me.

Chapter 73

Corgus sat in the chair by the window in my hotel room.

"Oh good! You can not only pop up unexpected in my office, you can show up other places to annoy me," I said to him.

"I travel many paths," he replied.

"I don't suppose you feel like traveling the path out of here?"

"I've come to give you good news."

"What good news? This is your last visit?"

"Nay."

"Shoot!"

"What is the good news?" Peasblossom tried to give the conversation some direction.

"The small may prod, but the large be spent." He pronounced.

"Oh, man, am I ever glad you told me that!" I heaved a dramatic sigh of relief. "You know I was really bothering me what the small and the large might be up to--aside from being sweater sizes."

"I think I understand what he means," Peasblossom said as she cast an inquisitive glance at Corgus.

We were interrupted as someone knocked on my door. I turned around and dashed to open it. Lenny Kanaka stood there.

"Hi, Lenny." I peered behind him to see if there was anyone else. The hall was empty. "You're alone."

"Yeah."

"Is the kahuna going to be here soon? Did you come along to handle the introductions?"

"No, man."

"When can I expect him or her here?"

"Right now. I'm the kahuna."

I stared at him. "Lenny, why'd you wait until now? Why didn't you just talk with us this afternoon?"

"I was working. I couldn't take time to sit down and chat. Now, I'm off duty. We have the time to discuss things."

"I'm glad you're here right now. There's somebody here you should talk to." I pulled him into the room, turned around to handle introductions, and discovered Peasblossom was the only one there. I wheeled on her. "Where'd he go?"

"I don't know," she replied.

"He was just here. Where'd he go?" I paced around the room, hoping I'd find Corgus behind the curtains or something.

"I think he left," Peasblossom supplied.

"Of course he did," I said in exasperation. "He always does that."

Lenny cleared his throat. I turned back to him. "Lenny, I'm sorry. I've got this little problem."

"The little man who isn't there?" he asked.

I stared steadily at him and nodded.

"As kahuna, I understand that," he said. "So let's get on with the reason you need to talk to me."

"I understand there might be some Trouble when I come

here next month for the meeting."

"Trouble?" he asked. "Who told you that?"

"The little man who isn't here."

Lenny eased himself into a chair. "I see. Does he have a name?"

"Corgus."

Lenny's gaze intensified. "I've heard of him. He's some big dude in the other world."

"He may be great there, but he doesn't put on a great show when he's here. By the way, right here," I said, pointing down, "is called Over There."

"Yeah, I've heard about that," Lenny said. "Why don't we put that aside for a moment because," Lenny turned his gaze around to Peasblossom, "I want to get to you. I recognized that you've got some special *mojo*."

"I'm here to help," Peasblossom said.

"Help?" Lenny asked.

"Yeah, help direct our magic," I explained.

"Your magic?" he asked, surprise flickering across his face.

"Yes. The four of us, Laura, Sidney, Joel, and me, have some sort of magical synergy."

Lenny whistled lightly. "You're right. Things sure have changed since I last saw you. You know any more about this Trouble?"

"There's some corporate type named Winfield who's trying to do a hostile takeover of this world, or Over There. Then there's some mage named Zorch who wants to become the big cheese in Over Here. They're working together to take over both worlds."

"And how are you involved in it?" Lenny asked.

"With this magic synergy thing we've got, we're the only ones who can connect with both worlds."

"You're in the middle?"

"Yeah, and the reason I wanted to connect with you was to find out what sort of local--uh--special people I might find here."

"Man, I don't know what I can tell you. You're already in contact with a whole bunch of folks I've never seen. As a matter of fact, I've not really *seen* too many of the folk at all. They're vague, almost-there things, but nothing concrete." He turned to Peasblossom. "Was there something happening when we were walking to the loading dock?"

"There were some little people attacking me. They were shooting and throwing things at me," she replied.

"What'd they look like?" Lenny continued.

"They looked like nothing, literally. They looked like the absence of something."

Lenny nodded his head. "Eepa. They're pixies. They harass people in the forest, among other things."

"Are they bad?" I asked.

"Not too. They're mostly just nasty, and when they're not being nasty to people, they're nasty with each other. They argue a lot."

"Tell me more. Who are the Fair Folk around here who might be able to help me; who might not."

"Okay. The biggest god around this place is Pele. She's sleeping, and you want to keep it that way. When she wakes up, she likes to erupt Kilauea or one of the other volcanoes. If you keep her awake, she gets angry and you don't want to make her angry."

"Swell." I turned to Peasblossom. "Good safety note: steer away from Pele," I said.

"That's a good general practice for getting along on this island," Lenny affirmed.

"Is there anyone else who could help me?"

"The Menehuneh might."

"Who are they?"

"The good gnomes; they build things."

"Sounds like they'd come in handy," I said.

"If you like the native style of construction."

"They do things differently?"

"Yeah, very natural," he replied.

"Are there any other special folk?"

"Too numerous to mention. We have an oral history. Nothing's written down, so stories deviate from teller to teller."

"That's swell. I guess I have to sit back and see what comes at me."

"Hey, isn't that what we do in our business, anyway?" he asked.

I nodded. "True. Listen, Lenny, it's good to know you'll be here to help."

"Whatever I can do for you, my friend." He started to leave.

"What exactly is a kahuna, and how did you get to be one?" I asked.

"I've memorized the definition of the word. It means, 'Priest, sorcerer, magician, wizard, minister, expert in any profession.'"

I furrowed my brow. "That's pretty much the definition of Convention Manager."

Lenny smiled up at me as he took his leave. "Now you're getting it."

Chapter 74

I was down in the bar with Peasblossom later. In Hawaii, she fit right into the drinking scene. Practically everything came with a paper umbrella.

"Is there any way you can translate what the hell Corgus meant by that comment about the large and small?"

"What he was saying is that we might get harassed by those little Eepa things, but apparently we won't have to cope with Zorch for a while."

"Why not?"

"He lost a lot of Preying Mansects when he tried to down the plane. He won't be able to try anything against us on the flight back. He's out of resources."

"So I won't have to turn the plane into a killer bird again?"

"That's right."

"Who's restricting him?"

"Those Who Count."

"Who's that?"

"They're the ones who keep track of the resources Over Here. They make sure that no one uses up too much."

"Are they the beancounters from Over Here?"

"Yes."

"Is everyone scared of them, just like here?"

"Yes."

I ruminated about something. Finally I said, "Tell me. How was Zorch able to make everyone on the plane completely forget about his attack?"

"It's a funny thing you do here in Over There. Whenever you're faced with magic, your mind rejects the thought that you've actually seen something supernatural happen."

"We won't accept something extraordinary?"

"That's right. The human mind will find every excuse to justify that events they've seen are absolutely normal."

I ruminated some more.

#

I was dressing the following morning, getting ready to go to the airport for the trek home. I had the contents of my pockets laid out in front of me on the dresser. It was a collection of the usual things: keys, change, wallet, comb, and handkerchief.

One other thing sat there that was not the usual; it was Echinacea's fruit/nut/seed. For some reason I thought it best that I carry it around with me. I didn't know why, but I felt she would have been angry if I didn't keep it on my person.

I didn't want to make a plant angry. Certainly not one that was able to swallow up bad guys.

Chapter 75

"Through the ages," Violet said to me over dinner, "alchemists have strived unsuccessfully to turn lead into gold. You take a flight out to Hawaii, and turn an airplane into a chicken." It was the evening after I got back from Hawaii.

"It was a fierce raptor," I protested.

"That likes to peck in the dirt?" she countered.

"Okay, so it was an *omnivorous* raptor."

"Ah yes, that's a rare breed, a terrifying bird of prey that's a vegan." She paused and reflected. "So you're going off to fight the forces of evil in Hawaii? How do you intend to manage that?"

"I guess it's going to be this Magical Synergy thing the four of us have."

"Do the other three know what they're getting into?" she probed.

"Well, kind of."

She paused and looked up at me. "What do you mean 'kind of?' You've explained what's in store for them, haven't you?"

I looked down at the table. "I intend to."

"You haven't told them?" She leaned in toward me.

"Not in so many words," I said.

"Why not? What are you waiting for?"

"I was waiting for them to bring up the subject," I said.

"You were waiting for them?" She raised an eyebrown at me.

"Yeah, but they haven't mentioned it."

"Why should that be?" she said, leaning back. "Let me see. You used to go into roaring, screaming fits every time the word *magic* was mentioned, so they haven't brought up the topic. How secretive of them!"

"Okay," I mumbled, "maybe I should have brought it up."

"Maybe you *will* bring it up. Tomorrow," she commanded.

"All right."

"What were you thinking?" she asked.

"I was trying not to involve them."

"You were going to do battle with the combined forces of evil all by yourself?" she asked.

"I'm fighting those forces against my better judgment. The other three don't really need to get involved. I *have* to. I've got my reasons. I'm under the IRS's thumb."

She leaned back in her chair and regarded me, skeptically. "You're making excuses. There's something else lurking in there. Despite your usually trivial behavior, I think I see something oozing out into the open, forcing its way in past your brazen exterior. You have a deep, dark secret." Her eyes widened as she stared at me. "There's something almost noble inside you!" She slapped her hand down on the table top.

"Don't you dare accuse me of that," I responded. "I'd lose all my professional reputation. When you're in business, you're only supposed to appear to be like Captain America. Deep down inside, you're in it for the money."

"No, there's something else there. I can feel it." Her eyes widened as a grin of realization spread across her face. "You're grandstanding in front of me. That's what it is! You're showing off for the girls!" She clutched her hands together and smiled at me. "How sweet!"

I frowned down at the table in front of me. The disturbing thought was she may have been right.

"I'm really quite flattered," she continued. "You've swept me off my feet." I got dizzy as she focused her world-class smile on me. She held that expression and gazed at me, expectantly. She continued to gaze. She cleared her throat. As the moments passed, her smile began to freeze on her face. One of her hands slipped down, and she began to tap a finger on the table. "I said you swept me off my feet," she repeated, forcefully.

I think I was supposed to be doing something.

Finally, she rolled her eyes to the ceiling, swung around and addressed the waiter, "Could you please bring us the check?" She swung her head back and stared hard at me with an underline beneath her words. "The gentleman wants to take me home now."

Oh! That's what it was!

#

"You live over the store?" I asked.

"Of course, it's been that way ever since Mom opened the business."

We walked up--there was no elevator in this building--to her apartment.

"This is an awfully old building," I said. "Doesn't it have a bug problem?"

"Oh, no, Daddy took care of that."

"How?"

"He taught the rats to keep them out."

"Rats? They're vermin! They bite and things."

"Oh, no, he taught them to behave."

"But they're filthy. They live in the sewers."

"No. Daddy taught them to bathe, too."

#

When we got up to her apartment, I thought things were going rather well. We were passionately wrapped around each other. Things were progressing quite well, I thought. I was beginning to tingle all over.

Except for one little technical difficulty I was encountering. I was starting to get a little fumble-fingered. I tugged at a piece of her clothing I was unable to remove.

Had Daddy fixed that, too?

"You know," Violet said, "the way you're struggling with those hooks is both good news and bad news. The good news: you haven't bedded every wench on the island of Manhattan. The bad news: I'm as eager as you, and I'm getting impatient."

I replied, "Mmrffll." I was having a hard time talking. My mouth was wrapped around some part of her body.

"Tell you what. Rather than just lying back and acting virginal while you fumble, let me help. Clothes have changed since ladies wore bustles."

Once she got me past the technical difficulties, things advanced from the tingling, and continued on to--I'm able to say it--magical.

Chapter 76

I was a little late arriving at the office. I had to go home to change my clothes. When I arrived, everybody else was gathered around the conference/kitchen table planning the meeting in Hawaii. I dashed over to the coffee pot to pour myself a cup and said, "Hi."

"Oh, thank God!" Laura exclaimed as she collapsed and stretched out along the table in front of her.

"What?" I asked.

"You got laid!" she said.

"Huh? Where do you get that?"

"Oh, it's entirely obvious from the way you act."

"The way I act? I just walked in here and said 'Hi.'"

"Yes, it was *so* obvious."

"It was?"

"I was at my wits' end trying to figure out what to do with you, the way you were barking and snapping around here. I kept trying to find one of my sluttier friends to give you a mercy-fuck and calm you down. I couldn't find a volunteer."

"I have been nothing but even-keeled and an island of calm in the midst of the storm of our business."

"No, that's not true," Joel chimed in. "You've been your

usual self: immature, hyper, and hysterical. The neurotic person we've all grown to love."

"I don't know who's been spreading these false rumors," I said.

"Your behavior," Sidney chimed in.

"If we can stop this petty bickering," I said, "I'd like to discuss a particular subject with you." It was time for me to live up to my promise to Violet.

"The show in Hawaii? We've pretty much settled everything on that," Sidney said.

"No. What I want to talk about is--magic," I said.

Laura, Sidney, and Joel all exchanged glances and shifted uneasily in their seats. They were too familiar with my previous, Mirabel-induced reaction to the M-word. Peasblossom beamed encouragement at me.

"As you know there have been a couple of strange things that happened around here," I said.

"Are you talking about your getting laid last night?" Laura asked.

"No," I said patiently, "things around this office."

"That's true!" Joel affirmed. "There've been times when you've actually been pleasant."

"Some things that have happened since Peasblossom came here," I forged on. Why wasn't I coming out directly with the subject?

"Yeah, the network's been humming along," Sidney offered.

"Okay, okay." I pointed a finger at Sidney, jumping onto his topic. "The network has been working so well, we got that email ahead of time from Wendell."

"Naw," Sidney said. "Wendell probably screwed up and had the time and date wrong on his computer."

"What if I said that was Peasblossom's doing?"

"Oh, you poor dear," Laura said to the Traffic Manager, "he's fixated on you." She swung her gaze around to me. "Harry, I told you that sort of thing has to be kept out of the workplace." She turned back to Peasblossom. "What did he do to you last night?"

"I wasn't with her last night!" I burst out. "I just so happen to have my own lady friend."

"Harry, you turned off all of my sluttier friends. I can't imagine you finding someone on your own," Laura said.

"Actually, I made the first date for him," Peasblossom said.

"Oh, you are such a darling," Joel said to her. "The three of us should take you out somewhere really nice for dinner. You've made our lives much happier."

"Is that what a Traffic Manager does? Get you laid?" Sidney asked, as plots began to boil around in his mind.

I raised imploring hands to the sky. "Why, why, why does the conversation always drift away? Can we please get back to the topic? I was talking about magic."

"Yes, Harry, I can see what you mean." Laura turned to Peasblossom. "You *have* worked magic with him."

"What I'm trying to tell you is that she really *has*," I said to the three of them.

"Has what?" Sidney asked.

"Worked magic," I explained.

"Harry, please," Laura said, "it's great you've found somebody who's attracted to you, and I'm pleased it's made you lose your hatred of anything having to do with Mirabel, but don't you think you're overcompensating now?"

I squared up on Laura. "What happened with your award?"

"She fixed it," she replied.

I turned to Joel. "How did Grumpy manage to turn into a color printer?"

"She modified it," Joel said.

Sidney's turn. "Where's the other hallway Peasblossom showed the guy to deliver the sofa?" I asked him.

Sidney didn't reply. He sat there, staring into space, tapping his pen on the table top. He was a little too logical to warp the laws of physics around what he saw and heard.

"Okay," I said, "what I'm trying to tell you is there's some magic here."

All three of them turned to regard Peasblossom.

"She's special," I said by way of explanation.

"Where are you from?" Laura asked, looking at Peasblossom.

"Over Here." Three sets of eyes swung over to me and six eyebrows raised and managed to say, "You see?"

"Let me handle this!" I took over the conversation. "She is from another world. They gave their world the name of Over Here. They call our world Over There."

"Let me see if I've got this straight," Joel said, with his eyes closed in concentration. "You're telling me she comes from that place," he pointed in the general direction of infinity, "and it's called Over Here. Those people there call this place," he pointed toward the floor, "Over There."

"That's right," I said, as Joel put his hands over his face. I continued, "If you imagine you're having a conversation with the most extreme corporate type, it begins to make sense then."

"I do my best to avoid talking to those creatures," Joel said, still holding his hands up.

"Which ones?" Sidney asked him.

"Either," Joel replied.

"Tell you what," Sidney interjected. "Why doesn't Peasblossom do a little magic right now, just to prove it to us?"

"It doesn't work that way," she replied. "You have to need the magic."

"Besides that," I said, "she can't do magic because she's

LAPH-ing."

Joel regarded Peasblossom's calm features. "Oh, of course she is."

"She's here for something different," I said.

"What?" Sidney asked.

"She's here to focus our magic."

"That was the other part he has to tell you," Peasblossom chimed in.

"Harry," Laura idly rolled her pen back and forth in front of her on the table, "did Percy open up early today?"

"I'm serious," I said.

"Would you like to give me an instance of how she's done that?" Laura asked.

"When we were going out to Hawaii, she helped me turn the airplane into a chicken."

The three of them sat there silently, staring at me. They wore smiles on their faces that they meant to be encouraging.

"Was I too terribly engrossed with the in-flight movie that I failed to notice that?" Joel asked.

"You know," Sidney reflected, "that's the first time I've ever *not* seen anything turn into something else."

"That's because the Evil Mage Zorch put a Forgetfulness Spell on you." That should explain it.

They stared at me some more. Finally Laura thumped her hand down on the table. "Boy! Does that ever explain why we don't remember it?"

"Is this Zilch character one of your little green men?" Sidney asked.

"Zorch," I corrected.

"By the way, why did this Zorch make us forget that you turned the plane into a chicken?" Joel asked.

"It was because he'd attacked the plane with Preying

Mansects," Peasblossom chimed in.

"Oh, well, I'm sure glad you explained that," Laura said. "That was a big sticking point with me."

"He made you forget that you saw magic," I said weakly.

"Otherwise, you'll suspect the existence of Over Here," Peasblossom said.

The three of them shared a glance together.

Then Laura clapped her hands together and said, "Okay shall we discuss what we learned in Hawaii? I think the three of us should handle the brunt of the work. Harry's obviously *very* stressed with his duties."

"But we have to talk about this magic thing," I said.

Laura turned to Sidney and ignored me. "Have we received the technical specs from the dancers and tiki drummers for the banquet?"

"You might need to know about our magical synergy when we get to Hawaii," I said.

They all paused and stared hard at me. It was one of those when-the-hell-are-you-going-to-leave stares.

I got up from my seat and muttered, "Well, I'm glad we cleared up all those issues."

Chapter 77

I decided it was time for me to see Augie the CIA guy again. My little chat in Hawaii with Mr. Thompson from the IRS had me worried about my balance sheet. Images were flashing in my mind of me dressed in an orange jump suit crudely lettered with the words *Bubba's Bitch*.

I dialed his number directly, happy that I didn't have to go through a calendar progression, gave him my bra size, and then, to navigate my way through Password Land, assured him that the early blossoms get destroyed by the late frost. "We've got to meet," I told him.

"We can go to the Starbucks on Union Square," he said.

"I thought we couldn't meet there. Winfield knows all about it."

"The location has been sanitized," he told me.

That probably meant the city's health inspector had been through. I felt happy in the knowledge that I could be killed there, but no cockroaches would stroll across my body.

We set the time for half an hour later. I got there first and settled down with a latte.

"Yes!" Augie had suddenly appeared beside me. Damn! How did all these people manage to sneak up on me? James Bond would have spotted this guy a block away and now have him in a deathly stranglehold. I was definitely failing in the secret agent business.

"Augie, do you know there are all sorts of people and creatures who've been trying to kill me? I never bargained for that."

"You're definitely accumulating points in the hazardous duty category."

"Can I redeem some of those points and exchange them for a retirement home? I mean these people are trying to *roll me up* and *smoke* me, *like a cigar*." I hoped he got the meaning of the subtext I was italicizing for him.

"Knew there'd be some danger involved, but you came highly recommended."

Who recommended me? "A lot of these people are trying to *box* me in." I kept italicizing at him.

"Agency's very pleased with your performance."

"I'm sure you're so pleased you're ready to *reward* me." If I kept stressing many more words, I'd lose my voice.

"Certainly," he said as he began to dig into his ironclad briefcase.

I beamed a smile in anticipation. It shrunk when I saw him pull out a small envelope, a number six-sized, not even a number ten. And it hardly bulged. I snatched the thing out of his hands and peered in. The pictures that greeted me were Ben Franklin's. I'd definitely lost a decimal place.

I raised my eyes to Augie to protest, and he said, "Cutbacks."

"But I've got Mr. Thompson hanging over me, and there's all that money that got eaten by the plant, and you need to give me that Collateral Damage Exemption, and I've got additional expenses like the new furniture in my office that got shot down by green fireballs, and people are taking my money right before they get eaten by plants, and there's all sorts of strange creatures waiting for me in Hawaii, and there's a lot of shit I've got to cover." I wound up my rant imploring the ceiling and the gods who lived there. "Augie, I've got to have...."

He'd gone. I'd turned my eyes away for a second, and he'd left. I looked around the Starbucks and out the window to see if I could locate him there.

"Hi there, fella." I turned around to find Winfield sitting across the table from me. So much for Augie's cleansing this Starbucks.

"Don't you go exploding my cup again. I need this latte," I said clutching the coffee to my bosom. "Besides my budgets are shrinking all over the place."

"I'm re-initiating a verbal approach to win-win status between the two of us, trying to formulate a work-together."

"Then why do you keep sending your damned goons after me?" I asked.

"Apparently you don't understand the workings of a hostile takeover."

"Yours is flavored with a lot of hostility."

"And you are very stubborn about the inevitable," he replied. He displayed a confident smirk on his face. "However, I find myself forced to relax my pressure on you a bit."

"Why's that?"

"I had a conversation with my Chief Financial Officer, and he had something bad to report. It seems that I've lost a certain number of assets while trying to deal with you."

They may have been goons, but it struck me as rather cold to refer to his people as assets.

"My CFO reported that there's been a rise in my Worker's Compensation rates. He's shut down on my ability to operate with impunity while you're here in New York. He wants me to wait until I get to Hawaii, where rates are lower and my power base is better established. Also sub-contractors will assume the

Worker's Comp responsibilities over there."

"He's telling you not to mess with me while I'm in New York?" I asked.

"Temporarily. Besides, you pose no direct threat to me here. There's also the chance you might come to your senses and not go to Hawaii." He stood up to leave. "However if you do, don't think I won't come down on you. I'll be at full strength out there."

Without another word he left.

Chapter 78

Winfield had been right. Suddenly nobody was firing guns at me or holding knives to my throat, and for his part, no plants were eating his people. The five of us were able to put our heads together and do all of the prep for the presentation in Hawaii. Everything was going smoothly--as smoothly as these things go, with corporate types changing their minds all the time.

The place was quiet. I was sitting in my office working on tactical plans on my computer. I'd made it all the way up from the Barrel Level to the Factory Level. My door burst open and all four of my employees entered. They stood in a rank in front of me. It was obvious that Peasblossom had been dragged along by the other three.

"This is another intervention," Laura announced. "We're all set for dinner at seven tonight."

"We are?" I asked.

"Yes it's at--what's it called?" she directed this at Peasblossom.

"*Lo Stregone Della Cucina*," she replied.

"And Violet, or Violetta whichever one it is, has already been informed," Joel said.

"I take it this is part of the Traffic Manager's duties?" I cut a hard gaze in Peasblossom's direction.

"I couldn't do anything else," she replied, flicking her eyes in the direction of the other three.

"Harry," Sidney said, "you've been dancing around the office like Gene Kelly for the past few days. The last time you did that was when you first met Mirabel, and you know what a disaster that was."

"So we thought it would be a wonderful thing if we were to meet this new lady of yours," Laura said.

"I tried to tell them not to worry," Peasblossom said.

"I must admit that Peasblossom's recommendation of Violet went a long way to quiet our fears," Laura said with a nod toward the Traffic Manager.

"But we need to meet her," Joel blurted out.

I looked at the circle of implacable faces in front of me. "I think it's a wonderful idea. All of us should get together."

If you can't fight 'em, join 'em.

Chapter 79

"I take it this is the condemned getting a last meal before her execution," Violet said as we headed for the restaurant.

"They really mean well," I explained.

"I'm almost touched by how they're watching out for your best interests, and I've got to admit they have good reason to be cautious. After all, your last choice was Mirabel, and I've heard all sorts of stories about her."

"They just want to meet you."

"And the Senate just wanted to meet Julius Caesar.

We were the last of the group to appear. The fact that the rest of my staff had arrived early showed they meant business.

Alfredo had already set them up with a bottle of wine and antipasti. Joel's eyes were slightly widened, a sure sign that he approved of the restaurant's fare. Peasblossom also had a drink in front of her. It was oozing a trail of paper umbrellas behind it.

Alfredo did his usual welcoming act for Violetta and brought us back to join "your dear friends."

The four of them stood up, Laura, Joel, and Sidney with cautious, diplomatic friendliness.

"You know, I'm really pleased to see how much you all care

about Harry," Violet said, and then took over the introductions. It was about three milliseconds before I was forgotten.

#

They melted like butter. I understood the feeling; it'd happened to me just a little while ago. In the space of about twenty minutes, she said--

To Sidney: "I think the Giants should draft that linebacker out of TCU. They've been weak at the position for half a dozen years. They should return to the tradition they established when they had LT at that position."

To Joel: "The American Ballet Theatre is the best company in the country, if not the world. Their latest production of *The Firebird* is breathtaking."

To Laura: "In the business world, you've got to adapt your approach to all the different personalities you encounter. I'm sure you treat clients differently from the way you work with Roadies."

In the meantime Alfredo was dealing out the meal. The main course was lobster *fra diavolo*. He also made sure that everyone's glass stayed filled. The conversation began to bubble about the table. Violet, with the help of Alfredo's wine service, had totally loosened everyone up. The party began to expand past our table to take in Vito and Vinnie and the rest of the patrons. The gathering was turning into a party that cascaded through the whole restaurant.

And the wine flowed. I heard various pieces of conversation.

Joel said to Violet, "Your eyes are so great. What you really need is to get some of Bobbi Brown's Peony and Python Palette eye shadow. The violet will perfectly offset your eye color."

Laura said to her, "I've got to get to your store to look at those books you have on Emotional Intelligence."

Sidney said to her. "You can't get any more head-banging sound than you get from Metallica."

The five of them clustered together. However, they also managed to include everyone else in the restaurant in their group. Vito and Vinnie had managed to buy a bottle of wine for two young ladies who had wandered in for dinner. Alfredo kept the service humming throughout the restaurant. Mama wandered out of the kitchen to hug everyone within range. We all strolled around the room, talking with everyone else.

"You'd better take good care of her, Harry. I know what a bastard you can be," Laura instructed me.

And so it went. Violet had become one of the group, or rather, she had totally absorbed the group into her sphere of influence. The five of them spent the better part of the evening with their arms wrapped around each other. They were all a little tipsy. Yes, somehow Peasblossom had managed to get a paper-umbrella buzz.

At one point Laura wandered up to me and said, "Violet just explained to me how Peasblossom managed to fix my award. I'm surprised you never explained the magic thing to me."

"My mistake," I said. "I should have laid it all out for you."

A little later Joel walked up to me and said, "I have to confess that I've been leaving a saucer of milk out every night right next to Grumpy. I wasn't all that surprised that the saucers were empty in the morning. After all, this is New York. But Violet explained to me what it was all about."

"Sure," I agreed, "it could've been anything drinking that milk."

"Is it true what she says, that I can do magic?"

"I think it's only under special circumstances. You need Peasblossom to channel it."

Finally Sidney walked up to me and said, "That's great shit, what Violet told me. I can do magic? Awesome, babe. Can I do shit like turn a bowl of Skittles into a bowl of pot?" He paused and stared into space, reflecting. "Wait a minute, if I've got a bowl of pot, I'll *need* a bowl of Skittles."

"Did she tell you the part about magic being a bit random?" I asked.

"That's out of sight. I *love* random. You should have told us earlier about this, dude."

They didn't believe me, but they believed her.

We wound up the evening with kisses all around, including the rest of the patrons in the restaurant who'd become our dearest friends. Vito and Vinnie used that opportunity to upgrade the intimacy of their relationship with the two girls.

Later that night, as Violet and I snuggled in bed, I asked her, "Did you like them?"

"I always have."

Chapter 80

We were putting the wraps on the preparation for Hawaii. Joel was the one who was most busy. He always had the last-minute emergencies, organizing the PowerPoint presentations. He had several freelance computer artists stashed around the office. I made sure that one was always working in the chair in my office where Corgus made his appearances. I hoped that would block the little guy from appearing there to bring even more confusion into my life.

Yes, Joel had managed to keep that damned chair in my office when he redesigned the room after the green fireball incident.

Sidney had arranged for the rental or construction and shipping of the hardware we'd need for the show. He'd also coordinated with the buzz-cut boys for the special stuff that was going into the Harbor Room at the hotel. It was all going to be air freighted to Honolulu and then shipped by barge down to Hilo on the big island.

It was the night before leaving for Hawaii, and I was at my place packing. Violet was there.

Uh--we were seeing each other a lot.

I stared at the empty suitcase in front of me, strolled over to the closet, pulled a jacket out, and meandered back, dangling the hanger over the suitcase. "I don't know, do you think this is right for Hawaii?"

A furrow creased her brow. "You told me you travel so much you can pack in five minutes."

"Yeah, but this trip seems different, somehow."

"What do you mean?" A small frown of suspicion crept across her face.

"Well, usually I know what to wear for each event, but I'm hung up about what to take this time. It almost feels like there's nothing for me to do," I said.

"How can you say that?" she asked.

"I'm sending the complete contingent: Laura, Sidney and Joel. Even Peasblossom's going along. Why do they need me?"

"What are you trying to tell me?" she asked.

"I feel like I'd be superfluous to the whole operation. Not only that, but who's going to be watching the office while we're out of town? I've got other clients who are going to be calling."

"Are trying to say you shouldn't go?" she demanded.

"I've got important things to do back here."

"You've got *really* important things to do in Hawaii! What about Winfield and Zorch? Who's going to handle them?"

"Peasblossom will be there."

"She can't possibly handle those people. You need to go to face them."

"What makes you think I can handle them? They're big time operators. How can I be effective against them?" I asked.

"Because you, Laura, Joel and Sidney have the Magical Synergy. Your wild magic can hold them off."

"You know, I don't hold much by this magic stuff," I protested.

She suddenly got very serious. "There's something else, isn't there?"

I was still holding the jacket over the suitcase. I threw it down on the bed. "Yes, there is, now that you mention it. This could be downright dangerous. Winfield and Zorch are both gunning for me. If I'm not there, they don't have a problem."

She stayed serious. "No, they can run free and do whatever they want to do. They can wltz right away with that power source."

"There's going to be big time security around that thing."

"But there's not going to be any Magical Synergy around there if you don't go," she retorted.

"A very *random* Magical Synergy that I don't trust all that much."

"A lot of other people have *en*-trusted it to be the primary line of defense," she said.

"I don't know if I'm ready to be the point person on that."

She got even more serious. "Is that the way it is?" She stared at me briefly. "Harry, there's many things about you that I find attractive. You've got a lively mind; you're fun to be with. But after that, you fall short. Once I get past that pleasant façade, I wonder if there's anything beyond--if there's any *you* back there. I can't have that, Harry. I can't have someone who's all show and no content--like a dog & pony show. I've got to have a real human being with me."

"I'm real," I protested.

"You may be real, Harry, but I don't know if you're genuine." She raised her gaze up to me. "I've got to have that."

She walked out of my bedroom, determination written on he face.

I chased after her. "I can be genuine. I can absolutely lead the league in genuine."

She turned back to me at my apartment door. "Harry, you've got to prove that to me."

"I will," I vowed.

"I hope so, Harry. I really do." She raised her eyes to me. "In the meantime, I don't know if I can stand being around a hollow shell, lacking the humanity that I need. If you chicken out on this trip, I don't think I ever want to see you." She turned and walked out the door.

The way she shut the door after her told me not to follow.

I paced around my apartment trying to figure out what it was I wanted to do.

What was wrong with Violet? Why didn't she see that I had some important organizational things to consider? Like how could my company operate if the head of it suddenly found himself dead? I was making a hard and fast business decision. It's not like I was scared or something.

Well, okay, maybe a little bit.

Well, okay, maybe a lot.

But what good could I do? I never wanted to have magic, and now I was supposed to use it in some way that I didn't even understand.

Yes, definitely I should stay here and not put myself at risk--or, for that matter, not put the rest at risk. After all, if I was there, Joel, Laura, and Sidney might get caught in some sort of magical crossfire.

I had to stay *here* to protect them!

My stroll around my apartment had turned into a march of determination. Granted, it was a definite march toward the rear of the battle lines, but there was certainly determination there.

However, after a few moments, the pace began to decrease. I was haunted by the vision of Violet's green-with-gold-flecks eyes. They seemed to be staring at me out of every corner of the place.

I began to consider the fact that I was charged by Corgus with the duty of stopping Trouble. He hadn't said Joel, or Laura, or Sidney. He'd said me.

And that's what Peasblossom had said. I led the magical synergy.

My wanderings had taken me back into the bedroom. I picked up the jacket I had been considering packing and put it back into the closet.

The question was: what could I do? I didn't see any sharp a definitive action I could take. After all, it wasn't like I really understood this magic stuff. I'd be flying totally blind if I went to Hawaii.

I didn't even notice that I'd wandered back from the closet with a couple of other jackets that I was dropping into the suitcase.

On the other hand, I reasoned, it wasn't like I had ever had a clearly marked path for me in the business world. I worked with Corporate America. Nothing was ever clear there.

Violet's eyes peeked at me from out of the suitcase. How could they have gotten there? After all, the only things I'd put in there were the two jackets and a few pairs of pants. Still her eyes were there, staring at me, telling me what I had to do.

I couldn't leave Joel, Laura, and Sidney to their fate. I couldn't trust that Winfield and Zorch wouldn't get into a little too much "high spirits" and hurt them.

I folded three shirts into the suitcase.

Violet was right. I had to go there. I didn't know how I was going to manage things, but I knew I had to do it. I just didn't picture myself as the hero type.

I looked down at the suitcase. I was most of the way through a five-minute pack.

I'd made up my mind. I was going off to Hawaii to be a hero. A fucking New York Lancelot!

Chapter 81

The flight to Hawaii was without incident. After the attack of the insectoids on the previous trip, I wasn't trusting anything, so I fidgeted through the whole long plane ride. Peasblossom tried to keep me calm, but I was having nothing to do with something as logical as that.

I was barreling across that line in the sand. I was heading to Hawaii where forces were mustering against me. I'd have to be alert for all of the people and creatures who'd be laying for me on the Big Island.

A whole flock of junior execs from Lambert was on this flight too. They had attached themselves to the project so they could travel a day early and leave a day late while taking care of a couple minor tasks--their usual work load when they were at the home office, only with palm trees this time.

Brad, the Boy Vice President with the influential uncle, was there, generating reports through his admin. My rough estimate had him killing off a forest a day. I wondered what the heck he had to do with this meeting. I hadn't seen him doing much of anything aside from his report-a-matic output. He was also the highest-ranking person in the advance group. I wondered if he might be the mole Augie told me about. After all, Wendell had seemed downright scared the day Charlie had walked in with my proposal and awarded me the show. He hadn't acted like he was the one pushing the buttons; he seemed to be taking orders form someone else, someone higher up in the company. I decided I'd keep an eye on Brad of the ever-flowing reports.

During the layover in Honolulu airport, Joel walked up to me and asked, "During the flight, were we attacked by a bunch of giant wasps that I forgot about?"

"No, Joel, I think if anything funny happens it'll be when we get to the big island."

"But they won't do anything dreadful will they? I mean like messing up the show?"

That was Joel. Dropping our plane into the middle of the ocean wasn't as bad as destroying anything he'd designed. However, he did get me wondering just what we were facing when Winfield and his friends showed up.

#

We arrived at the hotel safe and sound, and deposited our jet-lagged bodies into bed. We'd start organizing things tomorrow, while trying to adjust ourselves to the time difference.

Chapter 82

I woke up at the crack of dawn and fussed around my hotel suite as usual. I thought I'd call Violet to let her know I had gone, but only got her voice mail on both her home and cell. I tried the bookstore; somebody answered who was covering for her. That lady didn't know when she was getting to the store. I wondered what was happening. I'd never had a problem reaching Violet before.

The five of us met for breakfast and arranged things for the day. Sidney reported that all the gear had arrived in Honolulu and was loaded onto the barge. A tug had left at dawn to tow it down to Hilo.

"I just don't like this damned barge thing," he said. "I wish to hell those beancounters didn't insist that I do this."

"What could happen?" I asked.

"Hawaii's got those goddamned big waves the surfers love," Sidney said. "Can you imagine that barge getting caught in some of those?"

"This can't be that risky," I said. "Otherwise they wouldn't do it. We've got Charlie's top secret stuff on that barge. The buzz-cut boys wouldn't risk anything like that on a questionable logistic link. They're crack government people."

"Harry," Laura cut in, "are you saying we should trust the

government to operate like clockwork?"

"Yeah."

She shook her head. "Start with the Bay of Pigs, and work your way forward."

#

After breakfast we headed to the beach where they were setting up the opening night banquet. Lenny Kanaka was there, and we established the layout for that evening. Gordon Montbatten was also there, poking his nose into everything even though Lenny had things well handled. Tables and chairs were being set up, service areas for both food and drink were being constructed, Sidney's crew was setting up the audio and lighting.

Sidney's cell phone rang and he answered it. He spoke a few words and suddenly burst out with "Shit!"

"What's up?" I asked.

"The goddamned barge broke loose and it's been caught in the currents."

"How did it break loose?"

"The lines were cut."

"How did that happen?"

"Damned if I know."

Gordon Montbatten was oozing his way closer to peek in on the conversation.

"What are they doing about it?" I asked.

"The sea's too damned rough for them to retrieve it."

"What's happening to the barge?"

"It doesn't sound good."

"Why?"

"The currents are taking it toward someplace called Shipwreck Beach."

Chapter 83

Peasblossom looked at us and, in the most authoritative voice I'd ever heard her use, commanded, "Come with me!"

We tried to keep up as she dashed up the beach to a more remote part of the oceanfront where foliage offered concealment. Peasblossom surveyed us, as if measuring for some innate trait, made her decision and grabbed the back of Sidney's hand. He was initially surprised by the sudden contact, but then his eyes glazed over. He appeared to go into a trance, then opened his mouth, inhaled, and did something incredible.

Sidney started to sing.

I have heard Sidney sing before. He's tried to sing along with some of the heavy metal music he likes. It wasn't a pleasant experience. His voice has all the tonality of a rock.

What Sidney sang on that beach in Hawaii was entirely different. It was a lyric baritone that wound its way through the most beautiful melody I had ever heard. I couldn't recognize the words of the song. It was mostly vowels that flowed easily from one to the other. There were some consonants in there, but ones I'd never heard before.

We stood in awestruck silence, until Sidney finished the song. He then turned to Peasblossom and gave a solemn nod to indicate that he was finished. She withdrew her hold on his hand.

Joel reverently whispered, "That was absolutely gorgeous."

The mood was broken when Sidney's cell phone rang. That roused him from his trancelike state. His eyes focused, he looked up at us with his mouth screwed up in question, then he stared down at the ringing phone in his hand. He activated it, said, "Yeah?" and listened for a moment. His face registered surprise. He held his hand over the mouthpiece and glanced up at the rest of us. "The barge is being towed again. It's headed this way." Then he said into his phone. "Who the hell is towing it? You said you couldn't get it."

He listened for a moment. His face clouded over with doubt, then he said, "Okay," and disconnected the call. He stared out across the ocean in front of us with his brow furrowed. He finally looked up at us and said, "It's being towed from beneath the water."

Chapter 84

"It's the Nai'a," Lenny said.

"Who?" I asked.

"The Nai'a, the dolphins," he explained. He regarded Sidney. "You called them and they answered."

"That sounds awesome, man. I've always thought someone should talk to them dudes," Sidney said. He was himself again. "But how will they be able to know where to go?"

"Your song told them," Lenny replied.

Sidney raised his phone, as though he was going to call back to confirm what was happening, but then stopped and stared into thin air. Sidney's mind had been blown any number of times, under pharmaceutical influences. This was more than even he could comprehend. He needed some time to absorb that. We were all silent for a moment.

"Ouch!" Peasblossom blurted out. She was rubbing her calf.

There was cackling from the underbrush, and someone said, "Gotcha, elf lady." The Hawaiian pidgin was thick.

"Dammit!" Laura burst out. She was rubbing her shin.

"We smack all you *Haole* come here to our place," said another voice from the underbrush. Apparently *Haole* was used to describe a Mainlander. It didn't have nice overtones.

"What you do, little ones?" Lenny said to the little voices. He spoke with the same accent. In the meantime, he gave us the hands-spread gesture to indicate we should stand still.

"Hey, big ugly one, we teach you come here our place make trouble," was the reply.

"Yeah," came another voice, "old kahuna learn stay away."

"You fight with me, little ones?" Lenny said.

"Yeah we do, Big One, 'cause you too ugly. You nearly as ugly as Kuku here," said the first little voice.

"What you mean? Me ugly? You got face stop tsunami," said the second voice.

"I got fist make you face uglier."

"You think so?"

"You all sleep while you argue," Lenny cut in. "You fight each other, and you got big *Haole* sneak up on you behind bushes." Lenny gestured over in the direction we'd come.

"There you go, Lula. You fight so much, you miss spy come bother us."

"No, Kuku, you the one got big mouth."

"You still arguing," Lenny persisted. "What you do about big *Haole*?"

"We make him sorry he sneak up spy on us."

The undergrowth seethed with activity. The rustling in the ground cover made a beeline toward the bush Lenny had indicated. When it was at the far side of the plant a voice exclaimed. "Fuck!" It was Gordon Montbatten's voice. However, he had reverted to his origins and his Giggy Makowski vocabulary.

He tried to dash away but was promptly tripped up and toppled into the ground cover. The undergrowth surged around him, and he let out a series of shrieks as he was assaulted by the little creatures.

In that instant Lenny started running back the way we came,

gesturing for the rest of us to follow him. He dashed for the sand of the open beach, and once there, stopped. We glanced back at Gordon. He'd managed to escape relatively unharmed, although he was rubbing a few sore spots.

"What the hell was that?" I asked Lenny.

"The Eepa," he said. "Nasty little pixies. They hide in the bushes and wait to trip people up, preferably right at the top of a cliff. I haven't seen them around the hotel grounds before."

"When we came here on the first trip, they were here." Peasblossom said. "They were bothering me on the path around the back of the hotel by those landscaping rocks."

So the battle had started. They'd tried to shipwreck the barge and sent these little Eepa guys to harass us. I was certain there was more trouble to come.

However, we still had jobs to do. We decided to split up and take care of individual tasks. Sidney was going to track the equipment barge over his cell phone. Laura was heading into a conference with Eric and Emily about the video shooting schedule the next couple of days. Joel was going to organize the suites where we'd set people up for video and computer graphics editing.

Peasblossom and I were left with Lenny on the beach. "What's going on? There's got to be something happening, if those Eepa have come down here. Who could've sent them here?"

"Pana-ewa, the reptile man, is their leader. He's usually up to no good. Although he might be taking his orders from somebody else."

"Obviously someone further up the evil demon command chain," I said.

"Who might that be?" he asked.

"I've got a pretty good idea," I said. "It's some guy who likes to heave green fireballs at me."

Chapter 85

We gathered on the beach late in the afternoon, as the barge floated past the hotel. Our eyes confirmed what Sidney had been told over the cell phone. The tow lines angled down into the water, stretched tight, pulled forward by some unknown thing or things below the surface. Whatever was pulling it, the barge advanced directly toward the docks located further along the ocean front.

Sidney dashed off in the rental car to go to check the arrival. He had company. Several of the buzz-cut boys were racing in the same direction in plain, unmarked cars that managed to say "government" all over them.

With matters being handled by totally capable people, I lingered at the beach, trying to figure out what the hell I could do.

As I watched the barge head away to my left, another craft approached from the right. It was a yacht, a big one, a hundred feet in length. It dropped anchor in the water about five hundred yards out.

I could see the crew as they secured the ship. Usually a crew on a luxury vehicle like this one is composed of a number of suntanned people dressed in white who have a casual, relaxed, luxuriant air about them. The crew on this yacht was different. They were uniformly dressed in a red I found disturbingly familiar. Red cargo pants, red T-shirt, red shoes. Their heads were shaved, their musculature displayed a noticeable pharmacological assistance, and apparently membership on the crew had a two-tattoo minimum. The artwork for these tattoos was all chosen from the animal part of the biological spectrum, heavy on the fanged and the clawed.

The crew was also large in number. Modern vessels usually have enough technology to make them virtually hands-free. There was no outward reason why this one should be manned by what appeared to be a small army.

About a dozen of the shaved-head boys in red deployed the launch and boarded it. Someone else joined them. He wore an ice-cream suit with a panama hat, obviously the yacht's owner. The launch pulled away toward the shore. Appearing from the far side of the yacht was a second launch, inhabited by an equal number of the crew.

As the first launch approached the shore, I could make out who the yacht's owner was. He gave me a casual wave.

It was Winfield.

Chapter 86

With Sidney off securing the barge, I decided it might be a good time to check the Harbor Room. Charlie Lambert wanted me to pay special attention to it. I was convinced it was the focus of all the bad guys' efforts.

I brought Peasblossom along with me. Gordon Montbatten was not tagging along this time. He was undoubtedly in his hotel room applying some analgesic cream to the various nicks and bruises he'd received from the Eepa.

The place was humming with all the buzz-cut boys re-checking the security inside. They were all charged with leftover energy from the crisis with the barge. After all, the featured piece of equipment for this room had been floating adrift on the Beancounters' economy class transport.

Joel was in a corner working with a Marine Sergeant who was the assigned PowerPoint operator for this room.

The buzz-cut guy I'd talked to during the last trip came over to me. "Are you sure that--uh--gentleman," he said with a nod of his head in Joel's direction, "is all right to work in this room? We've got him on the list, but I'm a little worried about him." Joel's unisex outfit had a liberal flare that contrasted in the extreme to the conservative dress of everyone else in the room. "Has he taken a loyalty oath?"

"Government isn't a concern in his life," I explained. "He's more devoted to the color wheel. There's absolutely no reason for him to be disloyal."

I strolled over to Joel, who had gone to refresh his cup at the coffee urn in the room.

"Do you know this coffee has a security clearance?" he said to me. "Somehow making the beans take a loyalty oath makes them taste even filthier than most hotel coffees." His nerves were a little frayed. He was out of his element.

"How are you doing with Sarge?" I asked him.

"He's very sincere, but the only reason he's here is because he has the security clearance. I'm not allowed to touch the computer, so I've got to teach him the program to get anything done."

"Is it hard?"

"I'd prefer to teach a whale to tap-dance."

Chapter 87

I'd brought Peasblossom up to my suite that evening so we could lay out a strategy for the coming days.

"We've got to keep our eyes peeled for the bad guys. I'm sure they're going to attempt something with the thing Charlie Lambert's going to demo in the Harbor Room," I said.

"That's a dangerous thing," Peasblossom said. "They should stay away from Dark Energy."

I raised an eyebrow. How did Peasblossom know anything about the device's operation? "Whatever the stuff is, I'm sure Charlie knows what he's doing. We have to concentrate on Winfield and Zorch. We've already been harassed by those little Eepa things, we can expect more of the same," I said to her.

"Yup, yup," Corgus said from the chair over in the corner.

"And no sooner do I say we're going to be bothered by pests, then here you are. Let me skip the normal opening ceremonies of the Tolling of the Widgins and get right to the first topic: it comes in the form of a small reminder that you originally said you needed me to help with a 'little bit' of Trouble. That comes miles short of describing what I've found myself involved in this past month."

"Yup."

"I'm glad you agree, because I think we've got a lot of renegotiating to do on our bargain."

"Nope."

"What do you mean, nope?"

"Bargain's a bargain."

"I see. However, over here in Over There, we use this legal term in contracts, called the 'Excess Stress and Duress Clause.'" Made it up, of course. "It says that if your duties exceed those you signed up for, you can tell the other person to go whistle."

Corgus pursed his lips and pondered. "Good idea, but I don't feel like whistlin' right now, thank ye."

"I suppose suggesting you take a hike would only have you asking for better shoes. Let me lay out the crux of my complaint. I've got all of these bad folk trying to commit mayhem on me."

"Ye need to get rid of 'em."

"I know a great way. Get rid of my involvement with Trouble."

"Ye can't leave that."

"And what would you say if I told you I'm ready to leave, to walk out on this whole thing?"

"I'd say you be wrong."

"Why would you say that?"

"There be some'at make you change your mind," he said.

"Oh yeah? What might that be?"

He didn't reply. He just cast his eyes up to the ceiling, as though he was waiting for something.

There was a knock on the door to the room.

I kept my gaze on him while I retreated to the entrance to the suite.

I opened it, and Violet stood there. "I decided that since you came here, I'd come and see if I could help. So I flew out today."

"That's great. I've got a job for you already. I've got someone for you to talk to. Maybe you can make some sense out of him. That is if he's still here. Every time I turn my back on him, he disappears."

I led her into the room, craning my neck to see if Corgus was still there. I was surprised to find that he remained sitting in the chair.

Violet took one look at him and said, "Hi, Daddy."

Part 5

War at the Shore

Chapter 88

I stood stock still and stared at Violet.

"I do remember telling you I knew who he was," she said blandly.

"Do you think, by any small chance, that you were understating your relationship?" I asked.

"Has it ever occurred to you that one has to tiptoe around conversations with you're totally irrational about certain topics?"

I frowned at her while inwardly giving her points for successfully outdoing me at answering a question with a question. "I'm not irrational. I've never been irrational. The trait you're observing in me is the ability to make quick decisions."

Violet rolled her eyes to the ceiling. "You mean snap judgments?" She leveled her gaze at me. "We have to talk logically about this."

"Talk logically? Have you forgotten that Daddy, the king of illogic, is sitting right there?" I glanced at Corgus, who was totally unperturbed and stuffing his pipe with pencil shavings.

"Listen," Violet said, thrusting her fists to her hips, "I just flew all the way here to help you out, and all you're doing is arguing with me."

"I'm not arguing, I'm just a little surprised at finding out who your father is." I couldn't help but notice Peasblossom's reaction to our conversation. She was beaming brightly at us. I pointed a stern finger at her. "You have no right to be happy about anything."

Violet folded her arms and rolled her eyes to the ceiling. "Okay, I know this is much too stressful a time for me to drop the Father Bomb on you, but there's more to this than meets the eye."

"Or the nose," I said as I flailed my arms around me to clear the pipe smoke away. I turned to Corgus. "What brand of insecticide is that you're smoking?"

"It be a rare blend," he said.

"Not rare enough," I responded.

"Harry, we've got to stick to the topic," Violet said. She turned to her father. "Why did you come here?"

"To talk," he said.

I was ready to hit the ceiling; Violet remained patient. "To talk about what?"

"Travel to other places," he advised and disappeared.

"Well, boy, am I sure glad your Pop decided to come by and give us those detailed instructions. On the other hand, I think I'll take him at his word, pack my bags, and get the hell out of here."

"You know that isn't what he meant," Violet said.

"I never know what the hell he means. I'm just going to take advantage of what he said and decide it means I should head for home."

"You really want to go?" she asked.

"Yes."

"Even though people are depending on you?"

"What's there to depend on? Let's face it, I don't have a great record as a knight errant. I was right in the first place. I never should have come here. The best thing is for me to get the hell out of here and let more competent people handle the harassment."

Violet stared at me. "You want to leave?"

"Yes."

"Right now?"

"Yes."

She leaned back, and folded her arms over her chest. "Go right ahead. Go back. You're going to be very lonely back there in New York." She turned the stare up several notches. "All by yourself."

"What?"

"There are some very important things that are going to happen here, things that need to be handled by someone who is ready to shoulder the responsibility and take charge," she said. "You can go right ahead and tuck your tail between your legs and head back home, but you'll do it by yourself."

I stared around the room, looking for some sort of answer.

Peasblossom spoke up, her eyes bright with inquisitiveness. "Do you really have a tail?"

Her question broke my concentration. "That's the most ridiculous thing I've ever heard."

"Well, a lot of my friends do," she replied.

I shook my head to clear it, dismissed Peasblossom from my mind, turned to Violet and said, "I obviously can't catch a flight out tonight." I was equivocating.

"Do whatever you like," she said to me. She turned to Peasblossom. "Do you have a spare bed in your room where I could bunk out?"

I trailed along behind Violet. "You know, I've got a lot of space here."

The only response I got was an arched eyebrow.

"You know, your father told us that someone should make a trip. I was just trying to do what he told us." That was really lame, but Violet was grabbing her suitcase to leave.

"He didn't mean for you to turn and run. He obviously had something else in mind," she countered.

I interposed myself between her and the door. "Okay, okay, okay. I didn't mean it. After all, what was I thinking? I couldn't just walk out on a show and leave everybody else hanging, could I?"

"Are you sure?" she asked.

"Certainly. After all, it's my business."

"You're going to stick it out?" Violet asked.

"I promise."

"If you ever want to make your way onto my good side, just know that I only go to bed with heroes," she said levelly.

"That's a perfect description of me," I swore.

"Besides," Peasblossom chimed in, "Laura says that if he doesn't go to bed with you, nobody can carry him."

"Huh?" Violet asked.

"She means I'm unbearable," I translated.

I breathed a sigh of relief as she settled her suitcase back down. "You have only provisional status," she said. "I'm going to stay with Peasblossom. In the meantime, your behavior will be closely monitored."

"I'll be good," I promised.

"You'll have to be better than that."

Chapter 89

At breakfast, everyone fussed over Violet and hugged her, acting like they hadn't just seen her a few nights ago.

Laura, ever the matchmaker, eyed the fact that Violet had put Peasblossom in a seat between the two of us. I could practically hear the gears in her head meshing as she tried to figure out how to manipulate the two of us back together.

Sidney reported that the barge had been successfully docked and unloaded. Everything was stashed in a truck that was parked in the hotel's lot overnight, with several of the buzz-cut boys handling guard duty around it. The local crew was reporting at eight and they were going to unload the truck and start setting up the equipment.

There were multiple sites that needed to be put up: the oceanfront for tonight's banquet and luau, the ballroom for tomorrow morning's general session, and Charlie Lambert's special presentation in the Harbor Room for tomorrow afternoon. Further general sessions would take place during the rest of the week, along with all the breakouts that Gordon Montbatten was overseeing.

Sidney had been apoplectic when Lambert's beancounters had made us travel later, losing a whole day of setup. We were all going to split up and handle different jobs all around the site. Sidney would supervise the off-loading and split his time between the ballroom and the luau setups. Joel was going to divide his time between the three sites, making sure that everything had the proper look he'd designed. Laura would check the order of events for the banquet that evening, coordinating the staging with the fire eaters, hula dancers, and tiki drummers who were performing.

"What do you want me to do?" I asked.

Laura gave a brief cough; Joel looked up at the ceiling; Sidney studied the floor plan he had out in front of him.

Violet took them all in. "Harry, why don't you make sure that nobody from the Lambert staff gets in the way of things?"

The other three hastily agreed with her that it would be a swell idea if I made sure that nobody was getting in their way. Absolutely nobody. Present company included.

Actually, that was my job, keep the client from being underfoot. The fact that I wound up being out of the way myself was not lost on me.

Chapter 90

Since my primary client responsibility was to Charlie Lambert, I headed for the Harbor Room to check the setup on his secret project in there. I also believed that the power source being demoed in there was what Winfield and friends were after. I brought Joel along, since I figured that the simpler setup in this room would make it the first one ready for his touches. Violet and Peasblossom also joined us.

When we exited the elevator in the hallway outside the Harbor Room, we found a couple of the buzz-cut boys surrounding Brad, the Bright Young Vice President, and his admin. Given the size of the agents, two of them could probably surround up to a dozen people.

"I'm sorry, sir, but you are not on the list of personnel authorized to be in this room," one of them said.

"But there's going to be a company function here," he protested. "I should make a report on it."

"I'm sorry, sir, but apparently you do not have a need to know," Buzzo replied.

Brad gave him a my-uncle-is-going-to-hear-about-this glare and said, "I'm making a report about this."

"That would be good, sir." I gave the buzz-cut points. He was the picture of manners while telling the jerk to fuck off.

Boy Brad left in a huff. I wondered why he was so adamant about trying to get into the room. My suspicions grew that he was the mole that Winfield had managed to sneak into Lambert. However I'd still have to keep my eye on Wendell.

I'd forgotten about the security requirements here. I was about to apologize to Violet and Peasblossom and tell them they didn't have the proper clearance to get in, and that I'd catch up with them later. The words died on my lips when the guy at the door waved the two of them through.

"How did you get on the list of authorized people?" I asked Violet.

"Daddy fixed things up for us," she replied.

I was stunned. Could Corgus actually *accomplish* things, I mean aside from counting widgins and wodgins?

I dropped that thought as I spied Charlie and Eleanor Lambert. Eleanor had forsaken the lab coat she usually wore as head of the Research Department, and was wearing shorts and a halter top more appropriate to the tropical locale.

After I'd introduced everyone around, Charlie said," Okay, Joel, I guess you're the one I should talk to. We've got what looks like two of the same thing," Charlie indicated two chassis similar to computer CPUs. "Truth is we've only got one working model of this gadget. We've got a second one, that looks exactly the same, but there's nothing inside. It's just a chassis for display. You put that one up someplace where everyone can see it. Eleanor and I will operate the real unit."

"How do I know which one to put up?" Joel asked.

"The empty chassis is much lighter than the one that's got the guts in it. You should have no trouble telling which is which."

"I'll put it up, no problem," Joel said to me, "unless I've got to use a Marine platoon as the crew."

Chapter 91

My next stop was the beach to check the setup of tonight's luau banquet. However, since I was in the hotel proper, I decided to poke my head into some of the other rooms.

The first place I checked was the ballroom, where the general session was taking place the next morning. The lighting designer was handling things in there, making sure the truss was hung in the ceiling and the lights were mounted, cabled, and focused.

Later in the morning, once the lighting was finished and the platforms were put in, Joel would have to make sure the room was properly decorated with his tropical forest design. He had already equipped himself for the task. His shoulder bag contained a full spectrum of different-sized paint brushes for him to leap in and touch things up. He also had about a dozen little metal paint cans in there, filled with all the colors he had picked for the design of the show. He burned up a lot of calories carrying around his shoulder bag. That thing weighed a ton.

When we left the ballroom, I had some diligence to due on the breakout rooms my old buddy Gordon was in charge of.

I was a little disturbed to find that nothing much had been done in those rooms. The hotel's people had installed all of the proper tables and chairs, but there were no screens, projectors, flip charts--nothing in there.

Correction, in the last little room, way down at the end of the hall, I saw the Lonely PowerPoint Guy standing there, clutching his laptop and his projector, looking very distressed at being left in the lurch. He wanted a screen to focus his projector on so he could practice his presentation.

I beat a hasty retreat before the guy made me sit down and listen to his stupid speech.

Chapter 92

We left the hotel and went to the beach for the banquet setup. Peasblossom held back, reluctant to continue with Violet and me.

"Uh--I've got to go do something," she said. It was one of the few times I'd ever seen her show a desire to go off on her own.

"Why?" I asked.

Peasblossom looked hesitant. Violet cast a piercing glance in her direction, then said to me, "It's an elf thing."

"What?"

"If I said 'it was a woman's thing,' would you understand?"

What was happening? An elf/woman's thing? Was she coming into heat? I sure as hell didn't want to hang around her in that state. I already had Echinacea's fruit in my pocket. If I followed Peasblossom, I might find myself the father of a bouncing baby forest. "Sure you go ahead. Catch up with us later."

She scurried off.

When I got to the beach, Laura was plotting the sequence of the entertainers' presentation with Wendell. Sidney was setting up for the event.

"A couple of lifts are installed below the staging. Some

people are going to rise up, imitating Pele coming up out of the depths," he said. "I've got follow spots to hit them, along with general lighting. We're getting everything set up: audio, lighting, fireworks, and the banners Joel made."

The banners Joel had designed depicted the Lambert company logo intertwined with the Planning for the Future meeting theme. They were going to trail in the ocean breeze, and serve as a backdrop for the whole presentation.

I looked over to see Lenny Kanaka trying to rein in Sheila, the lady from Human Resources with the nut-cup fixation. She was dashing around after a busboy who was trying to set up the tables, doing her best to explain the theory of the Influence of Food Presentation on the Productivity of an Employee.

I went to see if I could help get Sheila out of the way.

Lenny was handling it. "I think the best idea would be for you to discuss your wonderful ideas with our award-winning Chef Pakula," he said to her. He turned to one of his assistants. "Robert, would you please escort the young lady to see the chef?"

The guy nodded amiably and led her off in the direction of the hotel building.

"Obviously, you didn't need my help fielding that pest," I said to Lenny. "By the way, what did the chef win an award for?"

"Meat cleaver throwing."

Chapter 93

Preparations for the meeting seemed to be going along smoothly. No problems had popped up so far. Violet and I headed back to the hotel to check on the status of the Harbor Room. The quickest way was through the non-public area, by the landscaping department and the loading docks. We were walking along the sidewalk, in a remote area of the grounds. I suddenly reached out a hand and stopped Violet from proceeding. I noticed a couple of people malingering on the sidewalk a few hundred feet ahead of us. They were two of the guys from the crew of Winfield's yacht. I turned Violet around to head back to the public area by the beach. There were two other crewmembers who had put themselves on the sidewalk back that way, blocking that retreat. I looked to the hotel to one side, but there was no entrance into the building there.

The bushes to that side of the sidewalk suddenly said, "Ouch!"

The rustling leaves gave out a cackle and said, "Gotcha!"

Peasblossom burst out of the bushes onto the sidewalk, rubbing at her ankles. She looked a little worse for wear, sporting some dirt smudges over her body. Since she had set off on "an elf thing," I didn't want to know how she might have picked those up.

"Where were you?" I asked her. "No! Never mind. Maybe you can tell me about that later. We seem to be in a bit of a jam here." I indicated the crewmembers that were now heading down the sidewalk toward us.

The only direction open was away from the hotel. We raced across the lawn toward the truck entrance with the four toughs in pursuit.

We emerged onto the street in Hilo. We were a block away from the beach. The street had a collection of stores and restaurants serving the occupants of the resorts on the beach. A glance to the right and left indicated more of the crewmembers heading toward us from those sides. The only way open was up ahead.

We crossed the street and continued heading inland, away from the ocean. We were traveling uphill along a narrow, residential street. Glancing back, I saw Winfield's crew members following steadily behind.

We continued along the street. The further we went, the more down-market the neighborhood became.

I'm not the most athletic guy in the world. The most stress I put on my cardiovascular system is hailing a cab. My breath was beginning to come in gasps as we raced uphill.

I hazarded a look behind us, and we had quite a collection of the muscled, tattooed guys giving pursuit. The collective expression on their faces was not friendly. Now that we were getting into the more remote, less populated part of town, I glimpsed them pulling hand weapons out of concealment.

The street we were racing up took a dip downward, bringing some relief to my legs that had been growing numb. However, the depression in the land had gathered the air into a hot pocket that oppressed everything around, absorbing both heat and odor. There was no ocean view in this hollow, and the houses here were small, dilapidated, and in some cases, obviously unoccupied.

We were faced with another problem in this little depression. Grouped in front of us was another contingent from the yacht's crew. We were trapped.

Peasblossom grabbed Violet and me and steered us into the yard of the house we were in front of. It was unoccupied, and the yard was overgrown with plants that practically choked our way.

We clawed through the yard and plunged into an arroyo thick with vegetation that backed onto it. We were now in the forest. We tumbled down one side of the arroyo then scrambled up the other. We found something like a path running uphill, and we headed in that direction.

"Ouch!"

"Damn!"

"Fuck!"

That was, respectively, Peasblossom, Violet, and me as we were stung about the ankles. We were also tripped as we did our best to race along the path.

"Got you, big one. You learn not come into our forest." The little voices taunted us from the undergrowth.

We could barely see ahead as we struggled our way through the growth.

A small clearing opened up in front of us, and we raised our eyes to see the rest of the crew of the yacht standing in front of us, blocking our way. They surrounded a figure in an ice cream suit. It was Winfield.

"Hi there, folks."

Chapter 94

We had been herded to this location.

I could hear the rest of the yacht's crew coming up behind us. I'm sure they had their Uzis trained on us, mirroring what I saw in front of me.

"I'm very disappointed about all of this," Winfield said. "I hoped we could manage a close-knit partnership to effect a long-term profit base."

He was babbling, so I nodded agreement, hoping to buy time while trying to figure out some evasive action we might take.

"I now find myself wasting valuable resources on this objective here while sending secondary operatives off to do the primary job."

"What's the primary job?" I asked.

"An object at the hotel, of course. My secondary task force is executing an acquisition of that power supply. While I'm here doing this: a takeover of a company only to liquidate its assets. That's a regrettable loss of a possible income-generating operation. I usually prefer to have forward-facing profit potential."

I hate it when absolutely batshit crazy people start using

words like "liquidate." I was going to have to figure something out. I glanced around, trying to see if there was anything that I could do in the middle of this tropical forest.

That was when Peasblossom pushed me.

I'm sure she meant to just get me started racing down the arroyo. I'm sure she only meant for us to go racing down the hill to get the hell out of the way. What she forgot was that the damned Eepa were right under our feet and they'd be looking for a chance to trip us up.

So we all went tumbling ass over teakettle down into the gulley. I don't know if Violet had also been pushed or if she knew what Peasblossom was planning, but she was crashing down into the arroyo too.

Gunfire erupted all around us, but our paths were too erratic for anyone to draw a firm bead.

When we came to a halt at the bottom, Peasblossom immediately grabbed me and shoved me under a bush. I rolled over a couple of times, righted myself to turn around and yell at her, when I discovered I was Over Here.

Chapter 95

Violet and Peasblossom were righting themselves next to me.

"How the hell did we get here?" I demanded.

"Echinacea," Peasblossom said.

"Huh?"

"She was there."

"How did she get there?"

"Wormhole."

"I should have figured."

"Didn't you see her?" Peasblossom asked.

"Strangely enough, there were other things dominating my attention, like bullets zipping around me." I looked back in the direction we'd come from. "What possessed those thugs to do something like that?"

"Bad guys have poor social skills," Violet said.

"They shouldn't do that," I said.

"Why not?"

"Because I really hate them firing at me," I turned to Violet, "and you."

"Why, how sweet of you to care," she said. "Don't tell me

you're actually starting to act human."

"Well, of course I care for you," I said.

"We'd better start moving," Peasblossom said. "They won't take long to figure out where we went and come after us."

This dragged me away from staring at Violet and focused my attention on our environment. We were in the other world, but it didn't look like Hawaii. If anything, it resembled the American Southwest, only with particularly weird plants, which included Echinacea. Peasblossom took us up the hill alongside us to perch behind a large boulder. Before she joined Violet and me, my elf Traffic Manager let out a ululation that sounded like a Bedouin on steroids. She immediately streaked over to tackle us, launching us backwards. It got us out of the way as the boulder we were hiding behind slid back in our direction.

It had been moved by some little dude who evidently lived underneath. He was an ugly little thing with a hooked nose, claw-like fingers and a warty skin. And he didn't look happy. He wasn't the only one. A bunch of these little monsters were popping up out of the ground, all fighting mad.

Violet whispered to me, "What Peasblossom just sang is something like saying, 'Yo' Mama's so ugly, she looks like a human.' These guys are pissed."

"Who sing 'at?" one of the little creatures asked.

"Man, I get 'at one and punch him up somet'in bad."

"Dey say bad t'ing 'bout my mother, I put her on 'em. Dey get bad bonk on the head den."

At that moment, one of the yacht crew rolled out from beneath Echinacea. All the little nasties began to scream and shout at him.

"Who are these little ugly things?" I asked.

"Mountain trolls," Violet said.

"Wait a minute," I turned to Peasblossom. "Didn't you say I

resembled these guys?"

Violet said, "You know there is a remarkable resemblance."

By this time, about half a dozen of the crewmembers had emerged from beneath Echinacea. They glanced at the little ugly dudes yelling at them, grinned, and raised their Uzis up. With cruel smirks decorating their faces, they squeezed the triggers--and a thick tan liquid came oozing out of the muzzles of the guns.

"What's happening?" I asked.

"The guns don't work the same in Over Here," Violet explained. "They don't fire out bullets. What you see pouring out of their muzzles is caramel."

"They don't pop out bullets? They just ooze syrup?" I asked.

"Yeah. I keep trying to get Daddy to get me one of those in chocolate, but I think he's trying to preserve my girlish figure."

The crew from the yacht had thrown their useless weapons aside and were mustering up their supply of steroids to face off with the creatures confronting them.

The mountain trolls quickly attacked as a coordinated group. They may have been small, but they were strong and had very nasty temperaments. Whooping out a chorus of ululations, they swooped down on the crewmembers, and almost before it began, the fight was over. The toughs were quickly overwhelmed and trussed up. The confident grins on their faces had given way to frightened bewilderment. The trolls gathered in a circle and quickly started chattering at each other, brokering some deals between each other. The crewmembers were grabbed by individual trolls and dragged off, screaming and shouting, back under their boulders. The last few trolls poked their heads underneath Echinacea, reached in, and emerged holding little black wiggling things. They stuffed what had to be several Eepa into their mouths, crunched down, and the wiggling stopped.

And just like that it was over. The last of the locals dispersed and vanished beneath their rocks. Everything settled back to the quiet we had encountered when we first came through.

I looked around at the other two. "Okay," I said, "important safety note: never get a mountain troll pissed off at you."

"Yeah, they're nasty when riled," Violet said.

"What are they like otherwise?" I asked.

Violet considered my question, then shook her head. "They're practically always riled."

I very cautiously stood up, looking around. "I think it might be a good idea if we got out of here. They don't seem to welcome tourists. But how do we make our exit?"

"Very carefully," Violet said.

We scrambled back down the hill, stepping over the pool of caramel on gthe ground.

Peasblossom stuck her head down toward Echinacea and said something that sounded like leaves rustling. She turned back to us. "She's got another shoot a couple hundred yards away from the one we used."

"That's good," I said. "We might be able to get away from Winfield that way."

"She said something else."

"What's that?"

Peasblossom looked at me. "She says she's happy to see you again, and she's pleased you're still carrying her fruit."

I felt the thing that I carried in my pocket. I thought it would either dry out or rot or something, but it just stayed the way it was.

Violet looked at me with a smile and said, "You romantic rascal!"

Chapter 96

When we got back to Over There from Over Here, it did look like we were about a block further down the arroyo. I hoped Winfield had concentrated his attention on the area we'd last been seen. We stood a good chance of getting clean out of here. There weren't any Eepa underfoot either.

As we headed downhill, I asked Peasblossom, "What happened to those thugs who were captured back there?"

"Those mountain trolls weren't happy," she said.

"I came away with that impression, too," I said. I watched that one munching away on what had to be a couple Eepa."

"I think they got taken home to Mama," Peasblossom said.

"Isn't that nice," Violet gushed. "Strangers in town, they bring them back to Mom for a nice home-cooked meal."

"Yes, that's right" Peasblossom said. "I wonder if they liked being cooked at home."

We made our way out of the forest into the back yard of one of the more up-market houses down the hill. We hurried our way past the barbecue and the swing set. I was happy to see this patch of domesticity didn't also feature a slavering guard dog.

When we rounded into the front yard, close to the street, someone was there.

"Yup, yup."

"What the hell are you doing here? Why weren't you up there where we were facing evil overlords and lots of guns?"

"Hi, Daddy," Violet said.

"I come to tell ya that some'at be happenin' back there."

"That's very specific, thank you very much," I said as we hustled onto the sidewalk continuing in our rapid retreat.

I took a glance uphill. A lone member of the yacht crew had been posted as a rear guard. When he saw us, he immediately raised his weapon, took aim, and fired.

As he squeezed the trigger, I went to leap in front of Violet to block her, but Corgus appeared in front of us, right in the line of fire. He absorbed the shots, fell to the ground and disappeared. I was pissed about being fired at. Involuntarily, my right arm shot up and pointed at him, and a blue beam lanced out at the tough. I noticed a golden beam emanating from Violet's upraised arm. Both beams nailed the guy like he'd been hit by a truck. He went flying back up the street, with his weapon arcing away about twice as far in the same direction.

I was sure that Winfield and his friends heard the shots, and would be coming down the hill after us. The three of us turned and pelted down the hill back toward the hotel.

As we raced along, Violet said, "Did you leap in front of me when that guy started firing?"

My brow furrowed as I realized what I'd done. "I guess so."

"Harry," she said, "that is so unlike you! You actually behaved like a hero!"

"Can I plead temporary insanity? I didn't know what came over me, but I just reacted instinctively when I saw him point the gun at you."

She cast a long glance at me. "Maybe there is hope for you."

I said, "Your father took one for us. Is he hurt?" What I didn't say was that was the first time I'd ever seen him actually *do* anything.

"The bullets are metal and The Folk have intolerance for metal, especially silver, but I'm pretty sure he'll be okay. He has special ways of overcoming problems like that."

"Can you translate what he said?"

"Something's happening back at the hotel."

"I guessed that." As we raced back toward the hotel, I considered what had just happened. "When he was shot, I retaliated instinctively. I didn't know what happened. Can I do stuff like that all the time?"

"No, only when you're in a high emotional state."

"I guess being shot at would raise the adrenalin. It did send him flying. Did I see you doing the same thing?"

"Yes, only mine was slightly different. It had a raised-knee flavor."

Chapter 97

When we got back on the hotel grounds, we met Joel, rushing up from the beach. "Harry, we wondered where you were. I came up to find you. They're getting ready to serve the appetizers at the banquet."

"That can't be?" I said. "We've been away for less than an hour." Then I noticed the sun had moved across the sky, dropping toward sunset. "What happened?"

"It was on wodgins time in Over Here," Peasblossom said.

"What does that mean?" I asked.

"Time moves faster Over There than it does in Over Here when it's on wodgins time. So what seemed like half an hour there, in Over Here, was several hours here, in Over There."

I started working it out. Okay here is Over There, and...

"They want you down at the beach," Joel interjected.

"I can't do that right now, Joel. I think there's something going on in the hotel that I've got to get to."

I dashed inside, waving Joel along with us. I dashed toward the Harbor Room. I knew Winfield was after Charlie's special machine. When the elevator opened in the basement, I was surprised to see the door to the room open and unattended.

I dashed inside and found all the buzz-cut boys lying

unconscious scattered around the room. Standing over them was the Evil Mage Zorch.

He painted a proper sneer on his face and said, "I've managed to put our friends to sleep. But don't think to retaliate, Chatham. I have covered myself with enough warding spells that I am entirely protected from any magic you might try to use."

"He's right," Peasblossom confirmed.

Zorch continued. "I'm sure Winfield will come trailing in here, having bungled your capture, to find I've managed to both secure you and the piece of--what do you call it?--technology in this room, filthy stuff that it is." He glanced over at Peasblossom. "Oh, but we've got a Drawback here. You can handle that kind of thing, can't you? There are two of them." He pointed at the two chassis. "Put both over here by the door, I don't want them confused with anything else."

Peasblossom carried the two chassis, both the real thing and the dummy, and stacked them on a table by the entrance.

"I've accomplished all of this and I even have a little time to play," Zorch said. Scrabbling and chittering came from the doorway and what had to be a whole bunch of Eepa came cascading in the room.

I saw them for the first time. They were about a foot tall and black, but not really. They were the color of a shadow, and were the ugliest things I've ever seen.

"Did you take care of things up in the big room?" Zorch asked them.

The Eepa let out a community cackle. "We tore it up big." "It taste good." "I go pee on it." "That taste good, too."

"That's wonderful," said Zorch. "Now you just have to take care of that mess over there." A black cloud scurried across the floor as the Eepa began to tear apart the displays that Joel had very carefully put together.

That was when Zorch got clocked.

Chapter 98

Zorch had protected himself from any magic Peasblossom or I could have launched at him. We carried no firearms, so we couldn't hurt him that way. The only thing that could have possibly hurt him was metal, and he'd made sure that Peasblossom was the one who handled Charlie's electronic equipment.

There was just one small possibility he'd failed to take into consideration.

That was Joel.

If there is anyone I know who is non-violent, it is Joel. His is the kindest, gentlest nature I've ever seen. There's no way you can make him angry.

Unless you mess with his art work.

When Zorch had loosed the Eepa on his display, he made Joel angry. The only thing Joel could strike back with was his shoulder bag.

The one filled with metal cans of paint.

The bag connected with Zorch's head and appeared to launch him all the way back to Over Here. He sprawled on the floor without a flicker of consciousness crossing his features.

Joel set off with his same bag, trying to flail at the Eepa. He had the element of surprise with Zorch having come up behind him, but the Eepa were aware of him and were experts at dodging blows aimed at them.

They were also very good at taunting and unleashed a barrage of insults Joel's way.

"Can't catch me, *Haole*."

"Big one no like when Eepa make things comfy."

"Me tear down faster than you put up."

"Oh, big one all fancy dressed."

One of the little creatures scrambled his way up the display wall, tearing as he went along. When he reached the top he turned his back and mooned Joel, squeezing maximum obscenity out of that age-old pose.

Joel had reached the boiling point. He stood in the middle of the room with his fists down at his sides, clenched in frustration. Peasblossom raced over to him, and placed her hand over his. He reached his other hand up and pointed at the Eepa mooning on top of the wall. A glowing beam in rainbow colors lanced out of his hand and shot toward the obscene little creature. There was a flash as the Eepa was struck by the bolt. He stood back up, a little dazed, and displayed a body that was polka dot, with lavender spots on a pink background.

The rest of the pixies began to laugh and shout and poke fun at the now-brightly-colored Eepa. In a fury, the spotted pixie leaped down off the wall into a group of jeerers and started battling with them.

Joel's eyebrows arched in triumph as he saw the pixies fighting each other. He began to swing his hand around, like spraying pistol shots, and lit up the individual Eepa in the room, painting them in varying patterns: stripes, plaids, checks, paisleys, swirls, tie-dyes, all in screamingly bright and clashing colors.

The Eepa settled into a free-for-all amongst themselves where they traded insults with some and battled with others. They'd completely forgotten their instructions to disrupt the humans.

The battling pixies skirmished in the middle of the Harbor Room floor, but as new, uncolored Eepa entered the room, the original group turned their aggressions toward them. The warring pixies migrated out the room and toward their normal habitat outdoors.

"Let's get the buzz-cut boys revived," I said.

Peasblossom dashed over to the closest agent and began chanting some sort of counter-spell to revive him. As soon as the first one had cleared the cobwebs out of his head, I told him, "Keep your gun trained on that guy," I indicated Zorch, "and don't let him move."

"Will the weapon work on him?" the agent asked.

"I'm pretty sure the lead bullet will do all right. You don't happen to have any silver ones, do you?"

"I think that's the Lone Ranger," Violet said.

"Whatever!" I waved my hand dismissively.

Peasblossom was getting the next guy revived, while Joel tried to patch together the torn pieces of his display. Zorch began to stir, and I pointed at him to the first guy, who leveled his gun at him.

"Don't move, Zorch," I said. "I think you know what those weapons can do in this world. And it isn't dispense sundae syrups."

Zorch started to respond, and Peasblossom cried out, "Don't let him talk either. He'll cast a spell."

Violet sped over and scooped up the shoulder bag Joel had left behind, and swinging it like a hammer throw, leveled another shot to Zorch's head. He slumped back down.

"I'm sure there's a roll of duct tape stashed behind Joel's display," I said to one of the other agents. "Use it to bind off his wrists and cover his mouth." He dashed to comply. I turned to the agent with the weapon. "Keep that thing trained on him, and don't be afraid to use it."

Zorch was disabled. The Eepa were having interracial battles outdoors. Joel was starting to effect repairs on the display.

I had ridden my horse into Dodge and defeated the bad guys. I had everything under control.

A laser beam shot out and hit the agent's gun, sending it cartwheeling off into a corner. I swung around to see what the weapon was.

A sighting dot swiveled around the room, menacing everyone who dared to move. The weapon targeting us appeared to be a video projector. It was being handled by the Lonely PowerPoint Guy. "Don't anybody move," he said. "I don't want to have to use this." He backed against a wall, keeping everyone in range. He continued to sweep the projector back and forth, making sure nobody made a move.

I had finally discovered the mole Winfield had placed in Lambert Industries. It was the Lonely PowerPoint Guy.

"What is that?" I asked, indicating the video projector. I moved to the center of the room, my back to the door, covering any escape route.

"It's a very special device," he said. "It's a fully functional video projector, but it also contains an assault laser that can be used as a weapon."

"Oh, yeah," one of the buzz-cut boys said. "I know about that."

"Does it really work for both functions?" I asked, keeping the Lonely PowerPoint Guy talking.

"Oh, yes, I've been showing presentations on it."

"No kidding?"

"That's right."

"You mean you could take that weapon and project a PowerPoint presentation with it? I'd like to see that."

His eyes raised up to me, hope flickering in the corners of

them. "You mean you'd like to see my presentation?"

"Sure."

"Really? It's got lots of good pie charts in it."

"I'll bet it has," I said.

"I mean they really show the market trends over the past twenty years."

"Boy, I'd like to see that."

I had him hooked. He set the projector down facing the screen in the room and began to pull the laptop out of the carrying case over his shoulder.

Violet tackled him.

She knocked him over; the buzz-cut boys secured him.

We had the situation back under control. There was a weapon trained on Zorch, Lonely PowerPoint Guy was subdued, and Joel was trying to fix the display with the glue gun he'd retrieved from his shoulder bag.

Everyone's eyes suddenly turned toward me. Then I realized they were looking past me to what was just inside the door. Violet said, "Harry, watch..."

The last word she said was, "...out!" but I didn't hear it.

I was falling down unconscious.

Chapter 99

Winfield and his crewmembers had entered the Harbor Room and get the drop on everyone with their automatic weapons. The agents in the room couldn't retaliate without taking massive casualties to both themselves and innocent bystanders in the room. Since those bystanders included Violet and me, I thought it was a great idea.

Being such a favorite of Winfield's, I got special treatment by being slugged unconscious. And doing the honors was my old buddy, Gordon Montbatten. I'd been pretty well convinced he was in on this in some way.

When I came to, I found myself being tightly trussed up by a thick hemp rope. Everyone else in the room was getting the same treatment. This included Lenny Kanaka, who arrived while I was unconscious. He'd been sent up from the beach when Joel failed to reappear.

Violet and Peasblossom were getting special treatment: they were being tied up with silver cable. Being surrounded by the metal made them totally incapable of performing magic. I could have attempted to raise some sort of magic on my part, but I was in the same fix as the agents. My magic was too random, and there were too many innocent bystanders. If I could get Peasblossom's support, I might have managed to properly channel the magic.

As I was regaining my mental bearings, Winfield loomed in front of me.

"It's really too bad we couldn't have formed a proper strategic alliance," he said to me. "I could have retained more assets that I lost on risk/reward ventures."

"I'm afraid some of your business associates play a little too rough for me," I said.

"I've put together a win-win outcome. We're just going to leave you here, no harm done. You'll stay restrained so you won't cause us any trouble." He turned to his crew. "Gag them. I don't want them heard shouting for help." He pointed at the devices Peasblossom had stacked by the door. "Take the heavier one of those. The other's just an empty chassis. Don't slow us down dragging that along."

They all moved toward the door, taking Charlie's device with them. Zorch lingered until the end. He turned back and smiled at me.

"I'm not finished with you, Chatham," he said. "I'll have a little surprise waiting for you in a little while. You destroyed a lot of my pets with your airplane. I think I'll make you pay for that."

Without another word he left.

I sat there, tied up and gagged, unable to do anything.

Chapter 100

Various sounds punctuated the room's silence. The agents grunted as they struggled to get loose form the hemp ropes that bound them. There were little groans of pain as the silver cord forced its magic-damping restraints on both Peasblossom's body and her spirit. Violet growled in anger as she tried to pull herself loose. Joel whimpered over the state of his display.

I tried the best I could to shed the ropes around me. I pulled to the left to try to loosen them. I pulled back to the right, with no success. I pulled to the left.

The rope pulled to the right.

I looked down to see what the hell could have happened. The rope was standard hemp, fibers of a plant that had been cut down a long time ago, dried, and braided together. It was nothing but dead vegetation.

Or was it? Was there one tiny spark of life left in those fibers?

I looked down. The rope was pulling me back to the right. One part of the rope at my side stretched out a thin tendril, extending from the tightly wound coils of the hemp. It elongated and probed down my body. It poked its way into my pocket.

Where I carried Echinacea's fruit.

The tendril stretched down until it touched the strangely colored growth. The whole length of the rope tied around me shuddered in recognition, as some communication passed between the two plants. Then the rope relaxed, slackened, and untied its knots as it fell away from my body. I shrugged off the coils and ripped the duct tape off my mouth.

The buzz-cut boys had seen me free myself and gave muffled shouts from behind their taped-up mouths to set them free. I ignored them. They weren't in pain. I leaped over toward Violet to liberate her from her restraints, but she jerked her head in Peasblossom's direction; the elf was the one who was most distressed. I freed her, then the two of us set about releasing Violet.

It turned into a tag-team effort as released people liberated their still-bound companions. When everyone was freed from the ropes, the agents formed up a posse to pursue Winfield.

"We have to recapture that device," the head buzz-cut guy said.

"But there's no..." Peasblossom started to say.

The agent silenced her, "That's all right, ma'am, they don't have that much of a head start on us." They went charging out the door.

"What am I going to do about this mess?" Joel wailed. "I could pull an all-nighter with some of the roadies to see what I could fix up. But I'll have to do both this room and the main setup in the ballroom."

"You need some proper help," Violet said.

Peasblossom got a determined look on her face. She strode over to Joel and did that thing of laying her hand on top of his. Joel's eyes glazed over, and he sang a short little melody of about half a dozen notes. When he finished, Peasblossom let go of his hand. His eyes snapped back into focus.

Joel had built a false wall to the display to cover the room's facing wall. There was nothing there, no entrance or exit behind his display. Despite that, little people began to creep out from behind the row of flats. They were native, about three feet tall, with simple dress and wide, open eyes. They didn't say a word, just stood there solemnly. The belts at their waists were hung with tools, ones that had never seen the inside of a Black and Decker factory, but they still looked like they could manage incredible feats.

"The Menehuneh," Lenny whispered.

"What?" I asked.

"They're the little people," he replied. "The builders."

I turned to Joel, "Can they do the trick?"

Joel was wide-eyed. In part he was astonished by the little people. But there was another part of him that had called the people here. That part knew what they could do. "I should be fine," he said with a nod.

We started to leave.

"Uh, sir," the remaining buzz-cut guy who was in charge addressed me, "I don't think those people are on my list of authorized personnel for this room." He indicated the Menhuneh.

Screw! I had to make my way around the government regs. "They're workers authorized by my company."

"I understand that, sir, but my orders are my orders."

"Agent, you've got to admit that we've got some special, emergency problems here."

"Yes, sir, but I have to have someone approve their presence in this room. Someone with authority."

Something clicked in the back of my mind. "I've got that," I assured him.

"Who would that be, sir?"

"Who?" I asked--both him and myself.

"Yes."

I sucked in my gut as I launched another lie out into the world. "Um--Mr. Thompson, from the IRS."

The guy's back noticeably straightened as he spruced up his appearance. "Oh--oh, okay. That's fine, sir. As long as Mr. Thompson approved it," he said.

"Good," I said. "We've got to get to the banquet on the beach."

Peasblossom turned to me, pointing to the agent. "I've got to tell him something," she said.

"I'm sure you do, Peasblossom," I said as I propelled her out the room. "But he's very busy right now, and we've got to see how the banquet show is doing."

I hauled her out as Violet and Lenny followed.

Chapter 101

The minute we left the hotel building, we could hear the audio system down on the beach playing Hawaiian themes.

"That's the music for the hula dancers," Lenny explained.

"So we're up to the after-the-meal entertainment," I said. "Well, the only thing I can do is make sure that the show goes off all right. I hope the agents are able to catch up with Winfield and get the power source from him."

"But--but--but..." Peasblossom started to protest.

"Peasblossom, not right now, please," I shushed her. "I've got to get up to speed on what's happening down on the beach."

We raced out from the hotel, reached the beach, and clambered into the booth in the back. Laura swiveled her head around and mouthed a "Where the fuck were you?" at me. She was totally frazzled, heading right into that dangerous territory known as The Angry Laura. Sidney was sitting next to the audio operator at the control table. The stage manager for the dance and drums group was on his other side.

Onstage the hula dancers were taking their bows. The audience was cheering and clapping loudly. They were into it, enjoying themselves.

The stage manager for the troupe said, "Okay, fade the stage lights and give me the Voice of God mic."

The audio operator handed over a microphone, slid up a fader on the audio board, and gave a finger point to the stage manager to indicate the mic was hot.

"And now, ladies and gentlemen," he announced, his voice booming out through the speaker system, "The Amazing Magic Tiki Drums of Hawaii."

Drums located around the perimeter of the stage thrummed out a slow, steady beat: single strokes that were accented by the silence between them.

The stage manager had returned the mic to the audio guy and said to Sidney, "Okay, bring up the stage right lift."

Sidney relayed the command over his headset, and a single silhouetted figure rose up out of the stage floor, standing stock still.

"Hit him with the follow spot."

Sidney gave the cue into the headset, and a spotlight shot out and revealed The Evil Mage Zorch.

Chapter 102

"Who the fuck is that?" the stage manager asked, staring at Zorch.

The little wizard loved being in the spotlight. He raised his hands up over his head and began to intone to the audience.

"Yes! The Magic Drums, the drums that bring magic into your lives. The bewitchment that spreads across this world. We bring it to you. We bring you the sorcery that changes your world. But be careful. You may feel the sharp edge of magic as it exerts its force on you."

He raised his arm, indicating the other side of the platform.

The troupe's stage manager looked at Zorch and said, "He wants to raise the other lift. Why not? If things are entirely wrong on one side of the stage, maybe things will be right on the other."

Apparently he didn't know that when life hands you a lemon, you should expect the rest of the day to be citric. He turned to Sidney. "Go ahead and raise the other lift."

Sidney shrugged and relayed the cue over the headset. The platform on the right side of the stage elevated another silhouetted figure with low-lying, inanimate objects arrayed around it.

Sidney gave a "Should I do it?" raised eyebrows to the stage manager. He shrugged a "why not?" Sidney relayed the command. A spotlight shot out and illuminated the new figure standing on the stage, surrounded by several very large tiki drums.

I gasped in shocked recognition.

Violet looked up at me and asked, "Who's that?"

"Mirabel, my ex-wife."

Chapter 103

Mirabel always had a figure, and she wasn't wearing very much, so there were calls of approval from some of the men in the audience. One thing she was wearing was bunches of jewelry. I was surprised she could hold her arms up with all the metal bracelets she'd installed their.

"So *that's* her," Violet said next to me, as she appraised my ex-wife on the stage. "Now I understand a bunch of things about you."

Mirabel was definitely enjoying being in the spotlight. She strutted her way across the platform. She looked up and started talking.

"I have studied magic for many years, and now I bring it to you."

"What the hell is she saying?" I asked Violet.

"I think somebody's taught her magic," she said.

"They couldn't have. She'd screw it up. She's never been able to do any of that shit right."

Peasblossom was on my other side. "You don't think Zorch has been foolish enough to give her some powers, do you?"

"If he did, he's handed an atomic bomb to a baby," I replied.

Mirabel continued, raising her hands to the sky. "And I'm going to bring it to you. I'm going to reach into the occult world and bring magic into your life. I'm going to bring enchantment down on you. I'm going to completely surround you by magic,--" sheswung around and pointed a finger at me, "--Harry!"

A green fireball shot out of her hand and lanced its way toward me. Peasblossom grabbed my hand and pointed it up toward Mirabel. A countering Blue Protector sprang up to meet her onslaught. The two beams clashed together over the audience's heads in a spinning, iridescent ball, shimmering in midair. The ball slowly rose straight up, then accelerated precipitously and rocketed in the sky where it exploded loudly, sending streamers off in every direction.

A larger branch of the explosion arced its way inland and shot down into the mouth of Kilauea, the active volcano above us.

When the streamer hit the bottom of the volcano, a loud groan emanated from the heart of the mountain. It was low and feral and--it sounded annoyed.

Lenny, behind me, said, "Oh shit." I shot a quick glance at him, trying to figure out what he was upset about.

Mirabel was raging mad at having been thwarted by my counter-magic. She raised her hands up high and brought them down, in a fit of pique, on the two large tiki drums beside her. Her hands still glowed with lambent magic.

The drums absorbed the magic glow, and the bass notes reverberated down into the ground. The audience cheered at what they thought was a great Sensaround show.

However, the notes didn't fade away or stop. They continued to reverberate through the ground and build in intensity. The earth began to shake, like a quake. Glasses and silverware on the tables rattled and danced around, some of them vibrating across the tabletops to fall onto the ground.

The low thunder under our feet swelled, rather than diminished. Joining its low rumble was an immense growl of anger coming from the mountain inland.

"Oh, double shit," Lenny said.

I turned back to him, "What is it?"

"It's Pele," he said.

Chapter 104

I stared at Lenny and said, “Briefly refresh me on Pele, would you?”

“Goddess of fire and volcanoes. Sleeps in the volcano. You don't want to get her angry,” he said.

“To my untrained ear,” I said, “the sounds emerging from the volcano resemble someone waking up on the wrong side of the caldera. Does it strike you that way?”

“Yeah, man,” he replied.

“I don't suppose there's any kind of kahuna thing you could do to get us back into the good graces of the goddess of fire, is there?”

“We can only hope we get some help in some way.”

“Where might that come from?” I asked.

“There's the Maidens of the White Mantle.”

“They're the snow on the peaks of the mountains?”

Lenny nodded assent.

“Can they stand up to Pele?”

“Not as far as I know.”

“You're not being much help, Lenny!”

In the meantime, the quaking had morphed into a new

sensation. It continued under our feet but seemed to have an echo back up by the volcano. The two sounds coalesced into one, insistent throb. It moved in our direction, approaching us. A shuddering in the bedrock that burrowed through the earth. It arrived at the beach, went under us, and continued out toward the ocean.

About a hundred yards out in the water, steam started geysering up from the ocean's surface.

The audience cheered wildly at this really neat special effect. They hadn't seen anything this great since the last Kiss concert.

Something grew out of the ocean in the midst of the jetting steam. A mass of glowing magma bubbled up from the ocean floor. The surface was dark, having cooled in the air, but veins of glowing lava bled out from the liquid core. The magma built up in a vertical column, defying the laws of gravity. It reached a height of about thirty feet and began to delineate itself into a human-like form with arms and legs and facial features twisted with rage.

It was the goddess Pele.

Chapter 105

The audience jumped to their feet, applauding the great special effect.

Zorch and Mirabel, realizing the ton of shitstorm they had unleashed, vaulted off the stage and went running off to hide in the underbrush down the beach.

Pele gave a roar of rage that was a rich mixture of both human and tyrannosaur. Her eyes glowed with molten anger as she cast her gaze around and focused on the Lambert people on the beach sitting at the banquet. She resolutely headed toward the shore in our direction.

Peasblossom stared at Pele's features, leaned in to me, pointed at her and said, "She's urinated."

I squeezed my eyes shut, leaned in toward Lenny, indicating Pele, and said, "She's pissed."

Lenny said, "I'll send for the cavalry, but I don't think they've got enough horses."

I felt a cool breeze wafting me from behind, in the direction of the mountain. I turned around to find its source and saw four ghostly shapes behind me, floating in the air. They were dim, transparent images that, strangely enough, looked alternately like young women, then snowy mountain peaks.

"Lenny," I said, "Pele feels like a blast furnace. Your cavalry reminds me of a room air conditioner."

He gave me a half-hearted shrug in reply.

Pele was making her way toward shore with murder in her eyes.

The maidens behind us tried to send a cooling breeze toward the fire goddess, a calming hand laid across a fevered forehead.

Pele responded with a blast of heat. An edge of the fiery gust turned the banquet's ice sculpture into a puddle. I looked back for the maidens, and they were receding, rushing away, looking very slushy.

Pele advanced onto the beach. When she came to the silk banner Joel had designed, she swept her arm out and immediately incinerated it. She also crashed down a light pole we'd set up. Sparks danced across the lights as they encountered the moisture on the beach.

I turned to Peasblossom and said, "Okay, desperate times call for desperate measures. I realize we've got a raging fire goddess stalking down on us. I'll just have to see what I can do to hold her back while everyone else makes their escape." I held my hand out for Peasblossom to touch and focus my latent magic powers.

Peasblossom raised her hand, approached, went past me, and walked over to Laura.

Chapter 106

Laura had been sitting at the table alongside Sidney, making sure that things went smoothly. Ensuring the show was wrinkle-free was Laura's job. She took it very seriously. There was just one cardinal rule for Laura: don't mess up her show. Some people had tried to screw up her shows and had been broadsided by her anger.

Brother Anthony of The Silent Monks of St. Susurrus, the Martyred Mime, knew of Laura's anger. He had formerly been known as Tony Skrinski of Handlers and Haulers Union Local No. 502 in Cleveland. He felt that the instructions of "handle with care" on the case he was carrying applied to other people, not him. Laura had "discussed" with Tony Skrinski just how wrong he had been. In incisive, cutting, cogent, and raging terms. Now Brother Anthony sought, in silent contemplation, to find the peace that dwelled way over on the other side of the spectrum from Laura's tumultuous anger.

Laura had watched Pele incinerate Joel's banner. She'd watched her knock over the lighting pole. That qualified as messing up her show. Laura had just started to raise her head in response, when Peasblossom came over and laid her hand on the back of Laura's hand. Laura got up.

And up.

And up.

Laura towered impossibly high. She was eye to eye with Pele, sharing a stare. She swung her gaze down to the ashy remains of Joel's banner, then brought it back to stare at Pele. The gaze she shot at Pele could have leveled the Himalayas. Pele's rumbling was suddenly picked up within Laura's chest. It was rage boiling up inside her. She inhaled deeply, filling her lungs. Then, in a voice that shook the mountains behind her, in measured words that slammed out like rounds of artillery, Laura roared:

"GET THE FUCK OUTTA HERE, BITCH."

Laura was, after all, a New York gal.

Chapter 107

Pele was definitely quailed. She had never met a force that equaled her own might. She tried to rally by sending a gust of volcano-hot air back at Laura. However, she was checked with a shock wave of elemental cold. Laura had launched her own gust back. It was the closest thing to absolute zero to be found. Born in the deep reaches of outer space, where lone hydrogen atoms tried to tremble out a dim glow of heat in the numbing emptiness, it had gathered the primal cold around itself and made its journey across the void of space and settled into the coldest bowel of iciness on Earth. It was the winter wind, slicing its way through the concrete canyons of Manhattan, turning everything in its path to frozen ash. It hit Pele with a force that sent her reeling back several strides into the ocean.

A high-pitched whine from the side forced its way into our senses.

Violet asked, "What's that?"

I looked over to the source of the noise and said, "Oh no!"

It was the launches from Winfield's yacht hightailing it back to the ship. Inside it were Winfield and that part of the crew who hadn't stayed behind for dinner with the mountain trolls. Gordon Montbatten was also going with them. An insectoid leaped out of the bushes along the beach, bearing Zorch and

Mirabel out toward the ship. Everyone was flocking toward the yacht to make their escape to safety.

"Screw!" I said. "That means the buzz-cut boys weren't able to intercept them. They're getting away with Charlie's device."

"No they're not," said Peasblossom.

"What do you mean?" I asked.

"That's what I've been trying to tell you."

"What?"

"They took the wrong one," she said.

"How could they mistake them? They had different weights."

"I put a Levitation Spell on the real unit, so it felt like there was nothing in it."

"What about the other one?"

"I weighted that one down," she said.

"How?"

"I put some stones inside it."

"Where did you get the stones?" Lenny suddenly asked.

"I took them off the pile over in the landscaping department."

Lenny leaned forward and gave Peasblossom a big kiss on the cheek, then he wheeled around to Pele, pointed at the launches, and shouted out, "They're taking some of Pele's Children."

Pele was reeling under the onslaught of Laura's attack, a force more elemental than she had ever encountered. She wheeled around and stared at the launches. She absorbed what Lenny said. His words gave her the perfect opportunity to escape what had to be an embarrassing setback to her superiority. She turned from Laura's attack and flipped her attention to the launches that were fast approaching the ship. She reached an arm down along the water and swept it out toward the yacht, sending a wave crashing away from the beach toward the ship. She launched herself out and headed with grim intent toward the yacht.

I glanced back at the table. The stage manager for the tiki drum group had collapsed his head into his arms. Laura had resumed her normal size and was sitting there quietly, still sending out a gimlet glare toward the fire goddess.

The wave reached the yacht as the launches approached. They went crashing into the mother ship, pieces flying in all directions. Pele followed, igniting flames around the yacht's decks. We could hear emergency klaxons going off all over the ship. The hull must have been breached; the ship showed signs of taking on vast amounts of water. Some onboard gas storage tanks were ignited and they exploded in flames that engulfed the entire vessel. I could make out figures leaping off the ship. It listed dangerously, spewing more people into the water, and sank out of sight in a matter of minutes.

I'm sure the ship had a lot of life preservers onboard, and it wasn't that far out from shore. I'm sure everyone out there could make it back. They only had to do one thing: avoid a raging fire goddess. Pele glared around in satisfaction, casting her eyes over the remains of the terror she had inflicted. Her face had lost the sharp lines of anger around it as the goddess's bloodlust was appeased. She cast a look of satisfaction at the wreckage around her and slowly sank back into the ocean, jetting steam as she went.

The audience was standing in a group and holding up their lit cell phones in tribute. Most light on the water was extinguished, and I couldn't make out what happened to the ship's occupants.

I said, "Well, Sidney, I guess you can start the fireworks."

He nodded reflectively and gave the order into the headset to the guys from Sparkle Plenty.

The fireworks were an anti-climax.

Chapter 108

The audience didn't leave after the fireworks were over. They stayed and continued to party. Conversation groups flowed from table to table. There was no reason for them to remain in the location; meal service was finished, the bar had been closed, but they were still talking excitedly with one another. They were really pumped. They'd decided we'd staged a show that was a combination of *Godzilla* and *The Attack of the 50-foot Women*.

Charlie Lambert was there, involved in an animated conversation group. He saw me and gave the thumbs-up gesture. I knew from that signal that I'd nailed the account down for years to come.

Sheila, the lady from Human Resources came by. She was beaming. "It was all because of my nut cups."

I checked my group at the table. Sidney was on the headset setting the lighting and background music with the crew. The stage manager for the tiki group had done a complete 180 and was taking credit for the great entertainment of the evening's banquet. Laura was sitting in her chair, alert but silent, looking like a tigress guarding her cubs.

"I think we're over the hump," I said. "I don't imagine we'll see any more of evil magicians, power-hungry industrial giants, or deranged ex-wives. We can turn our attention to other problems. We left Joel in a complete mess back in the hotel. Let's go back there and see what we can do with damage control."

I took most everyone back to help Joel, everyone but Laura. I couldn't possibly pull her away from her babies.

We found Joel in the ballroom. The place had been entirely restored--only better. He was wandering around in awe, with his hands clasped in front of him.

"They were totally wonderful," he said, referring to the Menehuneh. "I kept asking for things, and they kept giving them to me with extra touches that were absolutely splendid."

He was right. The place looked breathtakingly beautiful. It didn't look at all like a hotel ballroom. Instead it resembled some place from another world. I wondered if it could be someplace in Over Here. Violet took in the décor around her and mouthed a "wow" to me.

"One little thing," Joel said. "They never said anything back to me. I wasn't sure if they understood that everything should be temporary, that we should be able to take it down in a few days."

I raised my eyes to the ceiling and softly whistled through my lips. It sounded like I might need to do a bit of negotiating in the future.

"Okay," I said, "the place looks great. We're all set for the General Session tomorrow morning. I've got to run downstairs and inform the buzz-cut boys that they don't have an empty chassis down there, they've got the McCoy."

Peasblossom looked worried. "How are you going to explain about how it seemed lighter?"

"To them?"

"Yes."

"Easy. I'll tell them that information's classified."

Chapter 109

The Monday morning session was a big hit. The audience was totally juiced, and I'm sure that company morale had never been higher.

Once I was sure that things were settled in the ballroom, I headed to the Harbor Room to oversee that presentation in the afternoon. I knew it was important, so I wanted to stay on top of it.

Joel had adjusted the display to feature only one demo model, since the empty chassis was now at the bottom of the ocean with a few lava rocks inside it.

I prowled around the room, double-checking that everything was working and ready. I annoyed all of the technicians in the room by double-checking everything they'd already double checked. I even bothered PowerPoint Sarge. I marveled at how he was able to stand at attention while sitting behind the computer. I strolled past the power supply and started to reach out a hand to check it. However, too many buzz-cut boys tensed up when I got close to the thing, so I decided to leave that to Charlie.

I sat down in a chair that was behind our control table.

"Yes!"

I gave a start and turned around to see who had spoken. It was Augie, the CIA guy.

"What are you doing here?" I asked him.

"This is the important part. This is where we test the power supply."

"The important part is that you give me that Collateral Damage Exemption."

"We'll see," he said. "All depends on whether the power supply works."

"I thought the collateral damage thing depended on whether or not I had any hazardous duty. I've had guns fired at me, knives held to my throat, green fireballs flying my way, and a fire goddess trying to roast me. I think the 'hazard-' was particularly '-dous.'"

He scooted off to talk to one of buzz-cut boys, totally ignoring me.

I got up to follow him, but Charlie and Eleanor Lambert walked into the room.

I made myself noticeable in case they needed me, but they were involved with each other. Eleanor had changed into her lab-coat. They headed over to the power supply and fired it up. The thing gave out a contented electrical hum. There was a numeric display next to the gear, facing the audience, it flickered into life and settled at 122.9. Charlie and Eleanor nodded to each other and switched the thing off.

They were satisfied.

I was satisfied.

I forgot about Augie.

Chapter 110

The audience for the demo began to arrive, and I was impressed. I didn't personally know these people, but I'd seen most of them on the front pages of the newspaper. There were a number of Representatives, several Senators, a few Cabinet members, and a bunch of military types who sported enough scrambled eggs on their hat brims to supply brunch for a small town.

I understood why Winfield had tried so hard to lay his hands on this thing.

When everyone was gathered, Charlie began talking to the audience, giving a brief introduction of his R & D chief, Eleanor. She took over the demonstration and gave a description of dark energy and how they had managed to tap into it. She was aware of the scientific knowledge of the audience, so she kept her language well away from her Lab Coat Vocabulary.

As she headed toward the actual demonstration of the power supply, I became aware of somebody sitting next to me in the 900-Pound-Gorilla Seat.

Chapter 111

It's an old joke. Question: Where does a 900-pound gorilla sit? Answer: Anywhere he wants to.

We always have a 900-Pound-Gorilla Seat back at our control table. It's meant for our client to sit in so he can feel like he's part of the group running the presentation. In point of fact there's a number of clients with their own hierarchy, so the 900-pound gorillas have different ranks. Some 900-pound gorillas weigh more than other 900-pound gorillas. However, we have room for only one chair in the back, so the clients have to figure out who is the heaviest of the 900-pound gorillas.

In this case, the person sitting in the 900-Pound-Gorilla Seat was Corgus.

Chapter 112

"I'm happy to see that you survived the gunshot you took the last time I saw you. However may I ask what the hell you're doing here?" I asked.

"'Tisn't proper to deal with dark things," he replied.

"That's a good safety note. Are dark things worse than widgins or wodgens?"

"Them two be energies that differ from t'other," he replied.

"What does that mean? They need different rest rooms?"

"Yup. They discharge to separate places."

My attention was drawn away because Eleanor was approaching the power supply to demonstrate it. This was the crux of this whole meeting.

Eleanor flipped the power switch on. The same electrical hum permeated the room. However, there was suddenly a buzz to it, an overtone that grated along the edges of the noise. The numeric display, that had settled on a single number before, flashed insanely through an inchoate number of readings with a minus sign appearing and disappearing at the left of the numbers. Eleanor quickly dialed down a number of rheostats on the front of the chassis, but that didn't improve matters. The hum began to rise in pitch until it reached a shriek. A sudden blue-white flash of light shot across the room, a puff of acrid smoke emerged from the chassis, and then the sound faded down to that oxymoron: a thundering silence.

For a moment Charlie and Eleanor exchanged a questioning look.

"What the hell was that?" I asked as I turned toward the 900-Pound-Gorilla Seat.

Corgus was no longer there.

Chapter 113

I felt in the seat next to me to see if I could find Corgus hidden in some little crack in its construction.

He had disappeared. Something was tickling in the back of my brain. I was wondering if the two things were related. Had he accomplished what he wanted to do and left?

In the meantime, Charlie Lambert was attempting to make the best of a bad situation. He put on his most winning smile and said to the audience, "Well, I promised you a show of power, only maybe not the kind you were expecting. I'm sure you'll see in your handouts that we have made definite progress, but I did say that we were finding our way through unexplored territory."

Eleanor Lambert took over. "We have monitoring equipment on this demo, and we'll be able to find out what went wrong and initiate fixes on the problem."

Things wound down quickly from there. As soon as proceedings were over, most of the audience bolted out, heading to their private jets to get back to the mainland. A few, mostly the military, stayed to confer with Charlie and Eleanor, offering their sympathies, saying they understood how some things could go wrong.

Of course they understood how things could go wrong. They ran the government.

#

When the audience had cleared the room, I had the crew start taking down the audio-visual equipment. I made sure they did the stuff on the periphery of the room; Charlie and Eleanor were hovering over the demo equipment, looking at readouts on monitoring devices they had stashed behind the display. They were discussing things like "feedback loops" and "sudden power surges."

I stayed as far out of sight as possible. I didn't want my presence to link me to the failure of the power supply. I did feel a certain amount of guilt. I had the suspicion that Corgus had something to do with the blown demo. Why did he show up here? What did he mean when he talked about not dealing with dark things? Charlie had told me that this power supply tapped into dark energy. Was Corgus trying to thwart that?

If he was, I was truly pissed at him for blundering into the situation and screwing things up.

Chapter 114

After Charlie and Eleanor left the room, when we had torn down most of the equipment, Augie came scurrying through. He had a distracted look on his face.

I leaped up to confront him. "Hey there, Augie, how are we doing with that Collateral Damage Exemption thing? You know, the one I need for Mr. Thompson from the IRS?"

He frowned down at the floor. "Not good. Not good," he said.

"What do you mean?"

"Demo didn't come off. Not a complete mission," he said.

"What?"

"Can't list it as a win," he said. "Can't say mission accomplished." He avoided looking at me.

"Yeah, but we can say that a gun was held to my head and that the guy holding it was eaten by the plant," I countered.

"Has to be a win. Gotta show the agency a win." He pinched his lips with his fingers.

"How about we show a Nice-Try Exemption?" I asked.

"You'll have to do more."

"More?" I asked.

"Yes. Yes," he said, and scooted out the door.

"More? More? What do you mean more?" I shouted after him. "I've done more than I wanted to already,"

He disappeared and left me standing there, owing a whole lot of money to the IRS.

Chapter 115

Once we left the pall of the failed demo in the Harbor Room, we were swept up in the excitement the opening night had generated. There was an energy that pulsed through the employees of Lambert. The environment Joel and the Menehuneh had created in the ballroom sucked everyone into the mood. Gordon Montbatten had disappeared without taking care of his job of equipping the breakout rooms. With Lenny's help we were able to cover that.

It was Wednesday afternoon. Violet had escaped to the beach, and I was sitting in the lobby with Peasblossom, having a latte and going through the billing for this show and trying to figure out how I was going to cover all my expenses. She was questioning one of my budget cuts.

"Are you sure you don't have to send Mirabel any more acrimony payments?"

"There's no way in hell," I said. "She took sides with a group that was trying to put me out of business. As a matter of fact, I could probably get a restraining order against her for launching a green fireball at me."

"Yes, I'm sure a judge would agree with that."

I peered over at her face. Was this another example of her not knowing our world? Or was she learning sarcasm?

Just then, Lenny came up and sat down next to me. "I've had a busy day," he said.

"Really?"

"Yeah, first thing this morning I had to explain to Joel how it was impossible for him to legally adopt the Menehuneh."

"Oh dear. I hope you let him down gently."

"Yes. I told him that they were cultural relics for Hawaii, so they couldn't possibly move to Manhattan."

"Manhattan?"

"He wanted to put them on display at both the Museum of Natural History and then the Metropolitan Museum of Art."

"Joel visits both regularly."

"Well, no sooner had I settled that issue than I got a call from the front office," he continued.

"What'd they want?"

"Remember how Joel told us on Sunday night that he didn't think the Menehuneh understood about making everything temporary, so it could be torn down tomorrow?"

"Yeah."

"I took a look at it. I'll tell you, those Menehuneh do good work. That stuff is *permanent*. The rest of the hotel is going to fall down around it, but their work will stay."

"Problem?" I asked.

"Yeah, and sooner than I expected. The boys upstairs got wind of it, and they called me up to their offices. As they put it, 'this is a real problem.' They even brought in Legal, and those puppies never approve of anything."

"What do I need to do?"

"Not to worry. Remember, these are corporate guys. I asked them if they had actually *seen* it. Of course, they hadn't, so I hauled them down to the ballroom to take a look at things. I made sure that the Sales Department accompanied us. One look won Sales over, and I promoted it as natural native art. We're leaving it in."

"So we're not in trouble?"

"Not only that, they decided they wanted to contract you to do the rest of the meeting rooms in that décor."

"So I should start making out a budget?"

"One glitch."

"What?" I asked.

"Joel was there. They asked him for a price. Of course the only thing he wants is to work with the Menehuneh again."

"So he low-balled it," I said.

"Sounds that way."

"Shit! Tell them I'll get back to them with a formal estimate."

At that moment, Charlie Lambert wandered into the lobby. Time, and the mood of his employees, had healed the disappointment of the failed demo. There were a lot of other parts of Lambert Industries that looked like they were taking off. He spotted me and came over. "Harry, I just want to say you've done a bang-up job on this meeting--again."

"Thank you very much, Charlie," I replied.

"Needless to say, I want you to do all our meetings coming up. I've instructed Wendell not to even bother talking to anyone else. And don't worry about Finance giving you any sort of trouble about your budgets."

That last one warmed the cockles of my heart.

"I'm telling you, Harry," Charlie continued, "it's amazing the things you accomplish. You just do magic."

"Me? Magic? No!" I said humbly.

"I do Dogs and Ponies."

THE END

26548037R00218

Made in the USA
Charleston, SC
11 February 2014